Nylon Angel

THE FIRST PARRISH PLESSIS NOVEL

Marianne de Pierres

A ROC BOOK

ROC
Published by New American Library, a division of
Penguin Group (USA) Inc., 375 Hudson Street,
New York, New York 10014, USA
Penguin Group (Canada), 10 Alcorn Avenue, Toronto,
Ontario M4V 3B2, Canada (a division of Pearson Penguin Canada Inc.)
Penguin Books Ltd., 80 Strand, London WC2R 0RL, England
Penguin Ireland, 25 St. Stephen's Green, Dublin 2,
Ireland (a division of Penguin Books Ltd.)
Penguin Group (Australia), 250 Camberwell Road, Camberwell, Victoria 3124,
Australia (a division of Pearson Australia Group Pty. Ltd.)
Penguin Books India Pvt. Ltd., 11 Community Centre, Panchsheel Park,
New Delhi - 110 017, India
Penguin Group (NZ), cnr Airborne and Rosedale Roads, Albany,
Auckland 1310, New Zealand (a division of Pearson New Zealand Ltd.)
Penguin Books (South Africa) (Pty.) Ltd., 24 Sturdee Avenue,
Rosebank, Johannesburg 2196, South Africa

Penguin Books Ltd., Registered Offices:
80 Strand, London WC2R 0RL, England

Published by Roc, an imprint of New American Library,
a division of Penguin Group (USA) Inc.

First Roc Printing, July 2005
10 9 8 7 6 5 4 3 2 1

For Vicomte Henri Jaques Stanley de Pierres,
who loved adventure stories

PART ONE

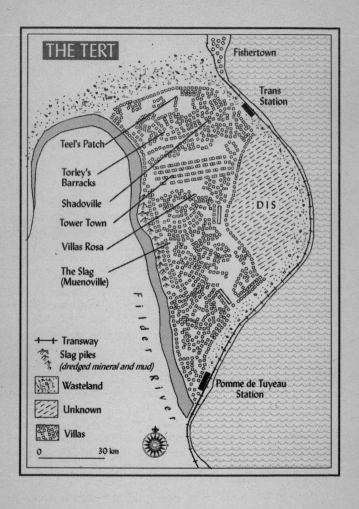

THE TERT

Fishertown

Trans
Station

Teel's Patch

Torley's
Barracks

Shadoville

Tower Town

Villas Rosa

The Slag
(Muenoville)

DIS

+—+— Transway

Slag piles
(dredged mineral and mud)

Wasteland

Unknown

Villas

0   30 km

Filder River

Pomme de Tuyeau
Station

Chapter One

If Jamon Mondo touched me one more time I'd kill him. And then they would be after me. His dingo-boys would hound me for retribution, licking up my blood as reward.

Parasites!

So what to do?

I stared across my plaster-chipped room at my translucent body replica, Merry 3#, and willed her to have an answer.

But she wasn't much of a conversationalist. Just a cheeky smile and a lot of see-through skin, who told me what calls I'd had and when my bills were due. No help at all!

See, Merry 3# and I were up to our heavily pierced ears in trouble.

I'd been working in The Tert—around Torley's—for three years or more. Bodyguard stuff mainly. Defending my own piece of the poison, living on stim and second-rate protein substitutes, scraping for credits or barter.

It beat the hell out of home. Home was a *hands-on* stepdad and a mother who was genuinely addicted to romance. (Neuroendocrine sims were the latest thing in the 'burbs.) When my sister, Kat, left home to play pro ball, *Dad* turned his *hands-on* approach to me. I left before I killed him and broke Mum's heart.

The Tert seemed the right place. Outside the city limits. A leftover strip of toxic humanity where, it was rumored, you could survive on your own terms.

I did all right there. Not many women of my large size were as handy with their fists and feet. I also cut a mean, hungry look when I wanted. I could take care of myself but I'd never make the front cover of a glossy, on account of my badly rebuilt nose and flattened cheekbone (courtesy of stepdad, Kevin). I could have had it fixed up, I guess, but it reminded me of what I'd left behind.

I was getting by—until Jamon Mondo came along. Well, noticed me really. He's been here forever. I was the new kid on the block.

When he hired me, Doll Feast said I'd hit pay dirt. *Parrish Plessis, bodyguard to the stars.* Well, to the dark prince anyway!

By the way the other babes on the Torley's stretch reacted, I figured she was right. So I went along with it. Anything had to be better than one more protein sub, or another soft-bottomed white-collar chump looking for his piece of the wild side.

That dream died my first night on Jamon's payroll. I was expecting the bodyguard drill. *How* he wanted to be protected, and from *whom.* Instead he took me to his barracks for a welcoming ceremony . . .

Dingoboys, panting, howling like the moons of Jupiter had lined up, in their uniform of dreadlocks, greasy skin and jutting teeth.

"Strip her down," Jamon instructed.

It took five of them to hold me.

I stared at him like some dumb, miserable animal gazing up the slaughterhouse ramp. Fear spiked through my gut, so sharp that I moaned.

It was not a sound to be proud of, but then this wasn't graduation night . . .

I tried to leave him after that but he had me followed and beaten. Once on Jamon's payroll, always on Jamon's payroll. A club you had to die to leave.

Why hadn't someone told me?

"Parrish!!!"

It took me a few moments to focus, weighted by my recent past. I checked my door, then automatically flicked to my comm screen.

It was Mei Sheong, her hair corkscrewing around her head in bundles of absurd pink curls. It cost her a week's pay out of every month's earnings to have it done. I'd suggested a straight replant, even genetic manipulation, but she reckoned that was bad karma. Who am I to argue with a chino-shaman?

She closed one eye and sucked on a curl. "I heard something."

My attention clicked in. "How much?"

She sucked a bit longer before she answered, "I tell you, but when you die I get your room."

I sighed. "Is it that good?"

"Yeah, it is. Anyway, I've got to plan for the future, Parrish. No control otherwise."

Control. The mother of illusions. But it didn't stop me wishing. Trying. Hoping my life might be mine again one day.

"All right, Mei. But I'm not planning on dying yet. So don't get any ideas about helping things along. Or you might find yourself closer to the spirits than you figured."

She opened the other eye wide in surprise. "You threatening a chino-shaman?"

"What's it sound like to you?"

"Sounds like you're in an evil mood."

I closed in on the viewer and her face. "The word, Mei. What's the word?"

She stepped away from her screen and glanced over her shoulder. "Hein's. Ten minutes."

Some nearly neo-punk revivalist had done Hein's insides out like a bunker, old-style, electrified grilles and concrete look-alike walls—the only concession to comfort being the tactile chairs. Hein's had a burnt look like it had been bombed and hosed.

Mei was perched on a tactile stool at the bar. Poured into a fluoro-pink bubble dress, red stilettos hooked around the chair's leg, she could have been Tinkerbell's kinky sister. The chair moaned soft ecstasy as she squirmed in her seat and flirted with Mikey, the barman's servitor.

Mikey was one of Jamon Mondo's Pets—a hideous result of illegal biorobotic experiments. The Tert was that sort of place. Mikey's proximity to my best source made me uneasy.

But—I reassured myself—that's why Mei was my best source. She could pry secrets from an autistic sheep.

I sat in a khaki tactile with my back to the south wall. It was a bit of phobia I had. Wherever there was a south wall, I had my back to it. It felt right.

The chair quivered a little and started whispering dirt to me in another language. I told it to be quiet or I'd stuff its chip somewhere unmentionable.

Mei giggled with Mikey a few minutes longer, then drifted out of the bar. This was part of her pattern. Disappear. Then reenter from another door. It seemed stupid, but it worked. Whenever I asked after her, most people would say, *She's just left.* I guess it helped that Hein's patrons were lucky to focus more than a drink's length in front.

Looking around, half a dozen faces were familiar and half a dozen were more permanent than the tactiles. A pair of 'goboys lounged behind the bar watching for trouble. I could smell them even without seeing their badge of dreads and elongated incisors. Their presence spurred my impatience.

Where was Mei?

I had to find some way to prise Jamon Mondo's jaws off me. Or there'd be two more bodies in Tert Town. His and mine.

"You sure are in a bad mood." Mei sidled alongside, her hair now stuffed into a dirty, pink knitted cap. Wisps escaped from underneath. It didn't do a lot for her sallow skin.

"Shows, huh? You going to tell me something to improve it?"

She grinned slyly. "What about your room?"

I couldn't understand her attraction to my tiny piece of rented air, but it seemed like a reasonable payoff—if the info was tight.

"Yeah, deal."

We sealed it, Tert Town style. Knuckles only. Crossing palms could get you dead or sick.

She whispered so I had to lean over to hear. "Razz Retribution is dead. Murdered on the Hi-way."

"Razz Retribution? The One-World journalist. So?"

"The cops are looking for a biker and his pillion. But word is that the rider was Cabal Coomera—and the pillion was some geek he'd picked up as a decoy. The geek is hiding out in The Tert. If you find him first—before the cops—he might know something about the Cabal. Maybe enough to get you in with them. Then no more work for Mr. Mondo." Her almond eyes gleamed knowingly under Hein's stained fluoros.

Am I that obvious? Or can she see inside my head?

I soothed my paranoia with logic. That's the other reason why Mei traded info for a living. She could make those leaps of understanding about people. You didn't have to be a genius to work out I loathed Jamon Mondo.

Still, I'd need to watch myself. I didn't want Jamon

to know what I was planning. "Who else you sold this to?"

Her face smoothed out. "Only you, girl. Mei knows who her friends are."

I laughed at the lie. "When did it happen? You got ID on the geek?"

"Hit was this morning. Word says he's petit crim. New 'round Torley's. Hangs out with another guy, named Dark."

"*Dark?* What sort of a name is that?"

She shook her pink curls loose from the beret and shrugged. "Takes all sorts. Now I got things to do. Don't forget our deal, Parrish."

"Call me if you hear more."

She grinned and drifted off.

Takes all sorts. Coming from a crazy pink and yellow chino-shaman in a bar full of total rejects—that tickled. But I had other things on my mind that weren't funny. Like the rumor she'd just leaked.

You see, I wanted *in* with the Cabal Coomera. *Who am I kidding?* I didn't just want . . . every fiber of me craved it.

Cabal Coomera were The Tert's real lawmakers. A mysterious, unaccountable sect who operated above the daily Tert politics. Some said they were descendants of the Kadaitcha, the feather-feet police of the original indigenous tribes, but that sounded like romance to me. More importantly, though, they protected their own. If I could gain entry to the Cabal, then Jamon Mondo wouldn't be able to touch me.

I wasn't totally inexperienced at their game either. I'd ridden with a vigilante group for a few months, before Jamon, but their race politics bothered me. So I concentrated on bodyguarding and building my own weapons cache.

You had to be able to take care of yourself in The

Tert. Most babes are chocked up with enhancements.
Wired so tight their buns act like capacitors!

I've got different ideas. Sure, some things you can't
live without—compass implant and olfactory aug-
mentations (olfaugs)—but the rest is pure me. Nearly
two meters of well-honed skin. In hand-to-hand combat I can match anyone.

Yet I didn't know much about guns. That was the
one small plus to being owned by Jamon Mondo. I'm
in good shape for fighting but it means fairy sprin-
kles if someone shoves a Smith & Wesson up your
nostrils.

When Mondo took over my life he insisted I train
in a shooting gallery with his dingoboys. For him
I'm just another cheap soldier in his muscle pool.

So why don't I take Mondo out?

Believe me I've thought about it. But it's not that
simple.

So I'm working on this other way.

"Parrish. Deep in wonder? Thinking about me?"

The voice was silky and heavy and sarcastic. I
knew it in my nightmares.

"Jamon." *Breathe, Parrish. He can't see what you're
thinking.*

"Where were you last night? I wanted you." He
reached forward and pinched my skin through my
clothes.

"Earning a living," I snapped, pulling away.

Undeterred he reached with his other hand and
trailed his fingers down my body to my crutch.
"Don't I pay you enough?"

I stared him full in the face, this time without
flinching. "You could never pay me enough."

He whitened at my jibe and removed his hand, but
his look of cool amusement never faltered.

He was shorter than me, fair and slender. Fine
boned. A holographic tattoo shimmered on his cheek-

bone, a naked girl on top of a man. Her head bobbed from side to side. One day I planned to gouge that implant out.

"Come, Parrish. You're the envy of the stretch. You have my protection. My attentions . . ." He kissed the tips of his fingers meaningfully.

I ignored the public display. Jamon's way. Like wearing his brand on my butt.

Lucky me! Luring a perverted death adder!

It wasn't the first time I'd pictured Jamon like that. The net's holo zoo featured death adders regularly on its Nearly Extinct Creatures series. Jamon had all the characteristics of one. Small, sinister, deceptive, deadly. You could mistake an adder for a harmless lizard, meanwhile it poisoned you in seconds.

A shudder rolled through me.

"Trembling with anticipation, little one?"

I arranged my facial muscles into a blank expression. I'd given too much away already.

Casting an eye over Hein's dismal crowd, he continued, "I'm entertaining tonight. Be there early. And wear something . . . interesting."

His eyes refracted then, like a crystal in the light. Something new. I wondered how much they had cost. Rainbow eyes. The idea made me want to howl. The one beautiful free thing left in this whole gray world was imaged in Jamon Mondo's eyes.

"Be there, won't you, Parrish?"

I nodded and hated my guts for it.

Chapter Two

The aged Trans-train limped out of the station and headed south past Fishertown where the view wasn't pretty. I often wondered who paid who to keep it running. Mostly its passengers were like me, locals taking the quick way from one end of The Tert to the other—Torley's to Plastique in a couple of hours. The rest of the passengers either couldn't afford the Hi-way bypass, or were bent on glimpsing real misery.

The Tert stretched for a hundred klicks or more between the sea and the snaking river, a turtle-shaped strip of land that should have been priceless. Instead, it harbored the wretched, the sick and the downright sicko. No dinkum *straight* would dream of going there, with its toxic soil and crazy population.

Years ago it had been a massive foundry and industrial site—whispers of long-buried tek as well—way out past the limits of the expanding city, Viva. Now, Viva was called Vivacity, one of the world's carnivorous supercities, spreading down the east coast of Australia.

The industrial structures had long since been demolished. A spanking plastic villa metropolis arose on its remains, complete with pocket courtyards, identical black lacquer front doors and palm trees.

It took fifty years of high-density living before the side effects of the poisoned soil became obvious. Now the long-termers in The Tert were either morons or nutters. Short-termers paid a fortune in protectives or took their chances with the rest.

The villa metropolis was no longer recognizable as distinct pieces of architecture, only a morass of living.

The seaside of The Tert was known as Fishertown, a gray stretch of ilmenite black radioactive sand. Slums huddled like clumps of seaweed along it, home to a miserable collection of fishing families.

Not the place for romantic moonlight walks.

I was headed to pay a visit to Minoj Armaments and Software, on the south side of The Tert. The "scenic" Trans-train was the quickest way there.

I found I was spending more and more time at Raul Minoj's, ogling his range of weapons. It gave me a kind of peace when nothing else would. Peace from things like my evening "date" with Jamon.

I stared at my reflection in the dull chrome piping of the train interior. *Wear something interesting,* he'd said. Well, interesting he got! I'd changed to a funky black nylon suit with lime pleats interweaved into the flared legs and a leather tank top underneath.

And dangerous. The tank had specially worked compartments into which I slipped evil-long poisoned pins. Handy in a fight! Underneath the pants I wore a string that stretched like a cobweb, front and back. Garrotting wires wound into the web.

Shoes? Well, I felt naked without my boots. The first pair I ever had were steel caps. Not much good for running. These days I wore titanium inserts. You could still kick the crap out of someone and sprint if you had to.

The train slid into the Pomme de Tuyeau on the southeast tip of The Tert and the doors twitched translucent before they opened. I found this a useful little bit of teknology. It gave you time to change your mind if the scene didn't look right. When you're my size, you're a target in any situation. I hated that. Being small had advantages.

The toll boys on the Pomme were Tert specials. Body-enhanced, skin-mixed, libido-jacked jerks. The latest craze in Plastique-ville was patchwork skin: Caucasoid, Negroid, Mongoloid with a splash of Albino thrown in for highlights. Infection rates were high amongst zigzags.

"Who wants to look like a frigging zebra?" Doll Feast would say to me. Her laugh sounded like a tracheotomy.

I cruised past the toll boys without paying. One blond giant with a piebald face and bulging triceps glowered at me but made no move.

How did they see me? I wondered. Doll Feast's lover? Jamon Mondo's whore?

Resentment squirted through my gut. One day it would just be about *me*, Parrish Plessis.

Inside the villa corridors and melded rooms anything and anyone that sells was for sale. Fishertown Slummers were everywhere, hawking shellfish aphrodisiacs and longevity oils smelling as potent as their scam. They had the voracious look of the half starved.

I silently counted my way to the hardware villas, reciting it like a litany.

Five villa sets north: Pharmaceuticals and Pleasure. No coin needed to pass through Doll's patch. The babes came here for fripperies and Doll was good to me.

Three villa sets east: Bodyparts, Replacements, Makeovers. Frigging zebra country!

One villa sets south: Stolen Tekno. Hmmm, tight ice. Who knows how far back that goes?

Then it's . . . *Hardware.*

I climbed up some battered stairs to the roof and across a planking arrangement, watching out for dayrats. Then down some defunct escalator steps to the fourth door along the bottom where I was scanned by security vid and optic ID, and decontaminated for blood residues and parasites. By the time Minoj's face appeared on the vidset I was tugging my dreads impatiently.

Minoj's greasy skin shone with angelic intensity; his grin was lecherous and rotting.

"Little thing"—he knew how I hated that—"waiting always improves your mien. Come in and play with the toys."

"You know if you weren't such a smart—" I began. "What's that?"

I stepped across the room and draped myself over his workbench to eyeball a gleaming spear.

"Special order, little thing. *Ne touchez pas.*"

I could barely breathe with envy at its sleek-lined sophistication.

Minoj raised a slicked, knowing eyebrow. "But what would *you* be needing?"

Ignoring him, I caressed its texture. "How much for this beauty?"

"More than your simple lifetime could afford. The latest in explosive tips." He sucked on his teeth, giving a weirdly excited whistle.

"It's for the Cabal Coomera, isn't it?" I said flatly.

"My perfect lips are sealed."

"Your perfect lips are as rotten as your teeth, Minoj."

"Ha, ha, Parrish." Minoj laughed like his gums—flappy and raw.

The ritual over, our banter shifted to serious haggling. I left with an ugly snub-nosed pistol and an upgrade for my hacker's "dream" pack. Bodyguards had to stay wired to the tek thing as well.

Cruising back along the same route, I lingered at Pharmaceuticals and Pleasure—P&P—checking out the latest erotic prolong syrups and sprays. The vendor offered me a free trial out the back, and I laughed in his lascivious face.

It was about then that I sniffed the tail.

It smelt of Jamon's boys. The 'goboys lived in a converted barracks arrangement like the old-styled armies, out the back of Torley's. The scent splintered through my brain like a migraine. *Semen on ferrocrete.* The 'goboy was imitating a punter by gawking at a nearby porn booth.

Jamon was having me followed again!

Gripped by panic, I ran, not stopping until I hit the tollbooths on the Pomme. Then I slung inside the first train headed north.

I didn't have much time to mull over why Jamon had a tail on me because Mei was waiting outside my room when I got back.

The suit itched and the cobweb of my string bit like second-rate bondage. I hauled Mei inside with me and sat her on my bed while I stripped, shoved my whole suit into the dry clean, and stepped into the san unit. By the time I'd cleaned up the outfit would be ready to go.

Aah, modern conveniences!

"What gives, Mei?"

The pink-haired shaman's face colored with excitement. "That guy, Dark, I've seen him!"

"How much?" Damn! I was running out of time. Jamon would have the troops out after me if I was late. In a way he already did. But this opportunity was too good to miss. Maybe things would work for me this time. "Hurry, Mei. I got a job with Jamon."

"I need to meditate. Can I stay here for a while?"

I sent her a sharp look as the san unit blew me

dry. *What was the thing with my room?* One tiny, over-priced firetrap of a back room on the top story of a run-down villa. It used to have a view into the identical room of the next villa but the window had been permanently sealed. No one in The Tert wanted to look in on their neighbors.

I knew decent digs were premium around here, but hell . . .

"OK, I guess. Don't touch anything."

My meager savings were somewhere she'd never find them and if she wanted to frolic in my underwear then good luck to her—most of it bit back.

"He's in one of Hein's sluice rooms."

I wrinkled my nose. Hein's sluice rooms were for those that preferred to do it by themselves with the help of inanimate objects. "One of those?"

She rolled her slanted eyes upward.

"How will I know him?"

"Very broad. No hair. Leather. Oh yeah, and a prosthesis."

"Where?"

She giggled. "It's all right. It's his hand."

I sprawled near the south end of the bar in Hein's, with a clear view to the corridor and the back rooms. The proprietor, Larry Hein, never spared me a flutter of his false eyelashes, but he gave me my drinks cheap 'cos Jamon was his boss too. He ran the keenest, toughest bar in Torley's. I had a lot of respect for Larry Hein and I sure envied his dress sense. The sorta guy who could make chiffon hip.

Torley's referred to Hein's and a multitude of bars, plus Shadoville and the whole strip of business that ran the north end of the villa sprawl. Jamon's patch. A lucrative but seedy spread that attracted plenty of Vivacity punters looking for a piece of action.

I was wearing my action. I patted my pins and felt

for the garrotting filament I had concealed down the
lengths of my web. Minoj's pistol lay holstered on
my waistband, barely disguised by my coat. I'd have
to surrender it when I got to Jamon's but for now it
felt good. Minoj said it was a Glock, but I had a
suspicion he had a cheap manufacturing deal with
an Indo business cartel.

If it shot straight I didn't really care if it was a
Barbie.

I was on my second drink and getting edgy when
a bald guy in black leather and a chain choker, fitting
Mei's description, filled the corridor. His bulk was
pretty impressive, even to me, his face clean-lined
and attractive, but his expression was mild. He sur-
veyed Hein's crowd for a vacant tactile, walked over
to it and slumped down in front of the large vid
screen.

Another guy trailed in behind him. Pale, skinny
with rusty hair, wearing R. M. Williams, a checked
shirt and yaaaahh . . . *moleskins!* Talk about the odd
couple! Bung Mei alongside and it could have been
a sideshow.

But, hey, who am I to talk in flared nylon and
webs!

As I mulled over my approach tactic, the One-
World news blared on the vid screen, a report about
Razz Retribution's assassination headlining it.

Dark and his friend glued their eyes to it like baby
animals imprinting.

The reporting bordered on hysteria.

*"One-World is devastated to inform all those viewers
on the public viewing net of the brutal and cowardly slay-
ing today of their beloved news anchorwoman, Razz
Retribution.*

*"Razz Retribution was rumored to be investigating
reports of illegal genetic experimentation, when her car
exploded on Hi-way 1049. Two men were cammed by Hi-*

way security fleeing from the site. If you have seen these men please contact your Militia buddy with the information.

"One-World needs you, its family, to root out this evil continuing to plague our new era . . ."

A close-up frozen image of Dark's rusty-haired companion led the segment into the break. He was gaping wildly from the pillion of a bike. The rider a dark, indistinct blur.

Then two things happened at once: The rusty-haired guy heaved his insides up on the floor, and his tactile shrieked in pain—the entire back section of the chair melting away where his head had rested seconds before.

I recognized the attack as a bounty hunter by the weapon, even before I spotted the creature. Ordinary humans couldn't handle the heat of their fire-stormers.

Hein's exploded in a melee of bodies as the clientele went to ground. In the confusion that followed I caught a glimpse of Dark propelling his friend along by the neck, protecting him with his larger body.

Sweet!

With a flick he tossed the guy behind Hein's reinforced bar and rolled his own bulk over.

The bounty hunter had missed the clear shot and vamoosed, but some nervous punters lost their bottle and shots sprayed everywhere. Jamon would be pissed off at the mess.

It's stupid to feel sorry for a chair, but I kinda did.

I slid along the wall in a half crouch with the Glock copy balanced ready, and edged for the bar. Dark and the moleskin guy weren't the only ones hiding there. Two Shrang cultists and a Fishertown Slummer were head-to-head at one end.

Damn! A religious war, that's all I needed.

Dark had his back braced against the wall and his feet wedged in under the bar.

"G'day."

He turned the same mild stare on me that I'd seen before. His eyes were the darkest brown, nearly black.

"Not really." His voice rang deep and I noticed the perfect shape of his clean skull.

He was right. It was far from a good day.

"Listen, we need to talk. And I can give you some space. Looks like your friend could lose a little heat?"

Shots zinged off the bunker walls as I held out the back of my hand in greeting.

"Parrish Plessis."

For a few seconds the docile look dropped away. He eyed the pistol and my web and my flares. Then he stared intently into my face, like a psy-spook.

As he held out the back of his hand to return my greeting a strange heat burned through me, like swallowing a bucket of caffeine caps on a stinking hot day. Sweat broke over my skin in its wake. The pointy knives of adrenaline running down my backbone switched to hacking great axes.

"What are you doing to me?" I demanded.

"Nothin'."

A question rose in his eyes but not the same one I was asking. Then the mild look settled back into place. He reached for his friend's shoulder and turned him over like a parent handling a frightened child.

"Stolowski. This girlie's going to help you."

Girlie!

I shoved the Glock copy so hard under his jaw that his thick neck jerked back.

"Let's get one thing straight," I snarled with raw sincerity, "don't *ever* call me that!"

Chapter Three

"But you said I could meditate!"

"Come on, Mei. This is my room. Anyway it's just for a couple of hours."

The chino-shaman narrowed her almond eyes until they passed for being closed. She was pissed off, I was pissed off, and if I didn't get my nifty nylon flares moving, Jamon was going to be dangerously pissed off. I could see why she didn't want company though, and why Dark was shuffling like an oversized teenager.

Mei was naked except for a swathe of pink goo pasted on her hair and a nail tattooing kit open in her hand. Girls' stuff!

Behind Dark, the red-haired, moleskin-clad Stolowski perked up like a dog about to score a biscuit.

"Get your gear on, Mei, and be nice to the company or I'll throw you out as you are," I said.

She opened her eyes, fractionally, and saw that I meant it. With an exaggerated sigh she disappeared inside, her bare butt dimpling like tapioca.

I shoved Dark after her. He seemed mighty embarrassed for a Goliath in black leather and chains. Red-haired Sto didn't need anywhere like the encouragement. His nose was practically twitching.

"I've got to work, but I'll be back after midnight, then we'll talk," I told Dark. "Don't go anywhere and you'll be safe. If you get hungry, Mei will dial in something for you."

I grinned to myself all the way to Jamon's. Somehow I didn't think Dark would have much of an appetite.

Jamon's gleaming mahogany table was set with silver service when I got there, ludicrous amongst the chipped plaster walls and dirty low archways. It should have been in a mansion somewhere in Vivacity, where the ceilings reached over ten feet and the guard dogs passed for bears. Instead it crouched uncertainly in Jamon's villa, covered in white napkins and a deluge of candles. One of his many affectations—Gothic meets tacky plastic.

Not that I don't like nice things! But I call it like I see it. No matter who Jamon thought he was, he lived in a run-down warren of villas built on poisonous earth. A real French-polished table didn't change it.

Then again, maybe I was jealous?

Four guests clustered at the other end of the room emanating the stench of shared chemicals. I heaped confidence into my step and strode toward them. As the faces turned, though, I almost lost it in surprise.

Jamon had two of his bitterest enemies in one room—a small one at that. *And where were their bodyguards?* I wondered.

"My dear, you are late." Jamon had his snake smile on, the one that made me nauseous. "Stellar you know, of course."

He slid his hand in underneath my coat between my shoulder blades, his fingernails stabbing into my skin.

I stared venomously across at a blue-haired bimbo. *Stellar the bodyshop bitch! Jamon's boy/girl.*

"Let me introduce you to the others," he continued. "Topaz Mueno."

Mueno, The Slag's main mover, bowed slightly and combed his plump fingers through his thigh-length hair. Tiny lights glimmered between its silken strands, like a Christmas tree. Heavy perfumes masked his body odor. Another soft, sweaty man. And vain. I summed him in that moment. Sometimes you can pick people's weaknesses in that first instance of meeting—before acquaintance tarnishes your judgment.

The Slag lay in the western quarter of The Tert, Plastique to the south, and Torley's on the north side. The Slag's western boundary was the poisonous Filder River where mud and garbage piled along the banks—someone's poor attempt to stay the inevitable landslides. Heavy metal slag.

"Road Tedder."

Tedder I knew better. He wrangled constantly with Doll Feast for control of Plastique's lucrative businesses, the bodyshops, hardware and tek. His deviousness drove Doll to distraction. She had him watched twenty-four hours of the day and still he kept his advantage—and his secrets.

Rumors say he murdered his first wife and ate her. Good hunting rule, I guess—eat what you kill.

Tedder lived in the 'burbs back then.

My favorite arms dealer, Raul Minoj, ran the knife edge between Doll and Tedder, though I suspected at times he hung more heavily over to Road's side.

"And of course . . . Io Lang."

An unremarkable-looking man offered his hand in greeting. It was cold and I caught a whiff of something . . . astringent, like antiseptic.

"Just 'Lang,' " he corrected pleasantly.

A huge spice worm of fear bucked in my gut. This man I only knew by reputation.

Lang ran the dirty heart of The Tert, a place called Dis—some said Dis harbored the root of all The Tert's industries, but I couldn't see it myself. No transport went that far in. No people ever came out. If you really needed to hide from the Militia it was the place to go, even if they dropped a bomb and flattened The Tert to get at you. Rumor had it that Dis went far enough underground to hit lava; or hell; whichever came first. The real crazies lived there, self-sufficient and secluded, a world within *our* world.

"And now, let's be seated for dinner."

Let's be seated?? Jamon really was trying to impress! In fact he seemed unusually excited about something.

"Parrish, you will attend Lang. Stellar . . . Señor Mueno." He seated himself alongside Road Tedder.

Even sitting, I towered over Io Lang. If I hadn't been so jumpy, I would have been embarrassed that I looked like his mother. I studied his appearance while Mikey, the Pet, served our meal.

Lang's brown hair was cut up over his ears and above his collar, military style. His milky skin made it difficult to place his age. A strange smile played along his lips. Not exactly pasted on, but not connected with the rest of him.

Only once during the tedium of the dinner did he look directly at me. I was thankful that it didn't happen again. If Mondo looked like a snake, then Lang reminded me of the worst predator of all . . . soulless Man.

To make matters worse Stellar, the bodyshop bitch, hung over Mueno like fake cologne. Mueno lapped up the attention, complimenting Jamon on his hospitality, while Stellar flashed her *I'm better than you, bitch* look at me.

A month ago I would have risen to the bait like a starving street kid. Now I just wanted out.

For the most part I kept my head down and listened to the tone of conversation—their words were carefully guarded. Instinct told me Lang was the dealer and Jamon and the others were buying. But buying what? Something valuable enough to get the four of them in one room.

When Mikey served the main course of cuttlefish I saw a slight difference in the color of the meat. Lang, Tedder, Mueno and Jamon's were an opaque, clean white. Stellar's and mine were a perceptibly darker, almost gray, color. If it hadn't been seafood I probably wouldn't have even noticed, but everyone eyeballs their seafood these days. Nobody, even the nutters, ate stuff caught in the Filder or off Fishertown. It meant sure death.

I glanced at Mikey but his robotic features gave nothing away. Nor did his darting human eyes.

"I presume the swordfish is imported?" Road Tedder asked.

Lang and Mueno stared at Jamon.

"Of course," Mondo replied hastily.

"Then you won't mind if I test it, Jamon."

"Actually, I do mind, Road. You insult me in my own home. Surely even you have better manners?"

The room suddenly stilled.

Only the shadows cast by the candlelight moved. I loosened my grip on the base of my glass so I could get my garrotting wire in a hurry. The 'goboys had taken my pistol.

Tedder reached with a slow teasing movement into his breast pocket. To my right I could smell the perfumed sweat on Mueno's soft body. Stellar's as well—hers was pure chemical.

"Understand that my *manners* have kept me alive, Jamon. I don't doubt your intentions. But tell me, did you prepare this meal yourself?"

With a flourish Tedder produced an object from

his pocket that sent me grabbing for my wire. Mueno and Jamon betrayed similar spasms. Only Lang seemed unconcerned.

Sniggering, Tedder dipped the object into his meal. A toxin detector.

I relaxed my fingers.

"In my place you'd do the same. Or are your good manners more important to you than *la morte vite*?" he asked.

Satisfied with the detector's advice he waved it across Stellar's plate and gave her a wink of assurance. Then he offered it to Lang and Mueno in turn. Mueno accepted and repeated the process.

"Lang?"

"Death before dishonor . . . isn't that the expression, Road? No, thank you. I trust Jamon."

Jamon's expression lightened at Lang's vote of confidence.

Lang was playing games, though. I'd caught the faint hum of his inbuilt detector, probably in his fingernail. He already knew his meal was within the safety limits of mercury contamination.

"What is the world coming to?" Stellar brayed to break the tension and then gulped down a large mouthful. Under the weight of her giggling inanities the moment passed.

As I sliced the offending fish and brought it to my lips, Lang looked directly at me for the second time that evening.

"Tedder lied about Stellar's food," he whispered. "My detector tells me that yours and hers are not the same batch as mine."

The fork clattered from my hand.

Sensing Jamon straining to catch our conversation, I forced myself to pick it up and smile back.

As Jamon turned back to Mueno and Stellar, I dropped the sliced fish into the palm of my hand

and stuffed it into a pocket to test later. From then on I pushed the food around the plate until Mikey came to clear the table.

Stellar had cleaned her plate and was busy licking her lips like a cat. Not just a plastic bitch, a dead one! I couldn't even feel sorry for her. Just angry. And sick. Sick of being caught in their twisted games.

When dessert came I declined it by claiming weight concerns. It was a bit lame considering it was genetically impossible for me to exceed a certain weight, but no one questioned my excuse.

I owed Lang for his warning—one I shouldn't have needed. Under the distraction of Mikey clearing the dessert plates away I touched Lang's arm. "Thank you."

He smiled his disconnected smile. "I need work done, privately. I'll contact you."

Chapter Four

I got back to my room a little before two a.m. Lang had excused himself and left around midnight—after some private talks with Jamon in his den—followed soon after by Tedder.

Jamon must have been pleased with the evening because he already had Stellar half naked in front of Topaz Mueno while he said his goodbyes. (There was nothing Jamon enjoyed more than another man's envy. Pure gold!)

With Topaz gone, he turned his attention to me, even though Stellar was in his lap.

"Parrish, come here."

Stellar pouted and stuck her tongue in the side of his mouth. "We don't need her."

At that moment I would have killed rather than let either of them touch me.

Fortunately for all of us, Stellar got her way.

"I'll save you for the morning, Parrish. After all, you are better to look at in daylight than Stellar."

The plastic bitch howled at his insult and lunged toward me, nails flexed like claws.

Laughing, Jamon tripped her and she fell hard on to her stomach. He grabbed a handful of her hair and yanked. As her howl of anger shifted to growls of pleasure, I escaped from Jamon's rooms, my breath tight and suffocating in my chest.

When I closed my door to the world, I found Mei curled up on my bed top-to-toe with the redheaded Stolowski. They looked like two teens home from a bad taste party. Mei was cuddling into Stolowski's skinny leg, unconsciously rubbing two fingers along the texture of his moleskins and sucking her thumb. Stolowski was snoring.

Dark sat in my only chair watching a news bulletin and studiously ignoring Merry 3# while she jigged and fluttered.

"You all right?" he asked, glancing up at me, his broad, smooth face shining in the glow from the vid.

He was attractive, in a *natural* sort of way. Not synthetically perfect like the genetically engineered. I could understand why he dressed the way he did. A guy had to have some defenses against the world.

I must have still been rattled from my evening at Jamon's because I had a sudden urge to throw myself on to his lap and bury my head under his armpit.

But in reality I'd given that up years ago. Especially with complete strangers.

"Nothing I can't fix," I answered sharply.

He shrugged, indifferent to my coldness, and his attention dropped back to the vid.

I warmed up a pro-sub to make up for the dinner I'd just missed and hunted through the cupboards for my detector. I found it jammed between some out-of-date vitamin patches and a bottle of imported water. When I scanned Jamon's fish for mercury, it redlined.

"How d-dare he!" I keened in rage, choking on my mouthful of pro-sub.

Dark turned and stared, then started out of his chair toward me.

I held out a hand to fend him off but he batted it away. With a quick movement he spun me around and slapped my back so hard I hit the floor. The pro-sub came loose in my throat and I coughed myself into the comma position.

"You all right?" He leaned over.

"Can't you th-think of something else to s-say? Or is that your complete r-repertoire?" I stuttered.

As I wiped the tears from my eyes, a look akin to frustration creased his face.

He grabbed my shoulders and hauled me upright into the chair.

Me!

I spat the remains of the pro-sub out and sprang away into a crouch.

"Don't touch me!"

A garrotting wire appeared in my hand like magic and I whipped it past his nose. I had the Glock copy in my coat pocket if I really needed to prove the point.

To my amazement he began to laugh. A deep, gut-twisting paroxysm that doubled him up.

My garrotting wire is not something that usually makes people laugh.

"What's going on?" Mei sat up sleepily and scratched her head. "Oh, it's only you, Parrish. Keep it down, will you?"

Then she stuck her thumb back in her mouth, rolled over and hung her dimply butt off the edge of the bed.

Stolowski never stirred.

Dark levered his bulk down onto the floor opposite the chair and motioned to me.

"Sit down, Parrish," he said, the edge of laughter still in his voice. "Let's talk."

I stepped over the remnants of the pro-sub, and thought, *Yeah, it is time to talk.* Only I stayed standing.

"Your friend, Stolowski, has been set up to take a murder rap," I said.

Dark nodded in agreement.

"If he tells me everything he can about what happened, then I might be able to help. Or at least keep the heat off him for a while."

"Why would you do that?"

"I need information that he might have about the bike rider."

Dark frowned, confused.

"You heard of Jamon Mondo?" I tried.

He nodded again.

"I work for him. We all do." I waved my hands around to indicate Torley's.

"You've been there tonight? With him?" he asked.

It was my turn to nod. What a pair of conversationalists!

Silence stretched the moment.

I tried again. "Look, Razz Retribution is . . . was a big-time newshound. If your friend has been framed for her murder then he's in deep trouble. The word around is that it's a professional hit. I just want as much information on the biker as he can give. In return I'll keep him safe."

"When you get your information, what happens then? Sell him to the nearest bounty hunter?"

This time I was able to shake my head for variety.

"Bounty don't pay subcontractors. It's not their style to share. If you and I make a deal, then I'll keep him safe until you can make other arrangements."

The big man opened and closed his hands. "What arrangements?"

"I don't know. Move intercity or something. Have a new face made. Use your imagination."

All signs of humor had left his face. "That costs money, Parrish. Sto doesn't have any money."

I could feel a headache building. "Can't you sell something? Everyone's got something to sell."

"He's got some family, somewhere," he mumbled. "Maybe they could help."

"Great. You find them and squeeze some money. I'll take care of him while you do. But remember, this is just breathing space. Not a permanent babysitting job. You've got a few days."

"How do I know that the information you want isn't worth a lot more?"

"There's the door. Take your chances out there. See how long your friend Sto lasts with bounty and Militia after him."

As if on cue another news bulletin headlined on the vid, with a replay of Razz Retribution's assassination. You could see the freckles on Sto's pale face. Behind him the rider was hunched over the engine, head low, back to the camera.

Dark sighed heavily, then stretched out full-length on my floor like an oversized leather couch. "All right, Parrish. I'll tell Sto. You got a deal. Make sure you take care of him."

Sleeping on the floor in your own room, while two people you hardly know snuggle on your bed and a third snores loud enough to knock chinks out of the plasterboard, is not the way to get a good night's sleep.

I woke early—had I actually slept?—feeling gritty, my heart pounding. I knew the bounty hunters wouldn't take long to link me with the disappearance of Stolowski. I had to get him to Plastique soon— away from Torley's—without anyone recognizing him.

Doll would hide him and me while I convinced her to lend me credit to buy Easy-tell. Easy-tell forced a crude gate into the hidden pockets of a person's memory. Made 'em spew out minute detail— everything the senses unconsciously recorded. Occasionally it messed with the taker's recall. It only happened to a few. Mostly they just ended up with a day-long killer headache.

My conscience kicked me—but I was desperate enough to risk it.

Then there was the small matter of Jamon. If he made good on his threat of a morning interlude, then a 'goboy could be on my doorstep at any moment. I reckoned my room had outlived its usefulness as a refuge by about four hours.

Four hours of desperately needed sleep.

I roused Mei first.

"Mei. Mei! Come on. Your bed pal has to go. Stuff is going to happen today."

She wakened quickly, making me wonder if she'd been asleep. She pinched the skinny redhead's arm. "You're cute. Wanna go out sometime?"

He screeched into wakefulness like a slapped baby.

At the noise, Dark surfaced from his dreams, flailing his arms like an epileptic King Kong.

Circus time and me the ringmaster!

The sudden banging at my door worked better on everyone than a bucket of water.

I knew right away the caller was no one I wanted to see and pointed to the ceiling.

Dark understood straight away. Whatever persuasion he muttered in Sto's ear worked, and without too much drama Dark and I pushed Sto up through the manhole in the ceiling.

The outside windows of my room had been permanently sealed off years before and the ceiling was the only other way out of the top floor. It led to one of the thousands of cut-throughs that interconnected nearly every villa—narrow, badly constructed passages through the rooftops of The Tert. There were problems with using that route but . . . one thing at a time!

"Dark," I hissed, "strip."

Mei started to peel off his jacket.

"How will I find you?" He stared at me helplessly, like I was disappearing with his only friend in the world.

As I levered up off the chair into the roof, I grabbed my spare comm spike from inside my suit and threw it to him. Don't ask me why I did it. The only other person who had one was my sister in the northern hemisphere. But a deal's a deal, and it was the only way to contact me when I was on the move.

Below, Mei gave a raw little cat growl at the dimensions of Dark's naked chest. She rubbed herself against him. For some reason that really peeved me.

"Use this spike in any link. I'll hear you." I tapped my cochlea implant. "And Dark . . ."

His eyes hadn't left me. "Yes, Parrish?"

"Move the damn chair!"

Sto crawled clumsily along the rafters. Every meter I sweated over him falling through the ceiling. At least he hadn't had time to put on his R. M. boots.

Small mercies!

We spent the first ten minutes avoiding my own booby traps. If we could get out that way, then others could get in, so I had the ceiling wired. I usually didn't sleep at night until I'd checked all my security. Most of the money I earned went into keeping these little gizmos operating in my part of the inner roof. I disabled the heat sensor by remote until we'd passed, then reactivated it.

Soon we were covered in grime, with lungs full of some pretty foul air. Sto started to make gagging sounds.

"Get sick and I'll leave you here!" I threatened.

The only noise I heard after that was gulping.

Inside the villa rooftops was not the greatest place to visit. For a start, normal-sized humans couldn't stand upright—let alone big people like me; second, if you got lost and came out at the wrong place, you'd likely find yourself in a room full of infected junkies who'd strip you butt naked and sell your gear (Titanium-capped boots were worth a mint. So was natural body hair and real nipples.); third, and most importantly, it was canrat territory.

"C-can we stop for a minute?"

Sto sounded shaky, so I relented.

With a jerky sigh he settled on a crossbeam and put his face in his hands. I switched off my miner's light and took some steadying breaths. The nifty light was part of my everyday traveling kit. It fitted across my forehead like a groovy headband. In The Tert you never knew when you might be in a dark place.

"Dark said you would protect me till he could get some money to get us out of here," Sto said from between his fingers.

"Dark? Yeah, well Dark's right, but you've got a part in the deal too."

"What do you want to know? I don't remember too much."

"How did it happen? I want to know every detail."

His hands dropped away. His voice was tight with the effort of remembering.

"I got a message to meet up with Dark at Con's pool bar. Thought I'd hike. Got picked up real easy, straight outside my squat. The biker never spoke or nothin'. I told him I wanted to meet a mate at Con's."

"And?"

"We got up close to this car on the Hi-way, a real beauty, expensive, with a babe driving it. He swung in real close and slapped a patch onto it. I recognized her. It was the news-grrl you see on all the TV shows. Razz. The beautiful one. I saw her face, then she . . . she . . . kaboom!"

He made a noise like a kid playing with war toys.

I'd begun to think he was a bat short in the attic when I smelled something that sent my adrenaline scooting. It prompted me to switch my light back on.

"You ever seen a canrat?"

He glanced about nervously. "You mean those dograt mutant things? They live on the roofs, don't they?"

"Outside, inside, wherever the food is."

"I heard they eat human flesh." His pale skin blanched as white as the static on a vid comm. His freckles stood out like a disease.

"Yeah," I said cheerfully as I started crawling, "but they prefer redheads."

Chapter Five

The bags under Doll Feast's eyes quivered suspiciously. She'd been a handsome *femme* once, but the stress of defending her piece of the poison was beginning to show in the gravel in her voice and the sag of her skin.

I knew that skin as well as my own.

"What use is he to you?" She jerked her head toward Sto.

He was yawning widely and watching porn vids in the back of her lab, his skinny, pale imperfections totally out of place among the benches of glossy, plastic half-faces and perfect bodyparts. After dragging his arse through a bunch of dirty Shadoville attics we'd ventured out and caught the Trans-train back to Plastique. I'd picked the newest carriage with the only functioning closed camera unit and hoped that'd keep the bounty hunters shy.

"I think the Cabal Coomera set him up on a job. One of them picked him up on the back of his bike. They blew up the car. Now Militia is after Sto as the accomplice because they got a clear shot of his face on the Hi-way vidcams," I said.

"Doesn't explain what you're doing with him."

"I figure he must know *something* about the rider. Y'know . . . twitches, missing teeth, something, how he smelled. Under Easy-tell . . ."

"*E-tell!* How you goin' to pay for that?"

"Could you loan me, Doll?" I loathed asking. I never had before, not ever, but desperation changed things.

She shook her head emphatically. "No. I want you to give up this stupid dream, Parrish. The Cabal Coomera is a men-only club. Kadaitcha stuff. They don't want the likes of you. Even if you hunt one of them down they'll never let you in. They'll never give you sanctuary."

"I've got to get away from Jamon, Doll. Can't you see that?" Anger rushed up the back of my neck. I added sullenly, "You're no help."

Her face sagged with resignation. "Come on. You know how it is, Parrish. I don't want a war with Jamon. As soon as Tedder knew I had trouble with Jamon, he'd be round to ambush me in a second. I'd be out of business. Think about it. Then you'd have nowhere to come. As it stands, I can give you some protection. Accept your life and deal with it."

I stared at her.

"Come on, Parrish," she wheedled, "you know how I feel about you. Listen, I got some free time now. What say we go somewhere a bit more private?" She touched my face.

I stepped back, suddenly sickened. In her own way she was just as manipulative as Jamon. I wanted rid of all of them. Her, Mondo, everyone who wanted a piece of me.

I was drowning.

"I need some time to think things over, Doll. Can you keep him safe for a couple of hours? You owe me that at least."

She nodded slowly, unhappy at the knockback.

"I'll keep him. But don't do anything stupid. You want one of my girls to watch your back?" Wariness creased her face.

Maybe she thought she'd really pissed me off this time.

She had.

"I can look after myself."

"Yeah, Parrish. Sure you can."

Outside, Plastique's business hub revved on full throttle. I found a cafébar crammed between The Toxic Sushi and a room selling fake IDs, and ordered a whisky latte. As the waitress brought me my drink I pondered over the amazing things people had on their nails these days. She had two tiny lizards lassoed onto hers. They squirmed and wriggled as she scripted my bill. What happened when she washed the dishes and wiped her butt?

"Cute, huh?" she drawled, admiring them.

"Do you believe in reincarnation?" I asked sweetly.

"What's that? Some type of devil worship?" Hope sparked in her eyes as she set the drink down.

I trapped her hand flat with the weight of mine and nicked the lassoes with one of my lapel pins. One lizard scampered free, the other one moved the wrong way and I sliced its head off.

"Hey, what you think you're doing?" she squawked.

"I read lizards for a job. In your next life watch out some asshole doesn't come along and cut your head off."

She snatched her hand away and stalked off muttering about the weirdos she had to put up with in this job.

I was pretty soft over creatures. Not just creatures. Defenseless things. I guess when you wallowed around for long enough at the bottom of the pile you worked out your own code of ethics. I'd been pushed enough, used enough, that the battle wasn't just a hobby anymore. It was a fucking crusade.

I sipped on the latte and contemplated getting drunk, but I'd made a deal with the incredible leather hulk that I'd babysit his skinny friend and I knew I couldn't trust Doll for more than a few hours.

Maybe just one more drink.

They sent a Pet to serve me this time.

"You any relation to Mikey?" I asked it.

"Sure, lady." A strange, resonant artificial voice. "We-all look-a-like. We-all brothers."

I couldn't decide if it was joking.

The second latte made me feel a whole lot better. Milk and whisky. Innocence and vice.

As I raised the glass to drain it, a scent filled my head. Caustic.

A preacher of some sort in a dusty black coat, collar and hat shuffled in and sat on the torn vinyl of my booth.

"It's taken," I said curtly.

"So nice to see you again, Parrish."

I peered at the preacher. "I don't know you." My skin prickled in uncomfortable waves. Arms, legs, scalp.

"Let us pray that you might remember." He bowed his head.

Caustic. Stronger now. I remembered the scent. *Lang? Io Lang?* I took a drink to disguise my right hand as it fished for the garrotting wire.

He chuckled. "There is no need for such . . . brutal measures, Parrish. This is simply a business meeting."

I stared at his profile, searching for something familiar. This was not the man I had met at Jamon's dinner party. The nose was too long and crooked, the skin reddened and slightly peeling, the forehead protruding. His coat was strapped with beads and crosses.

"Don't tell me," I said sarcastically, "you're Lang's identical twin."

"Look closer, my dear."

He raised his head so I could see full into his face and for a moment the entire composition altered. Skin tones, bone structure, expression. The man who had warned me against the poisoned seafood at Jamon's emerged. Unmistakable.

"How did you do that?" I whispered. Manufacturing a disguise was one thing, but this was like . . . like magic.

"Let's just say I earned it." His face realigned back into its disguise as a preacher. "Perhaps you can too."

His words kick-started a wild hammering in my chest. The possibilities of possessing such an ability rushed over me, leaving me trembling. I struggled to be careful, to be cool.

"What do you want?" I knew I sounded too eager. Next thing I'd be asking if he wanted me to roll over.

He handed me a miniature disk. "Here's an address. Bring me the contents of their computer files. If anyone sees you, kill them."

"And?" There it was again. Little Miss Eager. *Chill, Parrish, chill.*

"I can make you invisible."

I signaled the Pet and ordered a straight black coffee, no alcohol. I didn't want Lang disappearing before I could get my head totally straight. I took a gulp of my drink and scalded the back of my throat.

The Pet giggled, a sound like a boy wheezing in a tin drum. I told it to scram before I ripped out its resonator.

When it had rolled away, I fixed Lang with a flat stare.

"That's a handy trick, Lang. But what does it take for someone to become like you? Voodoo? Do I have to cut out my heart and feed it to the devil?" Then I tossed in one last question for good measure. "And anyway, why me? There must be a thousand hacks in The Tert that could pull a break and enter. It's not really my line."

What was I doing? Talking him out of it?

He waited a couple of heartbeats, as if testing the weight of his next disclosure.

"The contents of those files, delivered into the right hands, will send your esteemed employer to death row."

Mondo on death row!

Whatever his reasons were, he had me. Hook, line and ten-ton sinker.

I'd do it for nix.

By the time I got back to Doll's villa, Sto was asleep—drool stringing from the corner of his mouth, eyes rolling in REM—curled like a baby on a lab bench. I hadn't even used E-tell on him and he already had half the symptoms. He cradled a replica of a woman's head and torso in one arm. As I loosed it from his grip, I noticed the synth head had pink curls and almond eyes. And they say there's no such thing as love at first sight! Wait till I told Mei.

Doll was nowhere to be seen.

A faint thrumming started up in my ear, so I sat down in front of Doll's comm and answered my call. While it connected I played the usual guessing game people did as they answered their spike. Who was it? What lies would I need to tell?

I should have known.

"Parrish? Is that you? Is everything all right?"

"Who do you think you are?" I snapped at Dark's concerned face. "My freaking mother?"

"Is Sto safe?"

I sighed. "Your little buddy's fine. Now get on and rustle up his relatives. I'm busy."

"Have you been drinking?" His voice was sharper this time.

Have I been drinking? Who was this guy?

"If I thought it was any of your business, I'd answer that. But it isn't."

"Something's wrong?" He didn't give up easily.

I suddenly noticed that his chest was still bare. For some reason it made me even madder.

"Where are you?" I asked suspiciously. "Where's Mei?"

He gave a gut-deep laugh. "I could say, 'If I thought it was any of your business, I'd answer that,' " he mimicked my voice. "But that wouldn't get us anywhere, would it?"

Without the leather and chains he could have starred in an advertisement for men's aftershave: serious and clean-skinned; the kind of face every girl wants to rub her thighs over.

"There's a rumor around that there's a police embargo on crossing to the Outer. The cops want Razz Retribution's murderer. They've blockaded all the train stops. I don't think I can get out to find Sto's relatives."

It took me a minute to take in what he was saying.

The Tert had always been a strip of earth that the wealthy in Vivacity would like to have nuked (in fact they probably would have if it hadn't been too damn close for fallout), but there had never been any problem getting in and out.

Reason told me that it would be almost impossible to cut The Tert off. The Fishertown side alone stretched for nearly one hundred and fifty klicks. Then there was the Filder river access. How would they police such a huge, untidy sprawl? This embargo sounded more like a hallucination by one of Hein's more demented patrons.

"Aren't you too big for scary stories?" I sniped at him. His earnestness worked like a cheese grater on my psyche.

Frustration swept across his face. "Go and check it out yourself. See what I mean."

Pink fuzz appeared at the bottom of the screen, just below his jawline. Then the monitor tilted and Mei's face appeared.

"Parrish? Quit griping. He's right. There's an embargo at all Trans stops."

"What are you doing? And where are *you*?" I snapped.

She gave me that sly, eyes-half-closed look. "If I didn't know better, girl, I'd say you was jea—"

"Know better!"

A faint noise behind told me I wasn't alone anymore. "I'll contact you soon." I cut the connection.

"She's right about the embargo, Parrish! By the way, who's the beefcake? He looks familiar."

Doll stood in the doorway of the lab. The dull fluorescent light imbued her skin with a grayish tinge, reducing her expression to something callous and empty.

A flash of insight gripped me. A perspective shift. One I hadn't sought.

Doll—a tired, scared, selfish old woman. It left me marveling at what had ever led me to share a bed with her.

Probably the same thing that had sent me running from my stepdad. I'd thought men were the enemy.

Now I saw my mistake.

The enemy was anyone I rolled over for.

Ignoring the crack about beefcake, I rinsed my face off in one of the basins, patting it dry on some absorbent plastic. I didn't think Doll had it in her to do a jealous number, but I didn't want to find out right now.

Sto still snored peacefully on the bench top, one hand outstretched like he was reaching for something. Mei, perhaps? How could I mainline E-tell into someone who looked like they'd lost their favorite snuggly toy?

I couldn't.

Relief brought me out in a light sweat. Sto could keep what existed of his brain—Lang had offered me another way.

Doll broke the silence. "You need to go, Parrish. The whole world is looking for this jerk. Don't bring them to my doorstep."

"Sure, Doll." It wasn't worth an argument. I'd always be able to count on her for certain things, as long as I understood her limits. I did.

"Will I see you soon?"

"No," I said.

And now she understood mine.

I shook Sto awake and we left.

Chapter Six

We headed back to Mei's cubicle in Shadoville via The Slag, on a moped whose cracked solar panels wavered around on coils like deformed antennae. Solar 'peds weren't popular on account of their unreliability in bad weather.

Mostly Tert people used the more disfigured of the Pets if they wanted to travel distance inside the Tert, but I had an aversion to them. It didn't seem right riding on the back of a child even if it was the machine section that carried most of the weight. They reminded me a bit of a rocking horse with a kid's head—only the legs moved independently.

Not that I was naive about Pets! They had their own ways of taking care of themselves. Anyone stupid enough to hurt one usually wound up staked out on a poisoned slag heap somewhere. Pets might be low in The Tert pecking order, but even they had their defenses.

I took a route back to Shado through The Slag because I knew the Pomme de Tuyeau would be in chaos if the train had stopped. Plus I didn't like Sto's chances of staying unnoticed in the more commercial areas.

The Slag, Plastique and Torley's had distinct perimeter demarcations which, if you lived in The Tert, you learned to recognize easily. A network of monorails had once linked all areas of the villatropolis back to the Trainway that still ran down the eastern boundary. But the structures had been remolded and used to string up fragile hammock homes, or disassembled altogether.

Cramped living and lack of roads made for a crazy jumble of humanity. There were plenty of walkways—alleys big enough for scooters or 'peds or Pets—but you could get lost among them quicker than losing your virginity.

· Tert people used compass implants to get around. Some had maps overlayed onto their retina. I couldn't see the point in maps; once you knew the territories, you knew enough. The rest changed endlessly.

Every now and then you'd come across a precious parcel of space; usually the gardens that had once served a hundred or so villas as a community meeting place. Occasionally you'd also find the concrete guts of an old swimming pool, legacy of the days when Australia was still a country of backyards and mortgages. Mostly, now, the pools were built over with who-knew-what living underneath.

When Sto and I stopped at a demarcated entry point to The Slag, the toll had already doubled.

Topaz Mueno might be a vain lump of flesh but he wasn't stupid. I pictured him rubbing his soft white hands with pleasure at the extra revenue an embargo would create, forcing traffic along The Tert's easternmost strip.

The toll keepers in The Slag weren't like the jacked-up jerks that policed the Pomme de Tuyeau in Plastique. They tended to favor Topaz Mueno's look: long-haired, soft-bellied, thick lips. It wasn't a look to mess with. They could do things with knives that I only REM'd about.

Their homogeneous look was a type of vanity. I'd read somewhere that humans were attracted to others that resembled themselves physically.

Know thyself!

In The Tert you had to *know* people. You had to see and smell trouble. I've got better than twenty-twenty vision and the best olfaugs bodyguarding can buy, but my intuition's kept me alive.

Wrong! With Sto toe-to-heel at my back, I paid the Muenos' inflated toll, hoping they wouldn't look too closely at him; wishing I'd taken the time to make some superficial alterations to his appearance.

The keepers eyeballed him as he bent over to pick shrapnel from his foot.

"Who's the bunny?" one of them asked.

"Boyfriend."

"Where are your boyfriend's shoes?"

Mostly everyone wore shoes in The Tert. I lowered my voice to a conspiratorial whisper. "Caught him in bed with my mother. Thought I'd teach him."

They looked suspiciously from Sto to me, and back again. Sto's puny size against mine? I wouldn't buy it either—but I've said it before, it takes all sorts.

I turned my back to the toll keepers as they tapped queries into their comm.

"Get on the 'ped," I hissed between my teeth at Sto.

"But—"

"You want to make it out of here?"

He jerked his head up and down quickly.

"Jump on the 'ped. When I say . . . *Now*!"

We leapt for the machine at the same time. Five gold stars each for not ending up in a tangled heap.

I jammed the accelerator to full throttle and blasted through the toll with Sto's legs flailing out the back like streamers.

At top speed the 'ped only did twenty-five klicks. Hell, we might as well have got off and run! But Sto didn't look like he could *walk* more than two hundred meters before his skinny legs and tender feet caved in on him.

I turned every corner I could, and then some more, before we hit a cul-de-sac.

"W-what's wrong? What did you do that for?" he stuttered when we stopped.

If Dark grated on my finer feelings, then this guy gave me a dead-set migraine.

"Look, Sto," I said with patience I surely didn't mean, "there's an embargo on The Tert. Do you know what that means?"

"Cops?" he asked shakily.

"Worse. Cops *and* the media. We've been totally cut off from the Outer. Do you know what it's about?"

He swallowed as if he had a fist-sized marble stuck in his throat. "Me?"

I nodded. "They think you killed Razz Retribution. But you didn't, right?"

"R-right."

"No one kills a One-World newshound and gets away. The media are frigging royalty in this hemisphere. You've been set up to wear a murder rap by someone. Probably the Cabal."

"Who're they?"

I didn't even bother to reply because a noise above us triggered my body hair into a stiff salute.

Prier at twelve o'clock and descending—a media 'copter with military fruit but only a third of the size. Priers could land on a bald pate. They usually only carried one person—a journalist/pilot and a camera-mechanoid who doubled as a combat-model Interrogator.

Sto looked set to faint when I glanced back at him. If his skin got any paler, I'd be able to sell him for albino skin grafts. Shame about the freckles.

With Io Lang's deal burning a hole through my ability to think, all I wanted to do was steal the information he wanted and nail Mondo's arse. Stolowski, Dark, the embargo were all suddenly getting in the way of that.

I should dump Sto here! The Prier would pick him up in a few minutes—then I wouldn't have to worry.

Like an attack of conscience, a thrum started in my ear. My cochlea implant ringing again.

Guess who?

"Come on. We got trouble." I dumped the 'ped behind the remnant of a retaining wall and hauled Sto toward the nearest doorway. The Prier would already have a trace on the 'ped, sold and relayed by the Mueno toll keepers.

Well, if the media wanted us, they'd have to get down and dirty.

I dragged Sto to the last door at the end of the pavement, where the buildings loomed like decrepit bodyguards. The villas only ran to four storys, but add on makeshift microwave dishes and the wasplike sleeping cocoons glued onto the roofs, and it made for a neck ache looking up. From above I imagined it looked like a mutated beehive. Maybe one day I'd get a chance to see it from that angle.

I tore through a makeshift barricade and booted the door off its hinges so whoever lived there knew we were coming.

Inside a stench of something other than human had me fast-twitching my olfaugs to low sensitivity. From the gagging noises behind me I knew Sto was at it again. Some guys have just got weak stomachs.

I sympathized . . . for about a heartbeat.

Inside was empty apart from a few planks of discarded wood. Sto sagged onto a large piece, burnt at one end and fashioned roughly into a bench.

"Don't you know treated wood when you see it?"

I asked, neglecting to mention the mangy, zirconium-fanged feline curled up *underneath* the plank, licking its hair clean.

"Treated?"

"Soaked with pesticides. Burn it and sniff it and you're on a one-way trip."

He leapt up like I'd stung him.

The feline ignored us and started on its belly.

It was hardly the time but curiosity got the better of me. This guy was such a lamb. It didn't add up.

"Where are you really from, Sto? Born, I mean?"

His pale green eyes misted. His lip trembled and the words spilled out. "M-midcountry. I got press-ganged to the Dead Heart. We . . . I escaped. P-please don't tell anyone . . ."

Now I can take most things. But crying isn't one of them. Why dilute a good dose of emotion with tears is my attitude. When I feel bad, I get angry, but when runts like Sto cry in front of me, I get confused. Do I dump them where they stand? Or do I take care of them? I didn't like the fact that Sto was leaning me toward *Thou shalt cosset.*

Was that succor or sucker, Parrish?

He was an annoying little creep, but from what I'd heard, Dead Heart Mining Co-op made The Tert seem like a tropical paradise. Out there they used human labor because they were cheaper than maintenance on the mechanoids. Human underground work was s'posed to be illegal now, because the mines were old and dangerous, but no one really knew what happened outside supercity limits.

Or cared.

Australia had always tended to be a coastal country. But since they stopped piping clean drinking water in, the Interior had fallen to aridity and lack of interest. It was a place of feral creatures, snakes and some pretty brutal mining cliques.

Sto'd skipped out on the co-op and they'd have

their own people after him. But he was also media and cop bait, just because he hitched a ride on the wrong bike. Some people are born unlucky . . .

My cochlea implant vibrated again. I had to offload this call before my head turned into a tuning fork.

"Listen, Sto. There's a Prier about to land outside. We need to lose it and find a comm. Your buddy is giving me a headache tapping out my private number." I pointed to my ear.

He gave me a limp smile. And worse. Watery pale green eyes full of trust.

Damn it. I hate trust.

A muffled boom outside sent a wall caving in, and one of the feline's paws bouncing bloodily off my chest.

That was the first shot.

On the second, the blackened bench ignited like a bonfire.

Prier!

Sto and I hit the internal stairs at a lively gallop, coughing out fumes.

The Prier's pilot/journo could've easily blown the whole building to bits, so I figured the attack was just scaremongering. Otherwise Sto and I would be like the feline—body parts at all points of the compass.

I took that as a good sign. They wanted Sto alive. Probably so they could wring ratings on his trial.

Did I say trial? Make that execution. There'd be no trial for this skinny white boy. Maybe that's why I hadn't dumped him. I'm a sucker for long odds. That's all I'd ever had.

There were stories around of how the media used to work as "observers" of global events: no interference, objective views—an indispensable news source. Apparently they helped all of the lowlifes in the world get a fair deal.

Well these days the gloves were off.

Prier pilots had more firepower at their camcord-
ing, acrylic nail tips than the cops and the only people they had to answer to was the network credit
assessor. If the media wanted Stolowski dead, then
he was fried.

Judge, jury, executioner, photographer! *"Say cheese!"*

"Say what?" whispered Sto.

He crouched next to me, shaking, in the gutted
bathroom of the fourth story. His breathing came in
short, chopped-off gasps.

"Nothing," I mumbled. "Listen."

We could hear the Prier's propulsion unit whine
in the distance as the pilot probed the building.

"ATTENTION ALL WITHIN HEARING. YOU HAVE THREE
MINUTES TO IDENTIFY YOURSELF TO THE PRIER BEFORE AN
INTERROGATOR IS RELEASED. RESISTANCE IS AGAINST MEDIA
PROGRAMMING LAW."

The message blared out, replaying in several
dialects.

I'd always wondered when that three minutes
began exactly. From the end of all the messages or
the end of the message you happened to understand?
When you worked with no margin for error, like I
did, these things counted.

"Parrish? What's an 'Interrogator'?"

I pointed to the manhole in the ceiling and started
hoisting him.

"I'll make a deal with you, country boy. When we
lose this little piece of aggravation, you and I are
going to have a nice long educative chat. That way
you might live to see next week. Now, *up!*"

This time he did what I told him. Maybe he wasn't
a total dead loss.

That's it, girl, think positive!

I swung up after him through the hatch, my miner's light skittering along the ceiling like a disco ball,
and found Sto baled up by the yowling family of the

zirc-fanged feline. I didn't fancy telling them Daddy wouldn't be coming home tonight, so I shot through the ceiling to back the mother off and hurried Sto away along the main beam. I reckoned we had about ten seconds before the Prier's pilot let the 'Terro loose.

In five, we'd crawled through a roof cut fashioned into a tunnel. It led to the next villa set. In ten, the *maison feline* imploded.

So much for wanting Sto alive!

I counted us through twenty roof cuts, changing direction at random, before I dared to let Sto rest. Then I kept the miner's light on and my back against an upright to straighten the cricks. Being nearly two meters tall didn't exactly lend itself to attic crawling. And my hands were grazed and black with grime.

"Do you think they're still following?" he ventured. He hadn't complained but his feet were bleeding from snags and splinters.

"Yes." I could have lied but what was the point? Fear could get you to do things, things that ordinarily you'd balk at, and Sto wasn't exactly Mr. Risk.

Give the guy a break, Parrish, I told myself. *He'd escaped from the Dead Heart.*

Maybe that wasn't his idea though, maybe . . .

The dendrons in my brain fired and forged a connection. No wonder leather-and-chains Dark had blushed at the sight of Mei's dimply butt. He was a country boy as well!

With uncanny timing the vibration started up in my ear.

"Sto?"

He stared at me, eyes red-rimmed. If he cried again, I swear this time I'd toe-tag him for anyone who wanted to hawk his bodyparts.

"We're going to go down now and find a comm. It'll be more confusing for the 'Terro that way. Other humans to sort through. You never know, we might lose it altogether."

It was hardly a convincing speech. But I suddenly had the urge to talk to Sto's hulking friend. Right then, nothing in the world seemed more important.

Chapter Seven

"Where have you been?"

"Listen, you stupid hick," I hissed into the comm at Dark, "what in the great frigging Wombat's name do you think you're playing at? You're turning my head into a tune-up parlor."

I could feel Sto trying to see around my shoulder but I blocked him out with a sharp elbow.

We'd lobbed into a villa chock-full of Mueno clones. Greasy food-littered rugs covered the floor and bundles of feathers and fur dripping with fresh blood hung from ceiling and doorway.

A smell to forget.

With a little persuasion and some fancy finger language that bridged our dialect gap, they'd agreed to my using their comm. For money. Right now they crowded behind us in a semicircle of curiosity and suspicion. Not many visitors came in via their roof!

"What do you mean, 'hick'?" His aftershave complexion wrinkled into a frown.

"I mean, why didn't you tell me you'd come from the country?"

He ducked his head as if he was thinking quickly. "Would you be spreading it around if it was you?"

Patience isn't—would never be—my virtue. I lowered my voice to the barest whisper, though I felt like shrieking at him. "Well, what about telling the dope that's running blind trying to protect your mate?"

"Sorry." He gave me an odd grin, like something I'd said was really funny.

The conversation had gone about as far as I had time for; something told me the 'Terro wasn't far away. "I've gotta go."

"Where are you?" he demanded.

"Why?"

"Our deal, Parrish. I want to *adjust* it. I've found somewhere safe for S— our friend. Can you meet me at the south boundary of Tower Town tomorrow?"

Adjust it? What kind of talk was that?

He frowned like he was wrestling with a difficult problem. Probably how to untie Mei's bondage knots, I thought nastily.

"Things have changed for us," he said.

"Me too," I allowed.

"You'll meet me then?"

"Yes," I said. And I cut the link.

I paid one of the Mueno clones with the second last of my loose cred and made a signal to them that we'd leave through the downstairs door. Sto pressed up heel-to-toe with me again, closer than my shadow.

How I hate clingy men!

We edged out of the room and down a small flight of stairs. The clones crowded behind us at an even less comfortable distance. A whisper of fresher outside air cleared my head as I eased the heavy door open.

Nearly outta here, nearly—

Until a young turk amongst them shouted. A palm screen glowed in his hand. The familiar One-World news jingle blared through its tiny speakers followed by a description of Sto.

Typical frigging Tert! Typical frigging world! A filthy-poor voodoo squat with chicken guts for curtains, zero furniture and someone owns a micropalm.

I yanked the door hard to get us out of there in a hurry. It set a heavy-duty cluster of spirit feathers free from the top of the doorjamb. They fluttered down onto the top of my head. Fresh blood from them spattered my face. I tried to wipe it and succeeded in spreading it across my lips. I spat the taste away. But it was on my tongue.

The Mueno clones froze in their tracks, knives out, like a bunch of waxworks. There was something in their faces that I didn't like.

Awe.

A sensation crept over me; a fire that began on my lips, ran down into my stomach and along the length of my body as if I was being burnt from the inside out. As quickly as it ignited it faded, leaving me edgy and scared.

I tore the feathers from my hair and kicked them away. It made me feel better, until the Muenos fell to the floor, chanting.

About then my courage deserted me. I turned and fled, running and running, with a gut full of terror and the prickle of voodoo at my back. I ran till my lungs refused to breathe and my legs turned to burning lumps of flesh. I ran till a pain in my side forced me to stop and huddle in a dark corner like a frightened kid.

Only then, did I remember Sto.

I hate spirit shit.

You don't see so much of it around Torley's or even the south side of The Tert. The Slag, though, was full of it. Voodoo, animism, satanism, tek worship.

And then there's Cabal Coomera; although I like to think of their brand of spirit wisdom as something more pure.

I'd sure never felt anything like that sensation be-fore. And the taste in my mouth. No matter how hard I spat, it wouldn't leave.

And now I'd lost Sto.

I figured I must have run at least ten klicks, down narrow side paths and through crumbling court-yards, none of it in a straight line. I checked my compass implant and worked out the direction I'd come from.

Who was I kidding? Nothing on earth would get me back in that villa. Not Sto, not his hulking, hick friend.

No one.

Nix.

Hell, they'd probably just anoint Sto with chicken blood and welcome him into the fold. The 'Terro wouldn't be able to distinguish him from the rest.

The 'Terro . . . damn!

Giving Sto up to the voodoo Mueno clones was one thing, but letting a media 'Terro take him was another. Besides, I kinda liked him.

I sighed heavily.

With gloom stealing the last of the daylight, I hiked it back in the direction I'd just come and tried to ignore the sinister shadows lurking on the edge of my vision.

Running at night in The Tert is a recipe for disaster—things changed constantly. An empty walk-way one day may be home to two families the next. Pretty soon I was forced to slow, hindered by the dark. I fretted for Sto's safety. What would they do to him before I got back?

Bug-filled fluoros haloed light onto small sections of villa walls here and there; sometimes a plastic imi-tation candle lit a brief stretch of cracked pathway, or curtains leaked yellow pinpricks of light outside. Mostly, though, it was plain dark. I resisted doing my lighthouse impersonation by switching on my miner's light and moved along as quietly as I could.

The humidity climbed rapidly with the onset of dark, settling upon everything like a warm, sweaty hand. Moisture collected and ran off rooftops, spitting dirty raindrops on me.

Just to top off my general troubles, The Slag night noises started up, scary enough to send any self-respecting weirdo crawling back into their hole.

I fingered my pistol, listening to the screams, the fights, the chanting and the inhuman grunting—once I thought I heard a baby crying in a high-pitched, totally unnatural wail—but about three klicks from the spot I'd run out on Sto, a real commotion erupted.

I stole around the edge of a villa set to find a shadowy, circular space, occupied by—what looked like from the outlines—benches and tables. A single straggling gum tree rose above them thrusting up branches that resembled fleshless fingers. From what I could tell, at least ten or more villa sets spiraled out from the space like the spokes of a wheel.

Sheets of plas covered most of the area, blocking the night sky. A tiny glint of stars leaked in where the tree had fractured the makeshift roof. By the sounds coming from near the base of it, someone was in bad shape.

I don't buy into other people's problems. The Wombat knows I got a bucketload of my own. So I crouched down to assess the best way to skirt the perimeter unseen and vamoose.

Two voices and a victim, screaming.

"The bitch razored me! Cut my fucking dick!" yelled one.

The other one laughed roughly. "Yeah, like she could find it . . . move over . . . I've got two of 'em."

The victim whimpered, weak and desperate, like

a drowning puppy. The sound caught in my chest, stopping my breath. The fact that I comprehended their strange dialect didn't register. The only thing I understood was rape.

Understood. Smelt. Felt. Hated.

Relived.

Without taking a step I left that dank space in the middle of The Slag and faced Jamon's 'goboys again. But this time my hands weren't tied, my legs weren't pinned . . .

They didn't even know I was coming.

Wading in like the fists and feet of justice.

Afterward, blood thundered through my body.

I didn't feel bad. Or good.

Something tapped my thigh. Someone.

"Th-thanks, lady? You OK?"

With difficulty I tracked the voice. Had it been there before?

In the barracks?

"You go. Someone will come look for them. Them's Plastique boys."

Plastique boys?

The present crashed back. Two unconscious bodies lay at my feet.

The voice persisted, "Nobody ever done nothin' like that for me before."

I looked around. A young, small girl with ragged hair peered back. She had no arms.

"I had to." My voice sounded strange, distant, like someone else. I'd just beaten two strangers most of the way to death, with my bare hands, on their body heat.

The girl smiled wanly, hopefully. "Glad you did. Otherwise I be dead now." She tapped me again on the thigh and I realized she used her foot, not her hand. "You get out of here. I show you how. Put hand on my shoulder. I repay."

I did as she said.

She led me away from the blood, like a dog with a blind owner, down the narrow spaces between crumbling walls and into a makeshift hut hidden beneath a flight of rusted stairs. I squatted inside by the weak light of a solar torch while she cleaned blood from my hands with a wet rag, squeezing it into an old hubcap. Her feet were stained with it. Meticulously she wiped me, again and again, till the redness on my hands was gone.

My knuckles felt busted and swollen. I'd used my hands when I could've razored them—that's why they were alive. I was grateful for that at least. Revenge didn't make killing feel better.

She disappeared out of the kennel dragging the hubcap between her toes.

When she returned she gave me an uncertain look. Under her eyes seemed bruised. They reminded me of Doll.

"Where you from, lady? I never seen you round Rosa before."

"Rosa?"

"Villas Rosa."

Villas Rosa. The Slag slums. The slums in the slums.

Hysteria welled. I found myself talking quickly until it subsided. "I'm from Torley's on the north side. I'm protecting someone. A red-haired guy. Something . . . happened. He's back aways, two or three klicks. I've got to get him. *Now!*"

The uncertainty on her face changed. "It is you," she whispered with dawning excitement. "Me thought it must be."

"What do you mean?" I demanded. "Who do you think I am?"

Yeah, some sort of weird question to ask an armless kid living in a dog kennel in the navel of a slum.

But under the grime and the bruised eyes she seemed sure of herself.

Lucky her.

"Media's chasing you. And 'Terro. It's on Common." She nodded to a small, battered netset.

Anyone could broadcast on Common Net. It was like a CB with visuals. All you needed was a kit, some regular sunlight and the right frequency.

"Muenos talk, talk." She made gestures with her toes like a mouth opening and closing. "I listen. Muenos say the one who wears the Feather Crown will save 'em. They's singing for you now."

Wears the Feather Crown? Uggh! The taste of blood amplified in my mouth.

I forced myself to think forward, past what had just happened, the men I had beaten. I felt shaken, yet, strangely, no remorse. "What's your name?"

She shook her head in answer. Her eyes settled on mine. Gray and oversized in a thin face framed by clumps of matted brown hair. She couldn't have been more than eleven.

I tried again. "What do you call yourself?"

"No one talk me. No one call me."

No one talk me?

Call it a girl thing, but to live in a world where no one ever spoke to you . . . I couldn't help myself. "Well I'm talking to you. I'm Parrish. How about I call you . . . Bras."

Her face flowered into a look I'd seen recently and hated. Trust.

I stifled a groan. Sto was already one problem too many. Much as my heart bled for this kid, what could I do for her? How many kids like Bras were there in The Slag?

"Bras know where you find red-hair one. Bras help you." She took delight in saying the name I'd given her, rolling the sound over her tongue.

I reached out and touched her gently on her thin shoulder. The fabric felt stiff with dirt, the useless sleeves long since torn off. "Thanks Bras, but it's dangerous with me."

She pursed her lips stubbornly. "Bras belongs you, now. We eat, then find red one."

She fumbled in the corner of the hut under a pile of rubbish and unearthed a half-eaten scrap that once might have been a pro-sub bar. Solemnly she handed it to me with her foot. "You chew first."

I realized I hadn't drunk or eaten since my encounter with Io Lang earlier in the day, but the pro-sub didn't exactly tickle my appetite. Nor did the sight of Bras's ribs through her flimsy clothes. "You eat, Bras. Then show me where Sto is. I'll give you money." I felt for my last credit.

Bras sucked on the corner of the bar then took a small nibbling bite. She repeated the pattern two more times, softening it with her saliva before chewing. Then she shoved the remainder in her pocket. "Bras want no money. Others *kill* Bras for money. Bras stay with Parrish."

"But how do you get food without cred?" It was a pretty stupid question considering what I'd seen of her life so far, but some things you just gotta ask.

"Bras eat low food."

"Low food?"

She puzzled at a way to make me understand. Then she shuffled her feet under the little piles of rubbish on her floor, sifting it expertly. "Low food. Y'know, left when Muenos finish."

"Rubbish," I said slowly, "you eat the rubbish the Muenos throw away?"

Her face became indignant. "No rubbish, good food. Just low food."

"No offense." Then a flash of intuition hit me. "You're not Mueno blood, are you?"

She smiled sadly. "Not Mueno." Then she brightened a little with her next thought. "Bras know who Parrish is. Parrish is Oya."

Oya? I've been called a lot of things before but Oya . . .

"Bras, I need to find the red-haired one, soon. Can you help me?"

She smiled and beckoned me out into the night with a wave of her foot.

Bras moved expertly through the darkness and with an energy that surprised me. Even half-starved and handicapped, she was traveling faster than me, accepting her life, moving forward, surviving. I suddenly wanted to get her some decent food, maybe even some prostheses. I wanted to clean her up, wash her hair.

Bras's route amongst the darkened villas cut the distance I would have traveled without her in half. For the amount of people I knew lived here, the dark was strangely deserted. "Where is everyone?" I whispered.

"They scared of Big One. Stay inside. Bras not scared."

She stopped and nodded toward a villa outline. It looked so like all the others around it that I wasn't convinced.

"Are you sure, Bras?"

She clicked her tongue impatiently. "Yes. Sure."

The front facade was indiscernible from the next one, and the next. Only a thin stream of light from the first-story window confirmed the likelihood of inhabitants.

Without warning, Bras scuttled off across the courtyard, like a crab without its pincers, stopping frequently to listen. I figured her caution was from habit, till I noticed movement in the deeper shadows of a retaining wall that had once bordered a garden bed in front of the villa.

"Bras. Wait!"

But she ignored me, worming along to the high end of the wall, where she stopped. Whoever stood concealed there froze. A ripple up my spine told me that they'd seen Bras.

I had no way to warn her, outside causing a major commotion. I watched and hoped that the shadower had other things on their mind than a feral kid in the dark.

Since when did things ever go the way I reckoned?

The brief unmasked flicker of an LED display was the only warning before something reefed Bras bodily over the wall into the blackness.

My stomach banged painfully into my lungs when my brain made the connection.

The 'Terrogator had Bras!

I didn't wait to think about it. Fear for her spurred me. I let it drive my legs across the courtyard in a blur of speed. Then I launched feetfirst over the wall at the spot Bras had disappeared and aimed a high kick. If I got lucky I'd take out its CPU with my titanium insert. But I kissed air and nearly flipped flat on my back on to the jagged 'crete.

Hauling up into a less than copybook crouch, I flicked on my miner's light and performed a clumsy three-sixty.

The 'Terro had vanished. But a set of baleful, green eyes caught in the light.

Canrat! Huge, pissed off and hungry.

It leapt straight for me, drool swinging like wet ropes from its massive canine jaws. Twice the size of a large Doberman with a long rattus tail, it caught me square in the chest.

We toppled backward. One of its legs slipped down between my arm and body. Instinctively I clamped my arm to my side, trapping it. With my other hand I yanked my pistol from under my flimsy coat.

As it bared its teeth ready to slash deathly furrows in my face, I shot its balls off.

With an unearthly howl the canrat staggered off me, its tail furled protectively under its bleeding torso, and crawled away. By the time I climbed shakily to my feet, I could hear ferals—animals and human—squabbling over carcass rights.

So much for being inconspicuous, Parrish!

But where had the 'Terro taken Bras?

As if on cue, a zigzag of lights spilled onto the courtyard. Muenos crowded into doorways the length of the circular villa set, jabbering in excited voices. Some hung out of windows.

I caught the drift of their excitement. *The Big One is dead,* and, *Oya killed the Big One.*

Oya? The name Bras called me.

The door immediately in front flung open and Sto hurled down the stairs. A deputation of Muenos followed him out but kept their distance.

"Parrish. You came back for me." His smile, even in the shards of doorway light, was a beam all of its own.

I punched him sharply on the arm. A warm, fuzzy reunion with a naive redhead while generously spattered in gollops of canrat teste, surrounded by an audience of heavily knifed Muenos calling me Oya, I could live without! Anyway, now that I'd seen him, I was more worried about the 'Terro and Bras. Other than being a bit shaky, Sto looked fine.

"What's down?" I said. Casual.

He caught my mood. "After the blood and feathers thing . . . well . . . they think you're their warrior witch or somethin'. They watched me, but nobody hurt me." He glanced over his shoulder then back. "They've been waiting for you to come. Singing."

"They weren't the only ones waiting," I said more heavily. A stale, after-adrenaline ache burned in my muscles. "The 'Terro's found us."

I didn't bother to check Sto's reaction to the news. Instead I switched my olfaugs to maximum sensitivity. 'Terros had a smell like meaty bones and were quicker than any augmented human. If it was coming back for Sto, I wanted to know.

Somehow, though, I didn't think it would just yet. 'Terros cammed their experiences back to their pilots—who then fed the stuff on to the networks for the twenty-four–seven Kick shows. *Kick Arse, Get your Kicks, Kick 'em While They're Down, Kick and Whack*—the names changed, but they were all the same. Net, dedicated to real-time violence.

Reality viewing was nothing new, but Priers and 'Terros gave it a vigilante edge that juiced most viewers and sent ratings stratos. By now three quarters of the world had probably seen Bras kidnapped, and my pitiful attempt to rescue her. Perhaps that live feed would keep the 'Terro off Sto's back for a while.

Sorta like foreplay.

I swore softly to myself. Next time, audience or not, no titanium-wrapped microchip was going to make an idiot out of me on pay TV!

"Oya?"

An obese Mueno, bloodred silk pants clinging to his enormous thighs, stepped forward into the arc of my light. His long braided hair shone faintly and he smelled almost clean. Compared to Bras he was obscenely overfed.

"Oya? We have heard that you have come."

"What have you heard, Mueno?" I hedged. It seemed likely they'd somehow worked me into some old myth. Punters needed heroes—didn't matter what religion they gigged to. Muenos were worse than most. It had something to do with their particular mash of Catholic, voodoo, tek worship. God's in the heavens, the animals *and* the machine! Crowded, huh!

"Oya comes to lead the battle." He bowed his head. "Muenos follow, Oya."

Muenos follow Oya? To battle?

My world got crazier by the second! "What's your name?"

His thick face folded in a mixture of uncertainty and pleasure. I worried for a moment he was going to fall onto his knees before me.

"Named Pas, Oya. Houngan and Rate Keeper."

A houngan was the Muenos' equivalent of a witch doctor. *But Rate Keeper as well? In this stink hole? Talk about extreme free enterprise!* "You do this for Topaz?"

He spat expertly, in disgust, and nodded. "Topaz was a strong leader. Now he deals mojo with the Dis man."

Mojo with the Dis man? Mojo was black magic. The Dis man had to be Lang. I thought back to Jamon's surprise dinner and suddenly wished I'd known more about its purpose.

"Well, Pas, Rate Keeper. I need to get to Tower Town, pronto," I said.

He nodded thoughtfully. "We can take you to the borders, Oya. Further than that and they will fight us. Is that what you want?"

"No, Pas," I said, hastily. "The border is fine. Let's go." Thoughts of the 'Terro prickled me.

But Pas hesitated as if weighing something important. "Then what do you want from us, after you leave?" A band of tension tightened around the crowd, as if he'd voiced everyone's unspoken question.

I wanted to shout, "How the frig would I know?" But what do you say to a gathering of knifed-up Muenos who are worried about you leaving them behind without a cause? You adopt your most sanguine look and say . . .

"I'll send for you when the time is right, Pas."

He seemed happy with this. A ripple of murmurs signaled he wasn't alone.

Then inspiration hit me. It wouldn't help Bras but there were surely others like her, so I added it in for good measure. "Pas? While you wait for my word, I want you to do something."

Predictably, his chest swelled with importance. "Anything, Oya."

"I want *you* to feed all the feral kids without families."

Even in the shaft of doorway light I could see his shocked expression. "B-but there is barely food enough," he spluttered.

I smiled ferociously, hopefully in the manner of a good Oya. "I know, you'll find a way."

Sto and I and four Muenos headed northeast toward Dis. As we walked, I fretted for Bras's safety but knew it was fruitless trying to track the 'Terro.

It would find us.

It would also find that using Bras as hors d'oeuvres had been a bad call. When it showed its skeletal face again, I planned to pulverize it, viewing audience of millions and all.

How?

Well, I was still working on that.

Sto stuck so close to my heels through voodoo town, I could feel his breath fanning my armpit. I stopped myself from decking him by taking regular deep breaths. Call me Parrish Patience.

The Muenos that Pas selected as escort were nearly as corpulent as him. Their hair fell loose though, like slick veils.

Mueno women wore crew cuts. Much more practical to my mind. Long, loose hair is like jewelry in a fight—disastrous. I knew a guy on the north side who swore by his lucky ring. Better'n any knuckle dusters, he reckoned. One time he got it hooked up on a 'Terro. Tore his finger right off. Loose hair was the same sort of liability. That's why I wore my dreads tied.

By dawn, I was so tired my teeth ached.

Sto couldn't have been much better but he kept
up, spurred, I think, by fear that I might leave him
behind again.

By midmorning the crush of people on the pavements and the narrow walkways was suffocating.
Heat trapped under the makeshift roofs radiated like
microovens. The breath-holding stink of unwashed
bodies; the babble of everyday troubles.

I could only guess how far we'd come. But my
compass read a comforting northeast, which I reckoned would take us into the heart of The Tert.

I began to worry about my reflexes if the 'Terro
came for me now. Fatigue and crowds and heat. My
head swam. I called to the nearest Mueno.

They'd fanned out to form a loose guard around us.

"I need to eat," I said, reaching into my pocket for
my last credit. The one I'd offered to Bras.

He approached me, pushed my hand away, and
disappeared for a minute. Then he returned with two
enormous tortillas stuffed full of greasy meat and
unrecognizable lumps of other matter.

When you live on pro-subs seven days a week, the
taste was awesome. My stomach bucked at the as-
sault but I toughed it out.

Sto was less hardy. Three quarters of the way
through he threw the lot up onto his bare feet.

Wastage.

We walked on, heading steadily northeastward,
until the fading intensity of light told me that it must
be late afternoon. Several times I'd been tempted to
jump a 'ped or a Pet. But pride kept me walking.

One time a Gas-gas growled past at low revs. It
caught my eye because you didn't see many true
bikes in this deep. And because the rider stared hard
at me before nosing the bike off into the crowd. For
a brief second I wondered if it might be the Cabal,
but I was too worn out to dwell on it.

Sto hung between two of the Muenos like a slaughtered animal on a pole. Occasionally he moaned. I promised myself as soon as the Muenos left us I'd find a hidey-hole for us both to sleep. I wasn't far off falling down myself, but I didn't quite trust Pas's deputation to watch over us while we slept.

As it turned out we didn't have much further. I'd noticed a slight change in the architecture—if you could call it that—over the last half an hour.

Most of The Tert had been built in circular groups of buildings connected by walkways, courtyards and small areas that had been pools or parks. Those "gaps" were usually a patchwork of shanty tents or lean-to's. Some were left vacant—like the one I'd discovered Bras in—usually because the surface or pavement had cracked and let the poisoned soil through.

That pattern changed as we continued, until the circular altered in favor of rows. Rows and rows of tiny apartments stacked on each other like a kid's building blocks.

Tower Town.

"Oya?" The man who bought the tortillas approached me and bowed slightly. "We go no further."

We faced each other under the twisted remnants of a fire escape. I nodded and looked around for a sign of the customary tollbooth. How much was this going to cost me? "Thank you. Tell Pas I won't forget."

The two carrying Sto let go of him. He fell at my feet, pale and sweating. I'd need to get him some clean water. Being a country boy, his immunity wasn't likely to hold up to the slum food he'd eaten.

As the Muenos faded away like they'd never existed, I took stock. How to find Dark when Sto wasn't likely to move another step? I sighed at his quaking exhaustion, and hoped he'd pick up a bit or I'd have some explaining to do.

The image of the big hick dressed in leathers brought a smile to my lips. Not much else had lately.

Almost immediately a blotchy-skinned dealer with sharp features and dramatically molded hair approached us to peddle. "You two look in bad shape. I got stim, lark. You pay. You say."

His face was piebald, not typical Mueno, and his boots screamed *different.* Iridescent pink, thigh-length and high-heeled. Muenos went for jackboots. I wondered what he was doing so far from Plastique.

"How much for stim?" I knew Sto's body wouldn't handle it right now. Most likely give him a heart attack. Ordinarily that would be OK—revival is pretty standard stuff—but I had no money and no resuscitation kit.

No. The stim was for me.

"Three hundred."

"Three hundred!" I was tired, not stupid. "Fifty and throw in some 'lytes."

He curled the corner of his brown-and-white lip. "You know your stuff. Where you from?" The question came as he handed me a package and a derm written on in universal, labeled "electrolytes."

I squeezed a little from the derm onto my finger and tasted it. It passed the test so I jabbed it into Sto's arm. Then I unwrapped the package.

The dealer leaned across me and peeled off a thin patch from the wrapping with two shiny, needle-point fingernail implants. I imagined they came in handy in his profession. I'd seen others with them; they were usually blades though.

He gave me a confident grin that left me wary. "I tell you what. Since you're a long way from home, I'll let you taste the wares before you pay. Can't be fairer than that, now, can I?" He stabbed the patch onto my arm with a needle nail, quicker than I could see.

The rush hit me instantaneously and I knocked him meters on sheer reflex.

Then a moment later I realized the truth. The rush was all me. Instinct. The patch was a sedative. I went from hyped to woozy in the space of a couple of minutes. I pivoted clumsily toward Sto and tried to explain, but my tongue had swollen in my mouth.

Sto crawled forward to break my fall. *At least the dealer hadn't gotten up*, I thought. As I went down, I saw the Gas-gas parked across the pavement.

Chapter Eight

The Angel plummeted through my veins slashing away traces of sedatives with the sweep of its heavy, golden red wings. It seemed furious at the unwanted chemical invasion. I waited for it to pass close to my retina, struggling to see its face, to know it . . .

Voices cut in.

"Is she dead?"

"No, but I gave her a maxi dose. She'll be out for a while longer yet. I know what I'm doing, you know."

"What about Sto?"

"The 'lytes she gave him helped. His strength is improving. But his feet . . . ugh."

"Ugh?"

"Third-degree burns, blisters. Infected. It looks like he even puked on them."

I listened intently, gradually separating the images of the Angel from the conversation. My head was mussed but my body felt alive, *wired* by the Angel's touch. Craving more.

After a while I recognized one of the two voices. The lark dealer was one. And the other was familiar . . . but somehow different. I kept my breathing light and even, and listened a bit longer.

The dealer continued, "I've cleaned them up but he won't be able to walk for a few days. And my head has felt better."

I clobbered him, I thought with satisfaction.

"Keep him comfortable and out of sight, Styro. The last few weeks have been hard on him."

"Sure. But what about *her*? What happens when she comes round?"

"I find out what deal she's cut with Lang. It could affect our plans."

"He's dangerous, boss."

"There's something else as well. Topaz is losing support. Rumors saying he's dealing mojo. Sto said the Muenos are calling Parrish 'Oya.' "

"Oya?"

"Oya is their female orisa—spirit power. They have a *long-tell* story. *Whoever the Feather Crown chooses will protect their futuretime*. Sto said a bunch of chicken feathers fell onto her head while they were trying to leave a Mueno's place, sprayed blood on her. Now they want to follow her into a battle."

Styro made a gargling noise. "They just might get what they want. Does she know who you are?"

"Not yet."

Dark! I knew the voice, not the tone. This tone was confident and sharp. Nothing like the slow-speaking giant I'd encountered in Hein's.

Suckered. When would I ever learn?

"The fewer people that know you're back the better," said the dealer, Styro.

"Sure. That's why I let her take Sto. Thought she'd attract less attention than me." He sighed. "That was the plan anyway. Keep a check on Sto, will you? I'll wait for a while. I want to be here when she comes round, otherwise someone might get killed."

"That girlie is out of control."

Girlie! I wished I'd tossed him farther.

"I wouldn't call her that." Dark laughed. "At least not to her face."

Styro shut the door on us and I lay there seething. "It's all right, Parrish. You can sit up now."

I opened an eyelid; the merest crack. Dark was seated on a chair about ten feet away, propped against the wall of a small room, dressed in a T-shirt and jeans. His wired hand rested in his lap.

I thought about ignoring him, but cramping muscles urged me to move.

I swung my body up and my feet down, pivoting, so I faced in the opposite direction. Call it vanity but he'd scammed me and had me drugged; he sure wasn't going to get first peek at me with a queen-sized narc hangover.

I scrubbed my face with my hands. "Hick trades leather disguise for casual gang leader look," I croaked nastily with a mouth like glue.

"You're the one who added two and two and came up with a minus, Parrish. I'm not a country boy, never have been."

"Sto?" was all I managed in reply.

"Fine. When his feet recover. You should have got him some boots, you know."

"*I should have got him some boots . . .*" I spluttered, swiveling on the bed. "What do you think I've been doing for the last two days? Catching a few rays on Cable Beach?"

Dark laughed. "At least I got you to look at me."

Well if that's what he wanted . . . I stood and wobbled over to him, slapping my hands down onto his knees so his chair crashed to the floor. Then I eyeballed him, so closely our noses touched.

"Is—this—better?" I spat the words, hoping my breath was as bad as it tasted.

He put his hand up automatically for protection. There was no dumb look in those 'zine eyes. Just amusement. And a shadow of uncertainty.

I liked it when people weren't sure how far they'd pushed me.

He took a deep breath and blew it out in my face. It was pleasant and musky. "Would you like to use the san unit? There's one here. It's a bit crude but . . ."

I stepped back and stood upright.

It's one thing wishing your halitosis on someone. It's another when they politely offer you the san to rectify the matter. My desire to wallop him in his clean-skinned mug escalated by the second, but I held on to it. First I needed some answers.

"I'm fine the way I am. It helps keep assholes away."

He nodded like he agreed with me. Then he shot me a piercing glance.

"What deal has Lang offered you? I know you met him at Mondo's. What does he want you to do? What's Jamon got to do with it?"

I stared at him in astonishment. "Who *are* you? I've just spent two days lugging your sweet little buddy around The Tert, while you played me for a sucker. And you're acting like *you've* got a right to ask *me* questions."

He tapped the tip of one of his real fingers to his lips. In jeans and a crumpled T-shirt he looked like he'd been snipped clean from a centerfold. I could practically smell the aftershave. Stubble shadowed his ebony skull and I wondered what he'd look like with hair.

"Did Stolowski tell you where he came from?" he asked.

"Yeah. Sure. *Him* I believe."

"Well believe this. I was there too. Press-ganged."

"And you think it was Lang or Jamon?"

"Three years in the Dead Heart. Friends I made there died next to me. At work, in their sleep, one or two, every day. It taught me some things. Like what's important. Like how you need to look after your own. Before that I didn't really understand." His expression seemed haunted. "Let's just say Jamon Mondo and Io Lang don't look after their own."

"Cryptic!" I sniped. *Too cryptic for me.*

If Dark had scores to settle, then bully for him.

I just wanted to do my deal with Lang to get Jamon Mondo off my back. Then if the 'Terro hadn't found me, I'd go pick a fight with a Prier, till it did. Maybe Bras was already dead. But something made me think she wasn't. Either way a 'Terro was going to pay for using a helpless kid as a ratings hook.

"So you're from here. Before?" I asked.

A smile touched his lips. "You mean, 'before Parrish'?"

"I guess. Whatever."

He stood in one easy motion; not ungainly, the way he had at Hein's and then at my place. An energy burned in him that I hadn't seen before. At full height he had centimeters on me and a rangy, wide body. The Tert wasn't built for people like us; he could easily have touched the ceiling. I heard the faint echo of Mei's catcall as he'd stripped off his shirt.

OK, OK, so he was downright gorgeous. And not as naive as I thought.

That was good. He didn't need my help and nor did Sto while he was with him. It made my life a lot simpler already. I could really hate people I didn't owe or need to help.

"I want to see Sto."

He frowned at me. "Sto needs some rest."

"I kept my part of the deal and you lied through your pretty white teeth. Now I want to talk to Sto, *and then* I'm going."

"You're not going to tell me what you're doing for Lang?"

"Hole in one, baby."

He reached out and put his real hand on my arm. He might as well have jabbed me with an electric prodder. I jumped like a rabbit.

"I'm sorry about misleading you, Parrish. But things moved quickly when I got back. You gave me a way to hide Sto, temporarily, while I sorted out biz. I'd heard you were smart and tough." He shrugged almost apologetically. "You sort of fell into my lap. It was perfect."

I closed my hand on his wrist. His forearm was thick and strong and his skin was warm. His face wore an expression I recognized from his hick image of a few days ago, earnestness—the look that had suckered me totally.

Not this time.

"I want to see Sto." I could feel my jaw set.

For one long moment I thought he was going to refuse. Then he prised my fingers from his arm, stood and left the room.

I followed him out and into a long corridor. Light filtered down in chessboard squares from the high, barred windows. A warren of rooms led off the hallway. As we walked, the view from the high windows told me we were in one of the long rows of units that had been melded together like everything else in The Tert. My compass implant told me it was slightly north of where Styro had drugged me.

Eventually Dark stopped and entered a room. Inside, I was surprised to see an infirmary decked out with some quality med-tek. The interior walls had been knocked out and it stretched for a distance.

"Nice place."

"Just the beginning," he said, vaguely.

Sto lay propped by pillows on a clean bed, wearing shades. His feet were bandaged and a lump under the sheet indicated he wasn't alone.

I marched over and ripped the shades off. "Feeling better?"

His face lit with a grin. "Parrish? You're awake."

"Yeah. And pissed off," I confirmed.

With a tinge of embarrassment he slipped his hand under and tugged at the lump. "Parrish's here."

Mei stuck her head out and snuggled her pink hair under Sto's armpit.

"Hi!" she said.

"You little piece of—"

I lunged across the bed to strangle her, but she moved quicker than I anticipated, flicking a knife in my face.

The knife itself didn't deter me; only the movement as Dark came into my peripheral vision. His arms hung loosely at his sides like he was ready to step in.

"Don't hurt her, Parrish," Sto pleaded. "She only did it to help me."

I spared him a glance. "Talk. Quick."

"We grew up together on the edge of the three deserts. Her mum traded food and women to us dust farmers. We were—she was . . . my grrl. When I got co-opted to the Dead Heart, she ran away. Ended up here. She was helping me. I l-love her, Parrish. Please?"

Mei wrinkled her nose at his declaration, and I wondered how her version of the story would sound. Somehow I couldn't see Mei as anyone's grrl.

I used her distraction to twist the knife out of her hand, spraining her wrist. It was the least I could do.

"Right," I ordered, "everyone out, except Sto."

Mei stumbled angrily from the bed, nursing her wrist, and over to Dark. He put an arm around her. "Don't do anything stupid, Parrish," he warned.

"Get out," I spat.

He backed to the door, dragging Mei, his eyes

fixed on me. "Ten minutes or I'll come and get you myself."

I waited till the door closed then I sat on the end of the bed. For whatever reason, I figured I'd get the truth from Sto.

I put the knife down. We both knew I wouldn't use it. I'd protected him for the last few days and for the moment he was still safe.

"Start at the beginning. And don't leave anything out."

He relaxed a little, leaning back on his pillow. "Never figured to see Mei again when I got co-opted. But she ran away. Waited for me here. More 'n a year ago, Dark got 'ganged there as well. He told me he knew her. Promised to get me out."

"What did he want in return?"

Sto shook his head, smiling slightly. "That's the thing about Dark, Parrish. He don't want nothing in return. He used to be a mover here; a turk. His family is old Tert. Look at this place."

I'd never been into Tower Town before. You didn't visit strange gang territories unless you had good reason. I had to admit, though, the med-tek was impressive. But I didn't tell Sto that.

"So what was he doing out at Dead Heart?"

"Something happened." He lowered his voice. "Someone got him done over by a miners' press gang. Next thing he's in the co-op. Just more meat, like me."

"But he got out."

"His family bribed the gangers. Same ones as put him there busted him out. Me as well."

You gotta love biz! "Then you came here?"

"Not straight away. He's got friends. Lots of 'em. We hid out in Viva until he could set things up to come back. He wanted to slide back in here real quiet—"

"—but you went and hitched a ride with a hit man," I finished.

He managed a rueful grin and a shrug. "Dark's got enemies here, still. Maybe it was one of them. Maybe it was just bad luck."

I had my cred on the enemies. "So then I blundered in and took some heat off while he settled in."

His head dropped. "Somethin' like that."

We sat in silence for a moment.

"He's got plans, y'know, Parrish."

I knitted my brows. How much did Sto know of Dark's real ambitions? Zip, I'd warrant.

"He says his time in Dead Heart taught him to look after his own. Like his *old ones* used to. He's taken care of Mei and me real well. Now he's come home to take care of the rest."

He stopped then, exhausted.

"You don't owe him everything, Sto," I said. "Just because he helped you get out."

He shook his head, eyes watery again. "You should know, Parrish. People like Mei and me got no real chance in life. Well, maybe Mei, she's smart and pretty. But Dark's gonna care for us. No bad shit, regular food, medic when we need it."

I sighed. People like Sto *did* need someone. Up until pretty recently so had I. But now I'd crossed sides and I was giving some serious consideration to the motivations of the "Darks" in the world.

Jamon Mondo at least I understood. *Understood and wanted to kill.*

"You're carting some serious heat right now," I said.

His lip trembled in acknowledgment.

"I hope he keeps his promises to you."

He gave me a look of resignation. "It don't matter if he don't, Parrish. Leastways, now, we got someone to believe in."

"Yeah, well, we could all do with that," I said quietly.

He reached across and touched my hand; told me something I didn't want to hear.

"You're like him, you know. People believe in you."

Dark pointed northeast. He was standing in a foothold among the ridges of sleeper cocoons glued to the roof. Some of them were occupied, others padlocked as though the owners didn't care for the neighborhood.

"Follow your compass north, and you'll wind up back at Torley's."

I'd already figured that, but I let him bring me up top anyway. The view was amazing. Sometimes you forgot about the sky when you were in The Tert. Sometimes the only time you saw it was on the net. But up here it hurt your eyes with its bigness.

It also scared me a little, the sea of roofs, patterned like an endless, chipped mosaic floor. If you looked closer it fractured into millions of cocoons, spindly mic dishes and dirty plascrete. Like putting a microscope on skin.

It was a pink and gray early-morning sky. I'd wasted a whole day here. But in some ways it had been worth it, just to see this.

"Where's Dis from here?" I asked.

Dark turned to the south. You could glimpse the ocean on the horizon, the merest strip of tarnished silver.

"In between," he said. "No one goes there now. Our *heartland* ails."

Grand words, maybe, but they made me shudder.

Halfway up into the sky, in all directions, a haze drifted carrying the scent of The Tert. I had the urge to fly right out there and scoop the muck away. Like my dream where the Angel had swept the narcotics from my blood.

I'd barely given the dream any thought, but now the memory twisted in my stomach. What had Dark said about Oya and the Muenos? "Whoever the Feather Crown chooses will protect their futuretime."

Well, that was a gig I could live without!

Whatever they believed, I hoped Pas was taking care of the feral kids. And I hoped Bras was alive.

I must have had a strange look on my face. Dark had turned back and was staring at me.

"Be careful of Lang and Jamon Mondo, Parrish," he said.

"And that's all you're going to say about it, I suppose. No explanations."

He smiled. A force-twenty, devastating grin. "Would you believe me anyway?"

"Probably not," I agreed. *But if you keep smiling at me like that, I might line up in the devotional queue behind Sto and Mei.*

He handed me a comm spike.

"What's this?" I asked, surprised.

"In case you need me," he said casually. "Call."

A flick of my fingers would have sent it over the edge, into oblivion. I wanted to do that more than anything in the whole goddamn world. Instead my left hand tucked the clip safely into a pin slot in the tank top of my suit.

"Thanks."

Note to self: Cut off left hand, it's a tart.

PART TWO

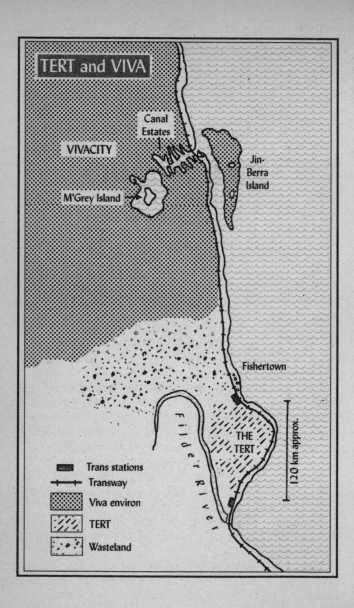

TERT and VIVA

VIVACITY

Canal
Estates

M'Grey Island

Jin-
Berra
Island

Fishertown

THE
TERT

Filder River

120 km approx.

Trans stations
Transway
Viva environ
TERT
Wasteland

Chapter Nine

The landlord had left an overdue rental jingle embedded in the door of my room. When I opened it, the damn thing sang Abba at ninety decibels. Personally, I'd rather six goons with semiautos waiting for me. But *Abba*?

They were touring Vivacity at the moment. Or, should I say, their clones were. The real Abba were long dead. This lot were about the sixth set of DNA replicas.

They weren't the only repros running around, either. The Rolling Stones had been and gone, the Beatles, Nirvana, and of course, the big "E." Something wasn't quite right with the teknology yet. Most of them committed suicide or died young.

Come to think of it, maybe they had got it right.

There was a constant stink about the ethics of it, but while it was selling music the performers' "estates" seemed to be in two minds.

Inside my room I stripped and cross-legged it in the san unit, letting the water blast over me till my skin wrinkled.

Then I got out and sat naked on the edge of my bed. I rifled through my dirty nylons for the disk Lang had given me. It had caught in the seam.

I cracked the casing and tried to recall his exact words.

Here's an address. Bring me the contents of their computer files. If anyone sees you, kill them . . .

The address printed on the outside of the disk was unfamiliar, the location—freaking impossible! Eighteen Circe Crescent, M'Grey Island, Viva.

Shite! How was I going to get there? I chewed on the problem till Merry 3# mouthed a drum roll and wiggled her latest dance routine.

I waited impatiently. The see-through girl was getting to be a serious show-off.

"You got mail, Parrish."

"Get on with it!"

I half expected it to be the landlord, who was one of Jamon's aging 'goboys. But the first was Jamon. His pale snake's face was livid and twisted.

"I don't like unexplained absences, Parrish. Be with me for the weekend or I'll set the dogs loose."

The second had no traceable sender and was a synth. "The goods are still required by Monday."

Lang!

A heavy weight found my shoulders. It was Friday. Jamon wanted me in his rooms tonight. Lang wanted me on a B and E in Viva.

Jeez, I always get the best choice of dates!

In this case, though, there *was* no choice. To be rid of Jamon, I had to steal for Lang.

I rummaged in my cupboard and found some dried food. Then I set about kitting up. I planned to be outta here before Jamon decided he'd waited long enough. No doubt 'goboys were already watching my door.

Into my pack went my 7.62 mm sniper rifle and the Glock copy. Two fresh pins slotted into my tank top. Then my pride and joy, my charm bracelet—payment from my most lucrative ever minder's job, an Equatorial trader with serious munitions connections who wanted protection while he surfed Torley's for suitable rough trade. The charms doubled as small stun explosives, apart from one, a cute mushroom, which sprayed a short blast of hallucinogenic gas. Worked well in small spaces.

My working kit consisted of a SOG that made the multitask knives around look like nail files and a hacker's "dream" pack—worm, gateway and password mole, now upgraded courtesy of Raul Minoj. It wasn't elaborate by most professional standards, but B and E wasn't exactly my line. At my height you were an easy target if you stuffed up.

Besides, I had a few moral problems with the whole concept. I didn't like to steal. It showed—in my opinion—a distinct lack of class.

I tried to rationalize Lang's job in my mind. In this case I was poaching information not goods. And to be honest, if it meant Mondo's backside locked away I would have stolen the King of Viva's gonads.

Only two suits hung in my 'drobe, khaki pants and working singlet, and my matt black velvet skintight. I chose the velvet. Call me vain, but a girl's gotta go to the city dressed up. I slipped gray overalls over the top. Flameproof, acidproof. My most expensive glad rag!

As I ran over my kit again, an image intruded, making it impossible to focus.

An angel with heavy, golden red wings. My Angel.

I sat up with a jolt.

My Angel?

Why was I thinking like that? Maybe this voodoo talk was getting to me.

When I'd gotten Jamon off my back I'd go check up on Pas, see if he was feeding the ferals. Then I'd find out some more about the feathers and the blood, what they really meant; and about Oya.

Mei probably knew something, but I didn't trust her anymore. Did I ever? Maybe I was being hard on her, but she broke the rule. Never double-cross your female friends—even for your man.

Not in my world.

On impulse I keyed Minoj's line on my comm. His mouth appeared on-screen first, then the rest of his face built around it. Glossy hair and white teeth. Weird!

"What could the most popular girl on the block want with me?"

I ignored the bait. "Anchor?"

The image froze while he considered my request for a secure line. Weighing my value.

"Wait," said the lips.

The screen blacked for a few seconds, then he reappeared, older and dirtier with decayed teeth. The real Minoj.

"What do you want, Parrish? This is a risk for me. You're hot property."

"When am I not?" I grinned.

He didn't laugh, so I plunged on. "I need some information about a guy. Used to live around here a few years ago. A would-be with a bit of a following, who suddenly disappeared."

Minoj gave an exaggerated sigh. "Do you know how many of those there have been?"

"This one's different. They say he's old family. Big guy, with charisma. Calls himself Dark."

Minoj scraped his finger along his front teeth. It was probably the closest they got to hygiene. "Sounds like love, Parrish."

I scowled at him.

He continued, "There was one. Tall, very thin. A user. Amphetamines and lark, mainly. Ms. Feast was his dealer back then. He vanished. He must have trampled on someone's toes."

Doll? "Whose toes, Minoj?"

"My memory doesn't work so good without the sweet oil of moolah, my little Oya."

My blood chilled. "Where did you hear that name?"

"The Muenos are building shrines to you in their simple homes. They pray that you think kindly of them." He rolled his eyes. "Topaz is not altogether happy about the competition. How unfortunate for him that an orisa manifests when there has been none for so long."

Topaz unhappy with me? Well he could get in the queue! "What'll it cost for you to tell me who vanished this guy?"

A strange expression crossed his face. "Are you in your room?"

"Yeah," I said suspiciously. "Why?"

"Oh, Parrish! And I credited you with much more sense."

"What do you—'"

A hammering on my door was short but emphatic.

"Au 'voir, little thing. Give my regards to the Dead Heart."

He cut his transmission.

The Dead Heart! Minoj's warning sent fear shooting to my toes.

I reefed the chair over to stand on it and throw my kit up through the manhole. But something was wrong. The cover wouldn't budge. I shoved as hard as I could. Nothing.

Someone had sealed me in.

I'd only been trapped, physically, once before . . .

My arms ached, stretched wide by two 'goboys; the inside of my thighs throbbed, raw with bruises.

"Turn her over," *Jamon ordered them,* "she looks disgusting."

For a second relief poured through me, as they loosed

*my limbs. Then they tightened them again, my face shoved
into the slick, hard floor. I think I stopped whimpering;
there was nothing left but a kind of numbness.*

*Jamon's breath slithered hotly around the side of my
face.*

*"You understand now, don't you, Parrish, that I am
the one who owns your life?"*

I emerged from my memories like a drowning person taking a breath. *No one* was ever going to trap
me that way again!

Hoicking my kit onto my back, I yanked my door
open. Abba strummed for one long second as I barreled straight over a peeping 'goboy. My knee kissed
his face. As we went down, he bit as hard as his
specially 'gineered canines would let him, locking on
to it.

I straddled his face, screaming, as he tried to lift
my kneecap off. In desperation I stuck three fingers
in the side of his mouth to prise his jaw open. Not
a preferred option—'goboys had hollow incisors that
funneled poison. I knew my overall would stand up
to the biting—if it didn't go on too long. But would
my kneecap stay attached?

He jerked his feet up, trying to rake my back with
his preternatural toenails. Mei reckoned they grafted
them off dead people.

Noise on the stairs told me others were coming so
I ditched the desperate idea and went for the guaranteed. Pulling my fingers from his mouth, I grabbed
a pin from my tank. When I shoved it into his eyeball
he howled in pain, freeing my knee. I was up and
hobbling wildly in the other direction before he could
howl again.

It wasn't pretty—what I'd done. But Jamon was
never going to trap me again, not alive. The 'goboy
would survive: eyes were easy to replace.

Chapter Ten

Normally, going from The Tert to Vivacity was a simple matter of paying a toll at the north end. A maze of enormous, discarded plastic pipes protected you from the poisonous soil. Walk through them, then catch the Trans-train to a Vivacity station. But that wasn't an option today.

Instead I had to leave from the northeastern stretch of The Tert. It had been natural bush once. A glorious stretch of tropical exotics and lushness that unfurled down to a sparkling beach. At least, so the archival holos said. Nothing much grew on it now, excepting a mud-colored fungus.

I jogged quickly over it to the last villa set. The buildings all faced out onto the brown waste. On the outskirts you could "feel" the weather more acutely and I zipped my collar up against the humid drizzle. It was actually stinking hot, but I couldn't stand having a wet neck.

I also didn't want Teece to see my black velvet underneath. He might think I'd dressed for him.

Teece owned an *alternate* way out of The Tert. It had been a lucrative number for him over the last couple of years; the quickest way to Fishertown, as the crow flies. Slummers were his main client base, but others used it too, if they were in a hurry or wanted to avoid the pipes.

Teece had been my first client when I moved from the 'burbs. I'd done a week as his minder while he set up his brand new biz. Turned out he was a biker with championship freestyle events to his name and enough sun-bleached hair to piss off any surfer. His sideline was cracking, so I took payment in bike lessons and 'puter crime. Being taught by a pro in anything never hurt.

These days Teece avoided Torley's. Too claustrophobic, he said. Nothing like a sunset over Fishertown, Teece reckoned. He'd even wanted me to live out on the edge of the waste with him. A business, sex and love deal.

It was the "love" bit that scared me off.

Anyway, I'm a city grrl. All that space gives me the creeps.

I found him sitting at a desk in his front office, overseeing a queue of unhappy customers. They were bitching about the price. It didn't surprise me. Teece was always quick to recognize a valuable commodity.

"This is double the normal fee," a thin, sun-dried Fisherwoman complained.

"And there are double the risks with this embargo on," he argued. "If my bike is destroyed. Poof! Where do I get the money to replace it? I am merely covering my costs. Insurance."

As if to back up his claim, the office rattled as a military bat swooped past overhead.

He smiled at her, teeth clamped around an overfat cigarillo. Wisps of smoke escaped. For a second, he could have been Raul Minoj's twin.

They were nothing alike really. Teece was as blond as Minoj was swarthy. He was strong, where Minoj

was withered. Yet they shared the same feral talent
for business.

The Fisherwoman seemed to be wavering. Teece
patted her shoulder sympathetically. "I think it is
wise to have second thoughts," he comforted, "the
waste is dangerous at the moment."

He'd read her perfectly. She slapped the money
down and marched out. A murmur echoed back
along the queue.

As Teece began the next negotiation, he spotted
me and signaled one of his men to take the desk.

"Parrish," he said aloud. "*Lovely,*" he whispered
as I got closer, embracing me fiercely. Teece was the
one person in the world who made me feel beautiful,
even though I wasn't.

We stepped into the back office—a comm cache
with a narrow view of the bike yard. A fan stirred
minute dust particles among the cathedral of hardware. Sagging lo-res prints of racing bikes decorated
the walls.

Outside the Fisherwoman fumbled with her kick-
starter.

Teece sighed. "My oldest bike. Due for scrap. I
hope some pieces are left."

I stared hard at him. "She won't make it?"

"She won't make it."

I swore softly, at Teece. I couldn't warn her, now.
She wouldn't listen.

"Don't you ever set me up like that, you bastard!"

He feigned hurt. "How could you even think such
a thing? Anyway"—he shrugged—"Militia aren't
damaging anyone. Just arresting them."

"What do you mean?"

"This embargo is a touchy thing, lovely. The Militia have to assist the media to find Razz Retribution's
murderer. On the other hand they don't want to be
seen as butchers. A situation may occur otherwise.

Riots. Spills from The Tert into Vivacity need to be avoided at all costs. We couldn't have the riffraff and the terminally insane mixing with the real people."

"But the media do what they like. They don't need the Militia. Those damn Priers are running 'Terros right into the heart of The Tert," I said.

"Aah. It's a part of life. We must accept it, lovely."

"I don't accept it," I declared, thumping his desk. "Governments full of crooked lawyers and businessmen used to run the world. Now it's frigging journalists. What's the difference?"

He laughed at me. "What do you prefer? Anarchy? I thought perhaps you would grow wiser with age, lovely. We *need* authority. It leaves us a simple choice. We fight it or we bend over. Either way there is meaning in life."

"Crap!" I said. "I didn't know you were so unimaginative, Teece. Don't you ever dream about anything other than this gutter?"

This time his hurt expression was real. "I like this gutter. What more do I need? I have money. I have a little power. For Chrissakes, I even have a view."

We'd had this argument before and finished it the same way. He went back to his life and I blundered along in mine. In Teece's mind I'd *chosen* to come here from the spanky suburbs and yet I wanted more.

For a moment or two I'd toyed with his offer of a partnership. He was kind, he was attractive, he had money; it would have been a way out of Torley's.

But that was before Jamon. Nowadays, even Teece wasn't offering.

"Can you hire me something that will make it across?" I asked.

His washed-blue eyes got vague while he considered my question. The even tan on his face and his bleached hair reminded me of the guys in old surfing 'zines. Teece, the mixed metaphor. The original bikie surfer!

"It's not a place to be going. Truly, Parrish."

"I believe you, Teece," I said, "but this is important."

"How are you going to pay for it?" He raised an eyebrow and gave a sly, expectant grin.

I wavered. It would be easy to sleep with him to cancel my debt. Payment in kind. But something had changed inside me. Something to do with Bras; and the night in the barracks; and Doll; and mostly Jamon. The physical act itself wasn't the issue— giving away my power was.

"Sorry, Teece. Not this time."

He eyed me intently. "Something's happened?"

I nodded, struggling to keep the excitement out of my voice. "Yes. I've got a chance to make my life my own again. And even some scores."

He stood up and walked around to my side. He only reached just past my shoulders but somehow he always seemed bigger.

Outside sirens wailed in the distance. He pulled me gently to the window and pointed. "See, lovely. *That* is your chance."

About a third of the way across the waste the Fisherwoman wove her bike frantically, dodging fire from a 'copter. Suddenly the bike skewed and flipped, catapulting her off. Within a few seconds a jaw-net lowered and trawled her limp body into the sky. The bike lay, throttle jammed on, screaming its guts out.

"You got enough bikes for those people out there?"

He nodded cautiously. "Yeah. So?"

"Then let's deal. And Teece . . ."

"Parrish?"

"I want one of yours."

Suspicion chased surprise across his face. I knew he had a private fleet. I'd never seen them, but he was a rev-head. Bikes were his passion.

"What's the payment?"

"A vintage Brough Superior SS100. I'll set up the deal."

"You *know* where I can get one?" His voice rose.

"Yes." I was lying.

He probably guessed it, but the slim chance that I wasn't made it impossible to ignore. I knew how to pique his interest. The Brough was one of the first superbikes ever made. The early ones had a JAP engine, Harley forks. There were probably only a handful of them in the world. I'd find him one, all right. I just wasn't sure how. Or when.

"How are you going to get across there? Nighttime's no better. They're scanning with IR."

I smiled. "Do we have deal?"

"You'll bring me back my bike unharmed. And set up a deal on the Brough?"

I nodded.

"Then we've got a deal." He rolled his eyes. "I must be crazy."

"Try this for crazy," I said and strode out of the room.

In the office the queue had dissolved into an unhappy clump of punters, discussing the fate of the Fisherwoman. I vaulted onto the table and addressed them.

"You want to get across?"

Mostly there were nods. A couple stared, hostile.

"Then I say we leave together. It gives us a chance. There's only one 'copter out there. Even if they bring more, it's not enough to stop all of us."

"What about the ones they get?"

I issued the challenge. "I'm willing to risk that. My business is urgent. What about yours?"

"What about the price?" a punter called out. "It's twice as much as usual."

I turned to Teece. "You going to give us a chance, Teece? Or are you going to watch your bikes wrecked one by one? Or go out of business, 'cos no one will risk the crossing?"

He picked at his fingernails, sensing the mood of the room change. They turned to him now, in support of my idea.

Eventually he raised his hands. "All right! But you each pay a hundred cred extra, as insurance. And if you don't deliver them to Mama, I'll hunt you down."

Mama was a humorless ex-Sumo toll keeper. He penned Teece's bikes safely on the Fishertown side and worked the system in reverse.

When it came to bike thieves, Mama didn't have a scrap of maternal compassion.

While Teece's men took DNA prints for ID and allocated bikes to bodies, he took me through the villa out into a back area covered with corrugated plas. In one corner a shed had been improvised. I could see the security sensors winking around it at various angles.

Teece tripped his fingers over a pad tacked on to the door, and lights flooded the inside. Six bikes gleamed at me like wary beasts. He caressed each one in turn, trailing his fingers over them with a lover's touch.

"Almost as lovely as you."

I checked to see if he was being flippant. His expression said no.

"They all have a name." He stopped next to a red, streamlined number with silver and black faring. "The last model Katana before the company was swallowed by Gerda. Eleven hundred ccs and wire wheels. I named her after you."

I waited for a laugh or a smile. This was making me uncomfortable. A joke, maybe, a lecture, a smart remark, anything . . .

Not that being likened to a bike juiced me much. But coming from Teece it was patent admiration.

"So which one will it be then?" I asked.

"Any except this one." He placed his hand on the red bike. "She's mine."

"But they're all yours," I said, puzzled.

"This one's different."

In the end I chose a dirt bike with a racing engine, white body and green and gold faring. I rode it up the line of about thirty bikes. Every punter had a helmet that recycled the air. Teece paid meticulous attention to helmet maintenance. A lung full of true waste dust was as dangerous as rolling naked in a slag heap.

Teece understood that a dead client was a bad client.

"Ready?" I shouted.

The engines growled in answer.

"Remember to stay in a group. If you go it alone, you're on your own!"

I pulled my helmet on and sniffed the ventilator. It smelled clean and good with a whiff of sunblock. Teece hadn't said good-bye but he'd given me one of his own helmets to wear. That was his way of saying "come back."

To signal a start, I punched my fist twice in the air. The small pack shuddered and surged forward.

I bunched in amongst them, shivers dancing up my backbone, hair stiff like it might snap if I touched it. I wondered, briefly, whether animals felt like this when they ran in packs.

We hung together tightly for the first couple of klicks, a minihurricane of dust and exhilaration. Sweat drenched my black velvet. I concentrated on staying upright, away from other foot pegs and tires, and kept my eyes on the helmet in front of me.

Before long a shadow flitted across us, and then

back, making a low pass. Panic rippled through the pack. The faster riders accelerated; the slower ones fell behind into a splinter group.

For a minute I faltered between the two, alone, like a straggling bird.

As the 'copter came back for another pass, I tucked in tight behind the faring and gunned my machine. It answered with the hunger of a racing bike coming off the bend into the home straight.

The 'copter missed its opportunity and peeled away chasing another target. I risked a quick backward glance as we regrouped. Behind us, zigzagging like hell on wheels, trailed a late starter.

Nice handling, stupid risk, I thought, tucking down.

We hammered along the next five klicks without a worry. Just open space and speed.

With the Trans-line only two klicks away, we'd nearly made it.

Too easy, I thought, *too damn easy.*

Teece would be watching us with his binoculars. I wondered what else he could see. I wished I had a psychic connection with him.

What's happening, Teece? Tell me what you see.

Nothing came back.

Then two Special Forces bats descended from nowhere and exploded a trench in front of us. I hit a hole and took the fall like a true pro.

Thanks for nothin', Teece!

The fall winded me but that was all. My overalls and helmet did their job, and I knew how to roll.

The bike wasn't so lucky.

Riders lay scattered around, a tangle of noise and confusion in a soup of dust. Some of the back ones rode over the top. To my right a rider lay still, hand trapped jamming the accelerator open, his neck at right angles to his body. I didn't wait to check for a pulse—by the angle of neck, there wouldn't be one.

I freed his hand and mounted his bike at a dead run. The bike's wheels hit the dirt spinning. My heart sledged against my ribs. Any harder and it would bust right through.

I wasn't the only one still upright. Maybe ten others pulled out of it. At a glance they all had the same luck as me, to be on the back of enduro bikes.

We scrambled out of the bunkers and automatically bunched together. The bats had gone but the 'copter was back.

Had the trailing bike got lucky?

The 'copter began firing in an arc behind us. Sharp sprays of dirt added to the whirlwind that dogged us. Its speaker blared a warning order, but my helmet muffled the sound. I didn't know what they were saying.

I sure as heck didn't care.

The Trans-line was in sight now, with the long snakelike gray of a Trans-train slithering along its tracks. A canopy of illegal aboveground electricity lines crisscrossed the lid of Fishertown beyond. The lines made it too dangerous for the 'copters to try and snare anyone in Fishertown. Once across the Trans-line I was safe.

Safe?

As the line got closer, the temptation to peel away from the others and break for it alone had me by the pants. A rider in front of me gave in to the same urge and veered right. The 'copter netted him within a hundred meters and winched him up. His arm dangled through the webbing like a branch broken from a tree.

Under a klick to go and the rest of us were suddenly cured of doing it alone. We stuck together tighter than a bunch of formation fliers.

The 'copter sprayed some serious flak in front of us but I was ready for it this time. I hit the first ridge at full throttle and jumped the width of the gully. Yeeha! It was the closest damn thing I'd ever got to flying.

We lost a couple in the jump, but we were closer to the line and the 'copter was running out of space. On the other side of the Trans-line power poles and humpies wavered in the heat. Call me an optimist; I swear I could taste ocean salt in the back of my throat.

My heart lightened with hope. Then two 'copters appeared, specks of black in the north sky. In the distance a long thin line stretched between them, like a towrope, only they were flying abreast.

Alarm damped my jubilation. I circled my fist and pointed, warning the nearest rider. By the time the message had spread through the diminished pack the 'copters were bearing down, bulbous tek insects flexing their tails. Deformed wasps. Pissed-off wasps, connected by some sort of weird birthing cord.

Then the cord dropped free into the shape of a giant net. They were going to trawl us all!

With only a hundred meters to go, I swore into my helmet, wishing to the great frigging Wombat that I was still on the racing bike.

Sometimes there's no substitute for grunt.

The 'copters veered slightly east over Fishertown and banked to come straight at us.

I realized I was holding my breath, waiting for everything to slow down so I had time to analyze detail and plot an escape.

But nothing slowed, no ideas formed in my brain, just the blur of objects on a collision course and a crazy wondering what it was like in a Viva jail.

Did they feed you pro-subs?

As the 'copters descended to drop their net, the bike pack exploded apart like fireworks. I arced slightly north, then started to weave frantically. The third 'copter chased me. I managed a spare second to feel sorry for myself.

Why me?

I redlined the bike over the last distance, mesmerized by the Trans-train. If I slowed now the 'copter would net me, if I kept my current speed I was going to hit the last carriage.

Choices! Choices! None of 'em good.

But I was so close. I just couldn't back off. Couldn't go to jail. Couldn't bear the thought of Jamon's snake smile when he heard.

Parrish, behind bars?

Decision made.

You always like to think you'll see things to their end; use your wits till the last possible moment. Maybe it was reflex, something out of my control, but when the crunch came—those last seconds when the gray carriage blurred into a wall of metal and the net fell to trap me—I closed my eyes.

Chapter Eleven

When I opened them, the world was upside down and in fast-forward. I'd made it, but without the bike. I'd missed the Trans carriage and the bike had flipped on the track.

It wouldn't have happened if I'd been looking.

For the second time today, I hit dirt.

This time the world went black.

When I came to, the first thing I registered was relief. Thank the Wombat my helmet was still on. I'd trashed Teece's bike; his helmet would just about ice it. I'd spend my life paying him off.

It also meant I hadn't gummed any poisonous dirt.

Only then did I pay attention to the pounding that hammered the entire length of my backbone and up into the base of my skull. When I tried to move, fingers of pain radiated out and over my shoulders. When I tried to breathe, my lungs burned.

Anxious images crowded on top of each other. Paralysis. Not being able to run. *Not being able to run.*

I forced myself onto my hands and knees, refusing to accept the possibility.

Someone touched me. It sparked a fire of agony

across my back. "Don't," I whispered, "please don't."

The same someone lifted me gently, as if I weighed nothing, murmuring a muffled reassurance. Part of my brain registered the impossibility of one person carrying me. I weighed ninety kilos.

The other part of me didn't care what happened as long as the pain stopped.

My helmet came off. Carefully. So carefully.

Then the side of my overalls pulled away followed by my black velvet. I heard it tear. I wanted to cry. My best outfit.

A cold feeling crept up my thigh and then the pain, mercifully, stopped . . .

Gradually my vision cleared. I was in the half dark of a Fishertown humpy. I knew that because I could smell smoked fish and see the jagged lines of stitching that held the tent together.

A voice spoke to me. "The painkillers won't last long. But I know a medic in Viva. I'll take you to her. I think you might have broken some ribs and your shoulder is dislocated." The voice laughed. "Spectacular fall, though!"

With an enormous effort I turned my head a fraction.

"You!"

Dark smiled at me. His teeth were toothpaste-commercial white against the gloom. How did he manage that, I wondered, on a diet of pro-subs and cruddy foods?

He continued, like I was interested, "I've got biz in Viva. Needed to get there in a hurry. Lucky for you."

Lucky! I had other names for it! "But who's minding the babies?" I whispered.

"Funny!" He tugged my clothing across my thigh. I suddenly realized I was naked from the waist down on one side. Even the string of my G had been torn.

"Sorry 'bout your clothes. They were badly ripped and I wanted to give you a maximum dose. Seemed the best spot."

I reached automatically to cover myself, trying to tie a knot in my G with one hand.

"Don't move," he snapped. "The drugs are masking the pain. You may have broken more than your ribs. I can't be sure."

I sagged back weakly. "Great!"

"Promise me you'll lie still and I'll get you to this medic."

"And how are we going to get there?" I sniped miserably. "Medivac?"

"Ahuh," was all he said, and left.

Note to self: Never joke about things you don't know the answer to.

I lay alone in the humpy, drifting in and out of awareness. Once I opened my eyes and stared into a woman's face. She was gaunt, leather-skinned and unhappy. Her hair was plastered around her sunburnt face in a dark, oily crop. I tried to say thank you for the use of her home, but the words wouldn't form in my mouth.

I wondered later how I knew this dingy tent was her place. Maybe it was the sour expression she wore. Kept for uninvited guests.

For a while I dreamt.

The Angel was back, working feverishly inside me; fighting infection, healing bone and tissue, cauterizing hemorrhages with the tip of its platinum sword. It seemed angry that I'd hurt myself. It needed me. "I'm sorry," I kept saying, "I had to do it. I had no other choice."

My cheeks were wet with contrite tears when Dark

roused me. He looked surprised, and then concerned. "Pain bad?"

I nodded, embarrassed. It seemed the easiest explanation. But in fact, inexplicably, the pain was less.

"The 'copters have gone but the ground search is starting. We need to move."

"But I've got to get the bike and the helmet to Mama's first."

"Mama?"

"Fat wrestler with a strap-on automatic."

Dark's forehead wrinkled with distaste. "We met."

"What's wrong, Dark?" I rasped. "Didn't your mama look like that?"

He ignored my jibe. "He's collected them already. Christ, Parrish, your bike was in bits! It could have been you."

"Least I wasn't crazy enough to ride across by myself. That was you trailing, wasn't it?"

He smiled this time. "Mama said to tell you you'd lost your insurance *and some.*"

It hurt to sigh, but I managed it. I also managed a quick prayer to the Wombat that Teece'd be collecting the *and some*—not Mama.

"Ready then?"

"Sure," I lied.

The woman with the gaunt face helped him carry me out on an old blanket. She was strong for her size and condition. Most Fishertown Slummers were tough from hauling nets and gaunt from their poisoned, mainly fish diet. People said they carried some sort of mutated gene that let them survive the heavy metals in their food. Whatever the truth, it didn't prevent most of them resembling beef jerky.

This woman looked pretty damn good—for a Slummer. And she wasn't too happy about me.

"Why are you doing this for her Loyl-Dark?" she hissed. "This your woman?"

Loyl?

A scorching, late afternoon sun had burnt away the drizzle. I squinted out at the curious Slummers crowding a short distance away, and waited for Dark to answer.

"No, Kiora Bass. Just biz."

Kiora Bass. I remembered Slummers named themselves after the fish of their area. Down the coast a bit they were Trevallies and Breams. Sounded stupid, but you didn't want to say that to a Slummer's face. They were as handy as Muenos with knives, only they used filleting blades.

A tinge of rage crept into her voice. "Don't believe you, you lie. She your woman, Loyl-Dark? You don't want me!" She followed with an obscenity that curled my toes and broadened my mind.

"Shut it, Kiora." He leaned over me and slapped her across the jaw. The whole sling sagged, jolting my shoulder.

"Hey, quit the domestic shit!" I growled at them. "Put me down or stop jerking around." I glared at the woman. "And quit with the insults. He's not my type."

What a stinking big lie that was, Parrish! Yeah, but look, it made her happy.

And it had. She bowed her head, a small satisfied smile playing on her lips.

I didn't look at Dark.

He'd hit her. I'd never forgive that in a man.

So much for The Tert town savior!

They bundled me along in silence, between humpies and past smoking fires, to an open stretch of beach. I could hear the sea lapping—an oily, flat sound. Then the high whine of something mechanical drowned it out.

A buzz saw?

When I saw what made the noise, I was damn near right. A buzz saw connected to a metal frame with wings and a pair of seats. A primeval ultralight.

I'd seen them a lot in the sky above The Tert. They always looked so frail and hesitant. Like they might get tired at any moment.

Kiora Bass and Dark rolled me onto the frame and strapped me to it in three places. My feet dangled over the end.

I struggled, gripped by panic. Jumping ditches on motorbikes was one thing. Flying in a mutated power tool was something else.

"No way am I going anywhere in this. Dark! Listen! Get me *off this thing!*" I tried to scream, but my lungs hurt too much. "For Womssakes, get me off."

The Slummers crowded closer, pointing at me. I saw Mama at the back, towering over them, his fat body quaking with laughter.

High point to his week, no doubt!

Kiora Bass smirked openly.

Fish bitch!

Dark ignored the whole proceedings.

Craning my neck backward, I saw him strap in, straight-faced, alongside the pilot.

The ultralight gave a little jerk and we accelerated along the sand. Next it hopped three or four times, like a demented frog. Then the rushing air and the engine drowned my moans. Two or three outrageous swerves cleared us of the power lines, and we were airborne.

I held my breath for as long as I could. And some more. My stomach turned inside out and then back, and tried to crawl out of my ears and nose.

As the wind tore at my clothes and blasted my face, I swore if I made it off this thing alive I'd never complain about my life again.

I followed that up by a string of stupid things you promise yourself when you think you're going to die—which you immediately forget as soon as you realize you're still alive.

A few minutes after that, my whole body began to shake with terror—great uncontrollable rigors. If I hadn't been belted in, I swear I would have bounced myself straight over the side.

My leg, where my clothes had torn, turned numb. Fear took me in a way I'd never known. I wanted to get my feet on the ground so badly I would have jumped. I moaned, over and over; no sane part left to tell me I was acting like an idiot.

I closed my eyes and begged some god—any god—to let me survive it. Just another day of life, another night . . .

We put down an age later on a potholed bitumen road on the rural sweep of Viva. Landing was like being stabbed by large steak knives. But my relief, so enormous after the terror, canceled out the pain.

The ultralight taxied along the road until a building came into sight. There was nothing else close by, apart from a bunch of trees that partially hid a house, some paddocks studded with dried plant carcasses and in the distance a four-meter-high perimeter fence made of solid ferro. Across the top of the fence a blue security light crackled like lightning in a thunderstorm.

I couldn't remember how long it was since I'd seen so much open space—apart from The Tert wastelands.

Dark came round to unstrap me. "OK?" he shouted over the engine.

My mouth was too dry to reply the way I wanted to.

He and the pilot hauled me inside a sleek building, through a dustproof door and deposited me onto a hard morguelike slab. Then they disappeared outside and the sound of the buzz saw soon faded into the distance.

For a moment I thought Dark might have gone with him and I struggled to get free of the blanket that had wound itself around me. It stank of fresh fish guts. No doubt Kiora Bass had lent me her best.

"Keep still until I've examined you," a cold voice commanded out of the darkness.

I craned my neck around to locate it, then fixed on a faint glow—the reflection of a screen. The outline of a woman sat behind it, tapping at a keypad.

"In a moment you'll be scanned. Loyl darling, can you remove her covering? It's imperative she *keeps still*."

Darling? Was she talking to Dark? I glanced up, relieved and annoyed. Where the hell was he? Where the hell was I?

He stepped out of the shadows and bent over me. "Parrish, she's a medic. Let me take the blanket away so she can check you over." He said it carefully, like he was planning to dismantle a bomb. "OK?"

I nodded slowly, resisting the urge to sink my teeth into his arm—just for the heck of it.

"Does it hurt much?" He smelled of wind laced with a faint musk, and his concerned tone took the sting out of my anger.

"I—it's all right," I allowed. Maybe it was a reaction to my first-ever air flight, or maybe I really was losing it. But with his face so close to mine, and me feeling so damn fragile, I suddenly mislaid my reasons for disliking him.

The gloom softened his face with kindness. Kindness wasn't a thing that featured on my life's highlight reel. I didn't know what to do with it.

"Stand away," the woman ordered sharply.

Dark tugged the last of the blanket from under my

legs and squeezed my hand for a second. "It won't take long."

The slab slid into a cylinder, covering my body like the lid and sides of a coffin. I concentrated on remembering to breathe and told myself at least I was on the ground, not hurtling through the air on the back of a buzz saw.

A few minutes later, when it retracted, I was shaking all over. My muscles seemed to belong to someone else. I drew a long steadying breath.

The woman operating the coffin stood up. The halo lights brightened.

"She'll live."

She walked over to the slab and peered down at me, taking in my torn clothes. "When did the accident happen?"

Dark moved to stand next to her. The top of her head was in line with his elbow. She looked breakable next to his size, though her pale eyes shone with a kind of fierce, cold intelligence. But it was the pigmentation on her face that stopped me. Two inflamed red birthmarks under her eyes, fusing on the bridge of her nose, gave her a tragic, bruised kind of look— like she'd been punched in the nose, or belonged to a bizarre cult. She wore nothing to cover them.

I sensed her natural antagonism to strangers— people who hadn't seen her before—and understood some of it. Sympathy stirred in me. Punters were paying a fortune for this kind of thing in The Tert. Being born with it was another thing altogether.

"Whenever I called you. A couple of hours ago. Why?"

"Remarkable," she said. "The scan shows fractures to three ribs—"

"Just what I thought," Dark cut in.

She placed cool, *he's-mine* fingers on his wrist. They were the same color as her hair—white as the moon when the smog thinned. "Yes, but the injuries are those of an accident that might have happened two weeks ago. The healing process is already well advanced."

"Impossible," he countered.

They both looked to me for an explanation.

I shrugged. I mean, really, what could I say? *The Angel did it!*

"Good genes?" I proffered limply.

"Drugs?" Dark said.

"No." The woman shook her head. "I tested that. Apart from her olfactory enhancement and compass implant there was only one other unusual thing in her profile, augmented or chemical."

"What was that?" Irritatingly, Dark beat me to it by a second. Whose flesh were we talking about?

"Her adrenal glands are showing excessive activity. But that may be a result of her high-risk lifestyle. I assume she's one of those body-for-hire types."

Body-for-hire types!

I could live with her description, not with her superior tone. Even Rene—my mother—didn't speak to me like that.

Rene!

I hadn't thought of her in a while. When I'd left the 'burbs, poor Rene's neurons were too saturated in happily-ever-afters to notice. Nor did she realize that Kevin only stayed with her for her allowance. NE addicts don't eat or spend much!

And Kat. Little sister Kat! I bet she didn't even know I'd left either. Kat the pro-ball player, the perfect athlete. People said we were alike. I couldn't see it myself . . .

"Parrish? Parrish? Are you listening?"

I blinked back into the present and abruptly swung my legs out over the edge of the slab. My knee banged against the medic woman's arm and she retreated like I'd contaminated her.

It made me want to cover my exposed upper

thigh—but shuffling modesty was not my style. I ignored it instead.

"Yes. I'm fine. In fact much better. What's this place?"

Dark expelled a breath of annoyance. He'd gone to some trouble to get me here and I was halfway to mended already.

"Parrish Plessis, meet Dr. Anna Schaum."

I bit my tongue and held out my knuckles, Tert-style. "Thanks for the help. 'Preciate it. Now how do I get out of here?"

One side of her mouth moved. It could have been a smile, but I didn't think so. She didn't return the shake. Instead she staged a whisper. "Where did you get this one from, Loyl? She's a healthier physical specimen than Bass, but her manners—"

My manners?

The flake of sympathy I'd felt earlier shriveled and died. The woman was talking about *me.*

Dark put a warning hand on my shoulder, intervening as smooth as a rat. Obviously he didn't want his precious little medic with broken teeth and a bent nose.

"Thanks for your help, Anna. But let's keep the remarks clinical."

"I thought I was." She gave him an innocent smile.

He patted her gently. "Parrish and I will be here overnight. Is that OK?"

She gave a tight shrug, then walked back to her screens and resumed working.

Call me paranoid, but I got the feeling Anna Schaum's instant, obvious dislike of me was totally personal. First the fish bitch, and now Dr. Ice Cold. Who else did Dark have on his lust list?

"Can you walk?" he asked me.

"Yeah." I nodded. "Can we get out of here? It stinks like a hospital."

He gave a strange laugh and showed me the way.

*   *   *

The sun was setting outside. I resisted an impulse to go fetal when we got into the open. I hadn't seen proper trees and grass for so long it was like a horror flick. Heat clouds bathed everything in a dull yellow. Even the ferro fence.

Dark placed his flesh hand lightly on my shoulder again, steering me toward a house partly hidden by white gums. I wanted to shrug him away but the feel of his hand was comforting. In the distance the noise from Vivacity droned, reassuring me.

"It takes a while to adjust to the space," he said.

We walked slowly. I might have been healing, but everything still hurt.

"Same as my first day in the Heart," he added.

"What was it like?" I couldn't help but ask. No one left the coast anymore. Living in Central Australia had gotten too harsh.

"Like? Barren. Hot in a way you can't imagine. Terrifying. Even underground. Too hot to breathe. They gave you cool suits but it didn't help a lot. Just kept you alive enough to work in the mine. In the evenings when you'd come out of the shafts, the sky was white with stars. I got used to the nights there, and how big they were. Coming back to The Tert, well . . . I keep wanting some space."

I looked around. "Anna's got some cred. A place like this must cost."

Silence.

I'd hit on one nerve. So I tried hammering another. "Funny you turning up in Fishertown like that. You never mentioned you were going to Viva."

"Nor did you," he countered.

"I didn't know—exactly. If I didn't know better I'd think you were following me."

"Maybe I am. Maybe I can't bear to be away from you."

My heart skittered for an instant.

"Or maybe . . . we're chasing the same thing," he finished.

My heart settled into an altogether different rhythm—suspicion. It quelled my agoraphobia. I suddenly remembered that he was a jerk who liked to hit women.

He stopped walking abruptly, like he could hear my thoughts. His breath fanned my face. A tinge of musk still clung to his body.

"Where are you going in Viva, Parrish? What are you doing for Lang?"

I stepped away from him, wincing from the sudden movement. It still hurt to breathe deeply, so I settled for panting. "What makes you think I'm here because of Lang?"

"He's offered you something important. Enough to risk leaving The Tert during the embargo."

"How do you know that?"

His eyes got calculating, his words measured for effect. "I know more than you think. I know that Jamon Mondo owns you and that you'd do just about anything to change that. I know you are pretty much alone and inclined to violence. I know you are impulsive and often irrational."

I stared at him, shocked.

Shocked. And then angry. Blazingly, pig-nosed, nutso mad!

My fingers grabbed to where my pistol should be. If only I hadn't lost my kit in the fall I'd shoot him where he stood.

"I have your kit. I took it in Fishertown," he said flatly.

I dropped into a less than friendly crouch. "Then I'd like it back."

He walked on, toward the house. "I'll give it back when you need it. When we get there," he said over his shoulder.

"What do you mean, 'When we get there'?" I shouted.

He turned back. The rising moon lit his smile.

"Wherever it is you're going."

I stamped after him, glaring poison at his back, struggling to get a handle on the man. He'd smashed another one into left field—just when I found myself softening toward him.

He'd gotten me out of a really tight spot. Now he was blackmailing me.

An Intimate showed us to a room with high-gloss imitation floorboards and four large chairs covered in pale green leather. The walls were adorned with well-hung artwork in watery tones, and a large bronze crucifix.

I wondered how often Dark came to visit.

"Hot food," Dark told the Intimate and slung himself into a chair.

Intimates were fashionable amongst the wealthy. Internally robotic, externally they took thousands of different forms—usually a beloved toy. Teddy bears were common. Dolls as well. So were naked torsos.

Anna Schaum's Intimate wore a party dress with heels. It told us its name was Lila. Its skin shone with pearly unblemished perfection.

"Wine as well," Dark called after it.

Wine? The only wine I'd ever tasted was like rocket fuel. Even Jamon served Bundaberg rum with his meals.

I sat down opposite him, and leaned back gingerly on my shoulder. I was still choking mad that he had taken my kit and was holding me ransom over it. Trouble was—how did I play it?

While I considered my options, the Intimate brought a bottle, two glasses and a plate of something I didn't recognize. Dark poured blood-colored liquid into one glass and handed it to me.

I swallowed the entire glass in one swig, bracing for the afterburn, but it was surprisingly mild.

Censure hung on his lips; he bit it back and poured me another.

"Artichokes?" He held out the plate like it was something he ate all the time.

I shuddered and shook my head. "I don't eat plants."

The second glass went straight to my head. I knew it would. Wanted it. Stim would have been better, but I'd take any port in a storm.

"Loyl Dark," I sniped. "What sort of a name is that?"

He sipped his wine slowly. "Loyl-me-D-a-a-c," he corrected. "It's a corruption of my gens—my family—name."

"And did your gens bring you up to hit women and blackmail people?"

He stiffened. "You wouldn't understand," he said.

My tongue felt sufficiently loose to help him *understand* more about me.

"Well you might believe you're some type of frigging Messiah, Loyl-me-Daac. But all you're really after is clout."

His face relaxed at my outburst. Not the reaction I'd expected.

"Power is an illusion, Parrish. I try and cover bases—that's all. The rest you have to live with. What's so wrong with wanting to make things better for your own people?"

I got up and poured myself another drink, the pain in my shoulder receding with every swallow.

"You don't get it, do you? Why are they *your* people? Who said they were? That's what's wrong with this stinking world. Everyone is trying to control everyone else. What makes you any different from Lang or Jamon Mondo?"

He frowned and said nothing. I'd hoped for more.

"So what's the deal here with Dr. Schaum?" I leaned on the arm of his chair. My torn overall fell away exposing my entire leg. I knew it wasn't wise to get this close to him but belligerence kept me there.

He looked away. "This is Anna's family home. Her parents were important people. She's a . . . friend. Most of her work here is research."

"Yeah? So why the tight ice around the perimeter?" I winced as I leaned forward to pull my boot off. Nursing my drink carefully with the other hand, I wiggled my toes.

His eyes were drawn to my foot, tracking like it was a dangerous animal.

"She's studying why certain groups have adapted genetically to heavy metals and toxins in the environment. Her research will save a lot of my people. Improve the quality of their life."

"Just your people—or are you going to share it around? Who decides who gets quality of life, Loyl-Me-Daac? *You?* Will Kiora Bass get it?"

He flushed, shifting in the constraints of the chair and threw me a strange, intense look.

"Kiora is dying. Anna has been studying her. Trying to understand what has given her better health than the others around her."

I drained my drink and removed the other boot. "You slap dying women around the ears often?"

"I lost my temper. Kiora is paranoid and hallucinatory. She thinks we are lovers. We aren't."

"Sure." I mustered up sarcasm I didn't really feel. This whole scene weighed a ton.

Without warning, he pulled me onto his lap.

Lulled by the wine I didn't struggle. Nor did I respond, curious about him, curious about myself.

He moved his flesh hand slowly up the length of the tear in my overalls, along my thigh.

An unwelcome tingle of desire trickled into my belly. Something I hadn't felt since Teece—back in the beginning.

He leaned forward and kissed me, filling my mouth.

I've never been kissed by anyone before. Not even by Doll. It was a quaint little rule I had. My mouth was mine, my virginity—to give to the right person. Besides, most people I knew had biological warfare going on in their saliva.

His sudden invasion sent my whole body rigid. Furiously, I wrenched away from him, grabbing my boots.

He moved to stand, puzzled.

But I backed across the room. "Where can I sleep?"

"Upstairs," he replied thickly. "Near the bathroom . . . I mean the san."

I nodded and backed away.

I climbed the stairs in four big steps and began crashing doors open. It made me feel better.

The house had gear I'd never seen outside adverts for Viva Hi-tels—the latest cons with some pricey old-world touches.

The room next to the san sported a giant poster bed you could fit most of Torley's in—if you wanted to. It frothed with a white lace spread and feather pillows.

I did one quick circuit, locking the door and the windows, then I curled up on the floor rug and fell into an edgy doze.

Sometime in the early hours a faint noise woke me. Voices. I fought off a moment of panic at my strange surroundings and got up off the floor to investigate. From the top of the stairs I could see Daac and Anna sitting together in the same spot I'd been with him earlier, caught up in a hushed discussion.

Peeping Parrish I was not—but some things you

just have to know. And some opportunities are just too good.

"How long will they take to replicate?" he asked.

Anna Schaum ran her hand through her hair. Her shoulders heaved silently. "I'm not sure exactly. I'm working off some of the old base notes. But the splicing sequences are all gone. They took my backup copies as well. Time—it will take time."

"Records?"

"Some are left."

"Which ones?"

"General notes on the side effects—all the specifics are gone."

"They knew what they wanted." Loyl stood and paced a little, his wire hand opening and closing in spasms. "I still don't understand how it happened. It can't have been hacked," he said. "Kiora Bass and I have been the only ones in here." He turned on her. "Haven't we?"

She shrank under the force of his stare. "Of course. Who else? It must have happened sometime while I was here alone."

He nodded, and resumed his pacing.

"Loyl, I don't know if I want to go on with this."

Daac stopped abruptly and came to sit next to her. *"Of course you do!"* He gripped her tightly, as if he might shake her. With obvious effort he gentled his tone. "Would it make you feel better to have someone else stay—permanently?"

"No!" Her voice sharpened suddenly. "I don't want anyone." She cuddled against him like a little girl. "Anyway, I've got Lila."

The Intimate appeared from the corner on cue and began to clean away plates.

Sweet!

Daac lifted Anna into his lap, leaning his face against hers.

My stomach clenched at the gesture.

I backed away from the top of the stairs and crawled to my room where I spent the rest of the night sleepless, disgusted by Daac's hypnotic effect on women, and wondering what the hell the two of them were talking about.

Chapter Twelve

The sweet scent of sandalwood wafted into the Emporium's storeroom where I sat staring at myself in the mirror. I hardly recognized the person who scowled back at me wearing an insipidly floral jellyfish creature that the label declared a "caftan."

Daac had suggested borrowing some new clothes from another *friend*, something *un*-me. On the ride into the city from Anna Schaum's compound, we'd barely spoken, certainly not about the night before.

From the smudges under his eyes I guessed he'd got about as much sleep as I had, but for different reasons.

The only thing that had stopped me from cutting out of *maison pastel* in the bitching hours was the knowledge that Anna Schaum's perimeter security was tight. Besides, I had no kit. It hurt me to even think how vulnerable I was without it. No fake ID. No hacker's pack. No arsenal.

After introducing me to his friends, Daac left me alone in the back room to re-create myself, with a direct "Do something different with your hair."

Although I could see the sense in that, I was fond of my dreads, so I rolled them up tight and stuffed them into a rather tasteless brown velveteen cap.

I could hear Daac in the shop front of the Emporium talking to the owners, Pat and Ibis. Fortunately, they were male and obviously infatuated with each other, which meant at least I wasn't going to have to watch them for a jealous knife between my shoulder blades. Anna Schaum, out there leaning quietly furious against the counter, was the worry.

The Emporium sold gems, healing stones, crystals, remains of 'riginal middens, fake gnamma holes, injun feathers and anything else that might catch the fancy of a spiritually dispossessed Viva citizen. The front window was crammed with so many giant lava and cascade lamps that they'd had to hire security to keep hypnotized passers-by moving along. Right now the Emporium was closed.

The Tert also had its fair share of spirit gear for sale, but not brilliantly polished and neatly arrayed like this. In The Tert, the stuff was likely to be soiled with traces of blood and other fluids.

Daac must have spotted me rubbernecking out the door, because he called me to join them. I loathed him for stealing my kit, but I had no way to replace it, so his blackmail carried weight.

As long as he didn't interfere with the actual job I was here to do, I'd agree to him coming for the ride. I figured he could watch all he wanted. He might even be useful. But once I'd downloaded the files Lang wanted, Daac wouldn't see me for dust.

I hiked my skirt impatiently around my waist, tucking it into my string. The clock was ticking on Lang's deadline, and the last thing I felt like was parading in this flimsy piece of repugnance in front of Daac's entourage.

Sometimes, though, bluff can go a long way, and my curiosity was piqued about Daac's strange network outside The Tert. How did he know these people?

Aside from Dr. Anna Schaum, Kiora Bass, Pat and Ibis were inconsequential, invisible people. No real money, no obvious influence . . .

I strode out, feeling naked in the unfamiliar looseness of the dress. Modesty wasn't my problem, just image. I wasn't the girlie type—and I didn't want to be.

Daac's stare didn't help matters. "It's meant to be worn long, Parrish," he muttered, eyes riveted to my thighs.

Anna watched his reaction, her pale blue eyes cold as a wax dummy.

"Darling. How divine . . . what legs," Pat trilled to fill the awkwardness.

Pat had a high, girlish voice and a compact physique. I knew if he turned around his buns would be as tight as fists. A workout junkie—I bet—with a bright, mischievous face.

I growled at him. If he hadn't fed me one helluva breakfast, I might have kicked his tightly toned butt.

"Heavenly," agreed Ibis, stuffing sugar-coated doughnuts between his plump lips. Ibis had probably never seen the inside of a gym; his buns, I bet, would be soft and malleable like two lumps of rising dough. No doubt he easily absorbed the impact of Pat's dense muscle. I imagined them in bed together—the rippling of Ibis's loose skin as they came.

Daac hadn't taken his eyes off me.

Anna's were on Daac.

"A frigging freak, more like," I snarled, completely ungrateful.

"You look like everyone else around here," Daac said.

He had a point. He was dressed in loose white pants and 3-D tie-dyed shirt. The spirals made me nauseous. Ibis wore a glittery disco jumpsuit and an outrageous red afro. Pat was in too-tight black with a swathe of gold chains. I'd heard Viva was in the grip of a major retrospective fashion groove—seeing it was something else.

"I think she looks awful," said Schaum.

"No offense, Anna darling, but what would you know about fashion?" said Ibis, wide-eyed and serious.

Schaum flushed the color of her birthmarks and tried not to look down at her severe taupe suit. "No offense, Ibis, but you're not just a fashion victim. You're a fatality."

The tension between them made me want to laugh.

"Shall we test the water first, Loyl-me-Daac? How about brunch?" Pat intervened.

"What's brunch?" I asked suspiciously.

Schaum sniggered.

Daac cast her an irritated glance. "Pat's suggesting we go out to eat, in public, test the climate."

"What climate? What do you mean?" *Who was I? The idiot no one remembered to tell things?*

"Your face is all over One-World, Parrish. First the 'Terro. Now your escape from the 'copters. Show her, Pat."

Gravely Pat replayed the latest news on the shop screen.

It was full of Razz Retribution's murder, the embargo on The Tert and *me:* an olio of inflammatory images concocting a dramatic tale about a crime of passion committed by a social misfit turned villain.

One Parrish Plessis.

I hardly recognized the photos of my old self minus the dreads, the bent nose and dinted cheekbone.

"Amazing," muttered Daac.

I wasn't quite sure which bit he was referring to.

There was more: vid shots of my home and footage of Kat playing pro ball in Eurasia, interspersed with mugshots of Rene and Kevin. Kevin had plenty to say. Words like *sociopath* and *nihilist* that he must have practiced for days.

My mouth fell open. Despite Anna Schaum's patronizing stare, I couldn't get it shut.

"They're making me out to be Razz Retribution's murderer," I gasped. "Me and Sto."

Daac looked guilty. "You were with Sto when the 'Terro came calling. Somehow the media's jumped on the idea you masterminded the murder and Stolowski was your accomplice. Your bike-bust out of The Tert across the waste seems to have fueled the idea."

"But I didn't do it!" I shouted, indignant.

"I'm sorry, Parrish. I didn't realize this would happen. That you'd get so involved."

My voice got louder. "I'm not involved, it's a stupid media beat-up." I sounded pathetic, even to myself.

You see, there wasn't really such a thing as a media "beat-up." A "beat-up" implied the possibility that you would be delivered, in the end, from the lies; that viewers might question what they saw.

But they wouldn't.

If One-World decided you were the perp, then you were. The truth wasn't relevant. Reality wasn't worth a canrat's teste.

I turned my anger on Daac. "Listen to me. I've got a job. How am I going to do it with the whole damn networld peeping up my caftan?"

He shrugged—a casual movement that belied his cunning. "Why don't you tell me what you're doing? Maybe I can help."

"Why would you want to?"

"Let's say it could be advantageous to us both."

He had me in a corner. Accept his help or no kit.

Maybe he didn't understand that being cornered made me do crazy things.

I lunged at Anna, jerking her toward me, catching

her around the neck. She was so light I lifted her clean off her feet, using her as a shield.

Ibis clucked unhappily and tugged Pat away from me.

"Get my kit or the medic will need some of her own help."

"Parrish!" Daac snarled a warning.

"Trash!" Anna Schaum spat over her shoulder at me.

I snapped her neck around as hard as I could without breaking it—though it wouldn't take much.

She wailed like a kid.

Ibis hid behind Pat, though he was half a head bigger. Pat stared at me with curiosity and, I guessed, only mild concern for the woman I was hurting.

Only Daac reacted in her defense. "Don't be stupid, Parrish. Let her go. You need us, right now."

"Need you?" The contempt in my voice was real. How could I possibly need two lava-lamp salesmen, an insecure scientist and the world's biggest jerk?

Daac kept talking, in his flat, measured, dismantling-the-bomb tone. I wondered if he saved it especially for me.

"Pat and Ibis can get you anywhere you need to go in Viva. Anna can treat any damage you do to yourself, and augment you with anything you need. I can protect you—"

"Protect! There you go again. Can't you get it through your head? I don't need protecting. Get off my case! Stay out of my life!"

"Loyl, please," Schaum gasped.

Daac eased a sleek, matt pistol from a holster under the flap of his shirt and raised it level with my head. "Parrish, let Anna go. There is no need to hurt her."

"No. There isn't. Just get me my kit and I'll be gone."

I could see the indecision in his face and I preyed

on it. "I'll break her neck, Daac. You wouldn't want that, would you? And if you shoot, you might hit her first. You wouldn't want that either. It might affect your precious research."

My last threat was right on target. Whatever Anna was doing for him was important enough to let me go.

He lowered his pistol in disgust.

At himself? Or me?

"Pat, get her kit."

Pat nodded and disappeared.

"You're making a mistake, Parrish," he said softly. "You'll never get what Lang wants and survive."

Pat returned and handed my kit bag to Daac.

"Slide it over." I bent my knees, lowering Schaum closer to the floor. "Pick it up," I told her. "Slowly." I never took my eyes off Daac.

His expression was surly. Pissed off. A *boy wonder doesn't get his own way* look. He gripped the pistol tightly but I knew he wouldn't use it. Not while I had his precious science geek.

I nodded briefly to Pat and Ibis. "Thanks for breakfast. Nothing personal, dig?"

Pat stared with interest, his eyes bright and alert. Over Pat's shoulder Ibis blew me a kiss. Some men are just born flirts!

I edged Anna slowly toward the door and double flicked the pressure lock so that it would take an extra few seconds to open when Daac tried to follow me.

Then I grabbed my bag and hurled Anna straight at him so that he had to drop his pistol to catch her. He recovered, but I was out the door and running.

By the time my lungs burned and my legs turned to jelly, I was hopelessly lost. My shoulders and ribs ached like torture, but I had my kit back, and despite the fact that the whole world seemed to have a warrant for my arrest, a weight had lifted.

It occurred that maybe I should forget Lang and Jamon, and just disappear here in Viva? *Not so easy!* I couldn't get work or claim benefits. I'd starve. The supercity was not an option for me anymore, but I daydreamed for a while as I wandered the wide leafy streets and used the glow-walks like everyone else.

Viva was an exquisite, neat, expensive carpet of humanity. You needed a minimum annual income of over thirty million credits to live there—and they were the poor types. Itinerants and visitors were welcome, but temporary lodging was heavily monitored and squatting a capital offense—as was vagrancy, homelessness, drugs—certain types anyway—and loitering. Viva was a safe city if you were a safe person. It was deadly if you weren't.

I was born in the 'burbs, just inside the rural sweep of the supercity; a place where you never saw your own earnings, and the bank put you through school, attended to your daily living needs and paid your taxes. In the 'burbs you were little better than a drone in a hive, serving the banking royalty of Viva and the media for the safe way of life.

Kevin, my stepdad, tried to addict me to romance, the way he had with Rene, jacking me in when I was asleep or drunk. But something deep inside me had resisted the notions. Maybe I was pragmatic by nature. Or maybe I saw too clearly what it had done to Rene. When that didn't work Kevin tried a more direct approach. Attempted rape in front of my mother, while she lay stoked up on happily-everafters.

I left before I killed him.

But not before he broke my face.

I told myself I didn't care about getting it fixed. But in truth I didn't want it fixed. I didn't ever want to forget.

The Tertiary—Tert—sector had been a kind of rebirth for me. No menu-planning twelve weeks in advance, no accounting for every single credit, no slick, greedy Kevin. In The Tert junkies were called junkies—not NE-reliant.

Tert people had an honesty about them—the sort you get when you've got nothing to lose.

But the grubbier side of The Tert inevitably ensnared me. I figured a place like that would mean freedom. Choices.

Not even vaguely. When Jamon came along, my options narrowed back to nothing.

But I couldn't return to the 'burbs, now. A misfit like me would be quarantined and rehabbed. No matter how bad things were, I could never live here again.

Yet if I wanted any sort of life in The Tert, then I had to cut Jamon out of it. I'd learned a lot of things in the last year or so.

Right now I was learning what I could do, when I had to.

A few years ago I might have fallen heavily for someone like Daac, joined his devotional, stood in the queue. Now I was learning to be my own fallback, my best resource.

I found a café with several entrances on a busy street, and sat at a table near one of them. Then I ordered a sparkling water and studied the city map on the back of the menu.

I paid the waitress with some fake ID cred courtesy of a stall in Plastique. I'd bartered half a year of hapkido training and a throwing knife to the stall owner for it.

The address Lang had given me was in the inner gyro of the city where most of the streets were on closed circuit. Worse than that, it was in a sparkling little marina called M'Grey Island—a tough place to B and E even for a seasoned larcenist.

Right now I would have given anything for Lang's ability to change appearance, or for one of Doll's twelve-hour reconstruction jobs. Somehow a lumpy velveteen cap and a see-through dress thrown over my tank top didn't feel the same.

I gnawed the tip of my finger and plotted several routes on the back of the serviette. Each angle I drew ended up back at the same place. There was only one way in. I tried not to think about Daac's comment that I wouldn't survive Lang's job.

Sighing into the bottom of my water, I stretched and tested my shoulder and ribs. They felt a little better and so did I, helped by the breakfast Pat had given me and the fact that it probably contained the first fresh nutrients I'd eaten in years.

I stared through the stained-glass windows of the café at the people on the street. Viva never seemed to be crowded. Not like The Tert. It smelled clean and good and I wondered if somehow they'd 'gineered some type of giant fragrance filtering system.

Just then, two men walked in the south entrance and up to the service counter holding hands. Pat and Ibis. I recognized their shapes instantly.

Adrenaline skittled up the back of my legs. They were looking for me, no doubt, and luck had brought them to the right place.

Folding the menu into my pocket, I picked up my kit and left quietly through one of the other entrances.

Out in the streets the crowds had built. People appeared from their businesses to lunch at the cafés and piazzas. Palms shaded the pavement and neatly trimmed bougainvilleas squeezed between them creating a beachside air.

The sun glinted on the reflective trims of apartment blocks. Each one seemed to blend seamlessly with the next and the next. After the cheap patch-work and filth of The Tert, Viva shone.

In the tourist shops you could buy replicas of Viva under miniature glass geodesics. When you pressed the button the sun rose and sparkled on the tops of its buildings, gradually casting a rose tint as it set.

It reminded me of those old movies that were so popular fifty years ago, where at the end of the story they all realized they weren't living on a planet but under a glass dome floating through space.

If the whole of Viva woke up tomorrow and found out they were on a comet scooting through the Perseus Spur, I doubted they'd care. As long as the streets were clean, the cafés served cappuccino and One-World was in their bedrooms and living rooms to greet them when they woke, who'd give a rat's?

Call me a cynic, but things were cushy in Viva.

The live-to-air media hunts outside Viva might as well have been happening on another planet.

That's why I knew I was already convicted of Razz Retribution's murder. The media had chosen me. The viewing public wouldn't ever know if I was an actor or the real thing. Which made for a clear conscience and a good night's sleep for them.

Entertainment without responsibility.

I'm all for it—if I'm not the main attraction.

I watched an intracity train slide slowly by. A fashion billboard covered one entire side of the compartment, advertising the One-World news.

Chills pimpled my body. I knew the face on the ad. A girl, young and gaunt, skin flawed, stance defensive. Not a Viva face.

Bras. With arms.

I wanted to run after the train and climb aboard to get a better look, but a police vehicle nosed past immediately behind it like an oversized centipede with as many eyes as legs. Automatically I bent down as if I'd dropped something and edged behind the cover of a public comm machine.

Police 'pedes filmed the streets constantly, feeding their images through ID programs to siphon for people like me. It was a truly random method; that's what made it so dangerous.

When it passed, I made a decision. If I hung around here much longer, I'd either run into Daac and his mates or be picked up by a police 'pede, so I swung onto the next in-city train and headed uptown.

Chapter Thirteen

The map told me that Eighteen Circe Crescent, M'Grey Island, was in a marina a hundred klicks from the nearest sea or river. But land had been scooped out and the water piped in and artificially colored to sparkle like no other blue you've ever seen.

The island contained maybe two hundred canals surrounded by a lake big enough for afternoon pleasure cruises and seeded fishing. The lake was for residents only and deliberately serrated retaining walls made it impossible to launch from the mainland perimeter. It gave the nervous rich the security they craved. Circe Crescent nestled in the center of the island where the canals got narrow and personal and very exxy.

I jumped the train at an earlier stop and walked. Just in case someone was expecting me. So far I hadn't seen much heat, apart from the 'pedes. That made me nervous.

Bras's face had appeared twice more on One-World ads on the ride uptown. Once on a floating billboard, the other time on the giant screen on the front of the Viva Bank building. Right alongside King

Ban himself. I figured that meant she was still alive, but the whys and wheres made my head ache. Maybe she didn't need my help anymore, but as soon as I got Lang's info back to him I was going to find out.

I walked along distractedly, like I really knew my way but was thinking about something else. In the inner gyro most people used private 'pedes. If you were strolling on the street then you were probably on candid camera.

I sloped into a mobile newsstand, my head averted from the servitor's receptors. The stand was an expensive one, sporting a hundred or more screens. But then M'Grey was a ritzy area.

"Which news do you require? One-World? Off-world? Common? Tabloid?" asked the servitor in a refined drawl. I wondered which famous newsreader they'd modeled it on.

"Just browsing," I muttered, consciously changing the inflections of my voice in case the stand was bugged.

The headlines scanned across all channels intermittently. Bras's face flashed up on each one, accompanied by nasal voiceovers similar to the servitor's praising King Ban's philanthropy in adopting the feral child into the royal family of Viva.

Bras in the royal family! A crazy stunt that'd send ratings, and pro-bank sentiment, rocketing. Why else would King Ban adopt a Tert feral?

When it wasn't Bras on the screen, it was me. I hated to admit it but Daac was right. If I'd kept my trademark hairstyle and skintight nylons, I'd be cooling my backside in a city quod by now. My stature was *way* too obvious—I might as well have been a flashing neon. At least with a lumpy head and a jelly-fish dress on I could be mistaken for a Viva type.

"Free browsing time is fifteen minutes. Your time

is now at thirteen minutes and thirty-nine seconds. You are required to insert your credit spike or please move along. Thank you for your patronage.''

Thank you for your patronage!

If my face weren't splashed across every screen in the global city, I'd have tickled its plastic and titanium gullet with one of my charm explosives. I fingered them, tempted. But for a change common sense prevailed.

I froze an image of Bras and got my one complimentary copy, then I quit the newsstand before the servitor pissed me off further.

Outside, private 'pedes scampered up and down the streets. A few couples ambled with no real place to go. So different from the hysterical velocity of The Tert.

My nerves jangled again at the sensation of space, but in Viva it was the norm and skulking in corners was going to call attention to me.

I slowed my pace and tagged behind a group of four strollers, following them to some open parkland by the moat. They laughed and joked and threw titbits to the birds and 'gineered fish that clustered around on queue. The two men wore safari suits, one in black, one in navy and the women wore white jellyfish like me. Their suntans were so even and their skin so clear it was impossible to judge their age. Anywhere from twenty to sixty.

Living in Viva with all its nutrient-rich food and clean water definitely had its advantages, but it wasn't perfect. According to Common Net reports, the rate of natural conception in Vivacity had dwindled to an all-time low due to the inconvenience of the whole thing. King Ban was plowing resources into fertility pharma and PURBs—portable uterine replica birthers—as the mainstay of future beautiful, healthy citizens. One for every home!

Ironically, in The Tert there was a birth explosion. They just didn't live for very long.

Nature's little joke.

Seems only the weird and the poor wanted to bear and raise their own children.

I sat on one of the park chairs and tapped the nose of a porcelain gnome who gave me the tourist rap.

"M'Grey Island is a beautiful example of how Viva citizens have been able to sculpt their environment. A 'gineered island, it is part-time home to many of Australia's most prestigious citizens. Such is the closeness of this small community that the entire island is on closed-circuit security. Tours are conducted through M'Grey on a monthly basis and tickets can be obtained from the conveyance station.

"M'Grey's moat and canal water is fed from underground pipes flushing recycled saltwater. Fish especially suited to this environment are a feature of the waterways and fishing can be enjoyed all year round. It is not recommended you eat the fish.

"One of the features of M'Grey is the picturesque sailing bridge which every evening disconnects from its mooring to hover above the moat until morning, giving the residents complete privacy.

"Between March and June, the royal family are often in residence enjoying the casual atmosphere and water sports of their 'oliday-prep-la-cite."

The gnome pronounced the last few words with a cutesy flourish.

I took the picture of Bras out of my kit bag and studied it awhile, keeping half an eye on the water lapping in front of me. Her face, though thin and angular, looked clean. And she had new arms. Real grafts or image-generated? I wondered.

The memory of her grateful expression, her willingness to share her last food bar, haunted me. How was she fitting into life in Viva?

A police water 'pede surfaced in the moat before me, splashed about like an oversized fish, then disappeared. A short time later it happened again. After an hour of moat-watching I knew I wasn't going to reach M'Grey that way.

Daac's words chased around in the back of my mind . . . *Pat and Ibis can get you anywhere you want to go* . . .

Had I been too hasty blowing him and his friends off?

Whatever gripe he had with Lang had nothing to do with me. What could it hurt if he tagged along to watch? If he could get me in there . . .

I reached inside the top of my caftan and fingered the comm spike he'd given me. Public comms were everywhere in Viva, all I had to do was call.

I got up and walked toward the closest one. I had the spike out before something stopped me. Something loud enough to be a voice in my head.

Don't trust him, Parrish. Don't trust anyone.

I put the spike away and hustled for a train. If I hung around M'Grey much longer a police 'pede would start running checks on me. I'd come back a little before curfew. In the meantime I needed to think in a place where I wasn't so obvious.

Time for another water.

Half an hour before dark I was back near M'Grey. So were a crowd of tourists coming to gawk at the floating bridge. I drifted among them, stooping, tagging on to groups so that I wasn't obviously alone.

I maneuvered close to the bridge, listening while it counted down and explained its own detachment procedure.

The main section, it said, was powered by six sophisticated aero engines with variable thrust control, and a bunch of fancy noise suppression gizmos. With the bridge aloft all night and a no-fly zone overhead, it cut M'Grey off from the rest of the city every evening.

The whole exercise was automated, though police manned a supervision booth this end. Nothing robotic for M'Grey Island residents—they could afford humans.

As I pondered hiding on the bridge itself, the tourist blurb informed me that the movement sensors could detect anything larger than a cicada.

Feigning innocent interest I examined the outside of the booth for possibilities.

It didn't offer a lot. The area immediately around it on the mainland side was featureless, affording no cover. The side connected to the bridge was decorated with electrified razor wire disguised as graffiti art.

I could be fried or just shot down in the open!

Agitation turned to knots in my stomach. How was I going to get across?

I fantasized about disappearing again, never having to think about Jamon or Lang or Loyl-me-Daac or Razz Retribution. But life's curlier problems never vanish—they multiply.

When the whole show was nearly over, a small land-to-air 'pede crawled up to the booth and settled outside. I guessed it was waiting for the guards to come off duty. The booth itself looked like it was designed to survive any type of blast or attempt at forced entry, so when the bridge detached they probably just shut up shop and went home.

A glimmer of hope dawned.

I swapped my attention from the booth to the 'pede.

Maybe . . .

The last group I'd tagged on to were middle-aged out-of-towners. One of them—a blond, smooth-faced woman covered in expensive gold tattoos with her hair molded in a replica of her own face—talked incessantly, in jerky, affected Northern Hem about how much better everything was where she came from. The others paid little or no attention to her conversation.

I smiled at her and altered my voice. "Fascinating though, don't you think? And imagine, *human* guards. Not robbies."

"No way, honey," she tittered indignantly. " 'Bout as real as my late husband's gonads."

I stumbled over the image, but plunged on.

"You want a wager?"

Immediately her eyes lit up. "How do we prove it?"

"Touch," I said decisively. "It's the only way."

She looked doubtful.

"Five thousand global creds." I produced my fake ID and waved it under her nose.

Greed and excitement supplanted doubt on her face. "OK. How, then?" she whispered.

"Those guards are about to knock off duty after the bridge stabilizes. All we have to do is wait around long enough for them to leave. Then we'll politely grope them. Whadyasay?"

She glanced across at her friends, then back at me and nodded.

She raised her voice. "Gregor, dahl. Take the others back to the Hi-tel. Be along in a while."

"If so, Prim." Gregor brushed her with a bored look then happily complied.

As Gregor and friends wandered off, Prim and I moved closer to the 'pede.

The bridge had detached now and looked close to its desired altitude. It hummed in the air like a huge dragonfly with silver-wire wings. The last of the crowd clapped enthusiastically at the spectacle, while Prim and I fine-tuned our plan.

"Leave to me, dahl." She patted my hand reassuringly and winked. "Done this sort of thing before."

I stared at her curiously.

She caught my look. "Customs. Frisked more men than you could possibly imagine."

Customs! My heart went arhythmic.

"Don't we both need to check the wares?" I managed.

She held up ten fingers. "Customs officer's promise. No cheating."

The guards left the booth soon after, checking the locks behind them and nudging each other as Prim swept over to do her thing. Under the cover of her approach, I snapped two charms loose from my bracelet.

She engaged the guards in conversation and I did my best to blend into the scenery.

A minute or two of Prim tittering and the guards thought they'd got lucky. I flicked one of the charms at the booth.

The mini explosion sent all of them scrabbling for cover. The guards automatically flattened, facing the booth, pistols drawn. Prim crouched next to the 'pede with her hands covering her head.

I sprinted to her side and crushed the second charm—the mushroom—between my fingers.

"Prim, suck this!"

Holding my breath, I let off a hiss of gas right into her nostrils. She wobbled under the wave of an instant hallucination and tumbled backward.

With Prim riding high, and the guards practicing counterterrorism, I slipped around behind the 'pede and forced my way up underneath its skirt, hooking myself into the body structure. With my caftan tucked tight into my string, I waited.

I'd gambled a lot on my expectation that once the guards decided the booth was intact they would inspect the island for anything else suspicious. With a bit of luck they might even assume Prim *dahl* did it.

My instinct proved right. After a fruitless sweep of the area and a brusque body search of Prim they slammed her in the back of the 'pede and charged off across the water.

Provided I could hold on against the wind and the vibration, stand the fumes and dust, and was just damn crazy enough, I might still be alive when the 'pede set down.

Chapter Fourteen

Eight hours later I watched Eighteen Circe Crescent, M'Grey Island, from my post in between the concrete pylons of a private jetty. A sleek powerboat was moored next to me, its canopy crackling with the blue light of security.

After the 'pede—complete with a 'cuffed Prim who was having an intense conversation with no one about the price of hair molds—had unwittingly dropped me on one of its island berths, I'd spent the rest of the night smothering coughing attacks from the dust I'd swallowed by hiding in the 'pede's airflow system, and skulking between CC camera units searching for the right address.

I found the house just before dawn, when my fatigue was greatest and my less-than-terrific ability to plan totally dysfunctional. In fact I couldn't think much past walking right on in, dumping the files I needed onto the disk, and getting out.

In the back of my mind it occurred to me that getting in here had been too damn easy, but denial is an insidious monster, so I skulked on down the driveway.

No one was around.

I broke into a side entrance. Basic dead bolts and a motion detector. Not a tough job, but messy because I was tired and in a hurry. No alarms. No dogs. No tek.

Inside, huge wall-sized portraits hung in the corridors, each of the same person, a face so famous that I recognized it immediately.

But I still didn't add it up.

Nor did I twig to the covered furniture and stale air.

It wasn't till I powered up the PC in the upstairs study and a muscular himbo crooned at me that it finally sunk in.

"Hi Razz, darling," himbo said. "I've totally missed you. Where would you like to go?"

My fingers seized above the keyboard.

This was Razz Retribution's frigging PC, in Razz Retribution's frigging house.

I was the idiot who must be under observation by the sum total of Viva's police and media. I scoured the ceiling and round the room for cameras and wondered when they'd stop rubbing their hands together and come out from behind their surveillance bugs to play. How often did a suspected perp turn up on the doorstep begging to be 'cuffed?

The coldest of furies gripped me. *I was going to get out! And I was damn well getting what I came for!*

Quickly I tagged my newly upgraded worm onto the operating system. The worm set about burrowing through the firewalls.

While I waited, I tried to focus on alternative escape routes. I sure as hell wouldn't be leaving the way I came.

But how then?

The worm breached the firewall and started squealing.

My fingers flew along the 'board trying to ride it

up over the huge security wave that loomed *behind* the firewall. Secondary vast ice of the like I'd never seen. It rose and rose and rose, smashing the worm downward into a long, hard gully. It countered every command I could throw at it.

Sweat made my fingers slippery. I'd heard whispers of this sort of stuff . . .

King Wave. Diadem. It had names.

A few seconds later the worm was fish mulch and I was back with himbo. He wagged a pixelated finger. "Naughty, naughty! Razz likes her privacy. You're in trouble." He turned and flounced huffily to the background of the screen.

Himbo and Merry 3# would get on a treat!

He was back in a flash in a sprouky white dress uniform and hat, and began reading my rights. The general drift of it was that I was about to spend my life in prison for attempting to breach confidential files of a member of the media.

I blew him a bigger than average raspberry and tried the backdoor approach. There had to be a way in. There was *always* a way in.

My fingers galloped over the 'board again using the normal routes, the way Razz would do it. I got to her organizer, which pulsed with a huge lock.

I deftly built a key—the way Teece had taught me—and began to shape it to the lock.

I lost precious seconds while I calibrated.

From the windows of Razz's study I could see the 'copters drifting in like buzzards to a still-warm carcass and setting down on the expensive, rolled lawns.

The 'pedes would follow soon. One would be a restraint module with neural disrupters and other various fancy paralysis tek fitted to the upholstery for safe escort to jail.

They say if you got a life sentence in a Viva jail you lived to be well over a hundred and fifty. All of it spent alone, in serious mental agony—relieved occasionally by bouts of serious physical agony.

The lock sprung and I shoved Lang's disk in the sleeve. While I waited for the download, I assembled the rifle.

More seconds wasted.

Each 'copter was spilling out four cops. They fanned out. I should have been flattered—all that for little ol' me—but right now all I could see were odds. Too many of them.

Another noise dragged my attention back to the PC. Not the worm this time, but himbo, shaking his fist and screaming serious trash at me. He seemed faint; see-through almost . . .

The download icons on the screen flashed normal but unintelligible data flow snaked through himbo, patterning his uniform. I instantly recognized the decoy. The files weren't transferring but . . . wiping.

Lang's given me a frigging wiper!

Diadem had been sedated and the hard drive was leaking information into the ether as quick as I could sweat.

I cold-slammed the disc from the sleeve.

Himbo got clearer again and blew a battle trumpet, but his walls were breached.

I ignored him and turned drawers inside out looking for something else to load onto. When I slotted a Zip disk, my hands shook with a rage beyond reckoning.

Precious more seconds passed, but I dumped everything I could scoop up onto it.

Then I shoved both disks inside my tank top and plucked my four remaining charms loose from the bracelet.

Two Wizards, a Trinity and an Angel.

I stepped across the room, keeping behind the cover of the slatted blinds. Two 'copters at south and east.

Two more at north and west and I had sixteen live bodies and all the points of the compass covered.

Two 'pedes slithered along from the nearest street intersection. If I didn't make a move before they got here it was going take a minor miracle for me to get away.

Who was I kidding? It was going to take that anyway.

I cut a large, rough hole in the security screen with my portable blowtorch and nosed the rifle through the bottom slat of the blind.

The security alarms went haywire.

I sighted on the south 'copter pilot as he leaned out of his machine. Unprofessional and stupid, I thought with grim satisfaction.

My shot was a perfect hit. Paralysis in thirty seconds. Then I swung around to the east but the pilot was safe behind his bulletproof bubble. I couldn't see him, let alone penetrate the casing.

I peeled the tab off the Trinity charm and one of the Wizards and kicked the slats wide open. The ground guys had about ten meters before they reached the house. I prayed that the ones at the back of the house were at about the same distance.

The Wizard took out the four from the east—unconscious but unlikely to be dead, unless they had weak hearts. The south guys had spread too far already and the Trinity only claimed two. I cursed having to use the other one on the same squad, but south was looking like my best chance.

As soon as I'd pitched the second Wizard I bolted down the stairs. If there were any left awake out there I'd have to take them myself; one moment longer and the north and west attack'd be all over my back.

I hit the driveway at three-quarter pace and accelerated into a full sprint as soon as I reached the lawn. The charm had done its job and the body count seemed right, so I flattened into a dead run over the final stretch.

Armageddon's mother broke loose around the back of the house. The two other 'copters had lifted off after me, leaving their groundies to follow up.

A heartbeat away from the south 'copter, a shot grazed my kneecap. I rolled the last distance in agony. If I'd been wearing my overalls instead of the jellyfish it would have deflected.

Frigging dresses!

I let off a return shot from my sniper and with difficulty hauled myself up over the pilot. His leg was caught in the safety harness, his unconscious body hanging out the door.

Inside the 'copter's comm band was crazy with orders. A sliver of satisfaction wedged in amongst my fear and pain. I was giving them some grief.

I stared at the panel of LEDs and touch-pads and panicked.

I couldn't fly this thing. I couldn't fly *any* damn thing!

The pain above my knee made it hard to breathe, let alone think. Yet the prospect of a life sentence in a Viva jail sent my fingers galloping over the panel of their own free will.

The machine can fly itself. All you have to do is tell it to.

The thought came through clear and strident inside my head like a voice—but not. Any other time I would have balked at hearing voices but right now I'd take any advice, sensory delusion or not.

" 'Copter, take off!" The 'copter bucked and lifted about two meters off the ground before landing again. Shots were beginning to rock the cabin.

You've confused it. It only follows a set pattern of commands and your voice isn't recognizable. It's not sure what to do.

Is it sentient? I asked my inner voice.

Of course it isn't, snapped the voice, *it's just a machine, not even a very smart one.*

Angel? I ventured tentatively.

It didn't bother to reply.

The pilot stirred and hope flared within me. Maybe I could force him to fly me out of here. I hauled him upright and screamed threats in his ear. But he went limp again.

Drop the pilot.

What?

Drop the pilot. You can't fly with him hanging from the door. Drop the creature!

Blind obedience isn't my strong point these days—especially to foreign voices in my head—but I could see its point. I flicked the pilot's belt clasp and he cartwheeled to the ground.

Now find the takeoff protocol.

I furiously scrolled through help screens, maintenance checks, configuration parameters—

"Got it!" I shouted and initiated the sequence.

I took a deep breath. " 'Copter, fly!"

Nothing.

Call it by its name!

What do you mean its name? I keyed for the start-up menu and searched. "Model Wasp, Keenu Class, Seventy-three A . . . Fly!"

Begrudgingly it lifted and nosed south, flying too low over the congestion of agitated 'pedes.

You need altitude, or one of those legged creatures will finish you. Get it up!

Get it up yourself, I hissed at my unseen copilot. The last thing I wanted was to be farther from the ground.

Two more are closing. A general alert is out. Deploy the incendiary weapons.

Incendiary? How?

With immense difficulty I forced my eyes away from the scene of my doom and feverishly scrolled through the manual pages.

I think it's—

You think . . . ?

The harder I concentrated on the words, the more unreadable they became. Panic had me. What happened to the cool, calm anger?

I took a deep, shaky breath and tried again. "It's got to be these."

Terror had paralyzed my mind, but my hands moved of their own volition, pressing in codes.

Four missiles deployed from the rear shoots. They went way wide of the pursuing 'copters, but it bothered my tailgaters enough that they dropped back and veered off. At least that was what I thought with a split second of relief.

ESCAPE! NOW!

A deafening explosion.

My top blades shot forward off the lid of the cabin, lasered neatly from the body like a hot knife through cheese. I bailed as the 'copter dropped like a stone into the moat.

How I survived the fall and the wreck is a total mystery. But I surfaced gulping and choking, caftan billowing like a parachute and burning debris scattered everywhere.

Engine noise.

Shouts.

I tried to tear my sodden dress off but it was bunched and twisted around my legs, and then there was the small matter of the speedboat powered up and heading straight toward me.

For a minute I thought it was trying to run me over and I gulped in air, ready to dive. But at the last second it slowed and swerved.

A figure stretched over the side, hands trailing like

a scoop in the water. I recognized the outline of the figure.

Loyl Daac!

Our hands connected in a watery slap, and as the boat started to move I was dragged like a fish thrashing on a hook as he gradually reeled me in.

Together we collapsed in the bottom of the boat.

"What the hell do you think you're doing?" I spluttered. My body felt numb from the fall and the buffeting of the water. My knee hurt. I coughed up water ungratefully. "I don't need rescuing."

"You didn't have to take my hand!" he muttered, extricating his legs from mine.

I watched as he slid away from me across the deck and slithered down the cabin steps.

The boat accelerated dangerously, slamming around the moat in a wild dash. I slid from one side to the other and cracked my head before I wised up and grabbed a rope hitch.

Ibis was in the driver bubble up to my left, his plump body molded like putty around the steering wheel. Daac had said he could get me anywhere in Viva. But could they get me out?

Why would they get me out?

I closed my eyes and gripped the handhold with all my strength. If I survived, I'd have plenty of time to ask questions.

The next thing I knew Daac was shouting at me. He slid what looked like a deflated octopus across the deck and barked, "Suit up."

I caught it awkwardly between my legs and then loosed one hand to grab it. My bad knee shrieked with pain. Holding on with the other hand I managed to hook my left foot in, then the right. I wriggled like crazy to get it up to my waist.

That's as far as I'd got when the first torpedo detonated near the bow.

A warning? Or a missed hit? Ibis slewed the boat in a radical sideways move, without slowing, and I vaguely registered houses looming on both sides. We were heading into the M'Grey Island canals.

Comprehension eased my dismay. The 'copters had to be careful what kind of artillery they employed in the canals. Wouldn't do to damage some toff's holiday pad.

From my position, spread-eagled across the bottom of the boat, I watched the 'copters descend on us like a swarm of wasps, squirting sprays of fire.

But Ibis was ready. The whole topside glimmered with the net of a security field. I recognized it immediately. This boat belonged to Razz Retribution.

Instinctively I ducked my head as the field crackled. The boat rocked dangerously.

"Parrish, get the suit on," shouted Daac. "The hood will seal and oxygenate. It hums when it's working. When I tell you, fasten it."

"What then?" I shouted louder, so he could hear me over the noise of the artillery.

He spared me a grin. "Hope you can swim."

I felt the boat slow marginally, then twist and turn. I tried to catch a glimpse of Ibis but I was being tossed around like a ball.

Suddenly the engine noise cut out.

So did the 'copters' fire.

We glided along silently on momentum.

Daac whispered, "Now," and crawled toward me. I scrabbled like crazy to get my arms in and press the seams together.

Ibis climbed down from his perch, wearing an identical suit. They each grabbed one of my arms and hauled me up onto the side of the boat. The security field crackled excitedly just millimeters from my head. Daac stooped so as not to contact it.

Ibis pointed over the side, and then indicated with

three fingers that he was going count us in. From the pocket of his suit he produced a small object. He released me, balancing the remote in one hand and holding the fingers of his other hand aloft.

We jumped on cue.

Correction. They jumped. I did a dead body impersonation.

By the way! No, I can't swim.

It crossed my mind as the water claimed me, and panic strangled my breath for the hundredth time in a few days, that for a bodyguard I wasn't much of a thrill seeker. Maybe I needed to visit Doll for some neuroprogramming.

Or at least a swimming chip.

Daac dragged me downward into the blue depths with him. When I thought I would finally pass out from oxygen dep, I took a breath. Just as he'd said, the suit was cycling breathable air and hummed steadily in my ear.

As my vision slowly cleared I attempted to stroke with one arm and kick, to help him.

Down this far, the water seemed crowded with distorted shapes and the dull tug of pressure.

At the bottom Ibis forced a salt-encrusted grating off a pipe inlet. He waved us to hurry, swiveling his head anxiously.

Checking for water 'pedes?

In the supercities canal living was not unusual for the very rich. The water 'pedes discouraged little escapades like ours.

Suddenly I wanted to get into the safety of that pipe as urgently as I'd wanted to jump out of the 'copter.

Daac went through it first, followed by me, then Ibis. He didn't wait for Ibis to pull the cover back but wriggled straight on down the pipe like a giant worm.

I knew if Daac's shoulders fitted then so would mine, but now I was inside the pipe . . .

Add claustrophobia to my desensitization list!

We squirmed along for an eternity. Daac's feet flapped in front of my face. I supposed Ibis had the same angle of me, but it was too cramped to turn and look.

Several times we jackknifed at pipe junctions, changing direction. I tried to estimate the elapse of time and the possible limits to my suit's air supply.

Neither calculation made me feel good. I had to trust that Daac and Ibis knew what they were doing.

Trust! What a shitty word!

I was so busy whining to myself that I head-butted Daac's feet.

He'd stopped. Something was wrong.

A moment later Ibis whacked into me.

I waited between them, not knowing why.

The water grew colder and colder. The chill penetrated my suit. It started at the tip of my nose and spread across my body. The only sound was of my own teeth chattering. Even the suit's transparent mask clouded with ice particles. A cold shadow appeared at the edge of my mind, spreading. Conscious thoughts began to fade.

Then a jolt of adrenaline stirred the faintest warmth inside me. I had a vision of my Angel melting ice with a torch.

Warming my body, especially my feet. Tapping them warm . . . Tapping the soles of my feet . . .

My feet? It was Ibis!

I scrubbed at my faceplate and looked for Daac's feet, but the water above me was empty. How long had I been immobile?

I lurched forward, frantic that we'd lost Daac. Ibis must have been thinking the same thing, nudging me along every time I slowed down.

After a few minutes we reached a T junction. No sign of Daac. I cursed him for not noticing we'd dropped off the chain, and myself, for losing us.

If only I could ask Ibis the way, but the width of the pipe didn't allow for friendly chinwags. In desperation I wedged my knees up as close to my chest as I could, reached down with my hands and began making frantic hand signals.

Eventually Ibis responded by tugging my left hand. I had no idea if he understood what I was trying to say. My own senses told me we'd been moving steadily west and the junction lay north-south. His guess or nonguess would have to be better than mine.

The left junction led south so I slithered into it with the small comforting thought that The Tert lay in that direction. The idea of getting back to Torley's and my own tiny room seemed like the best I'd ever had.

I slithered and crawled along so desperately that in the end I almost missed the way out. A shaft of light in the water, enough to make me look up.

Where the smooth top of the pipe should have been was more water. Carefully I reached through. Another, wider pipe, ran vertically from the one we were in. A rung jutted out of one side, and the whole diameter felt rough in texture like it had been made from a different substance.

Something inside said, *Here.*

I thought about doing my Kamasutra act and trying to explain what I'd found to Ibis, but I knew it was the right place.

I climbed steadily for about twenty meters hoping that Ibis would either follow me or wait below at the junction.

My legs shook with the effort of climbing and I could hear my own breath rattling, ragged and uneven. The last week had begun to take its toll. So had dropping eight meters from a 'copter into a moat, and being tossed around like popcorn in the bottom of a boat.

Suddenly my head burst free of the water. I blinked as water dripped off the faceplate. Daac peered anxiously down into the mouth of the pipe.

He smiled a force fifty at me. Then he reached down and hauled me out. My feet barely touched the last few rungs.

He dumped me on the floor of a well-lit basement.

I stumbled and turned back anxiously for Ibis, but the plump figure emerged seconds behind me.

Not bothering to hide my trembling hands, I tore off the suit and gulped in some real air. For a moment I thought Daac was going to kiss me again, but he settled for a bone-crunching squeeze. I sagged heavily against him.

"What happened to you?" he demanded.

"Th-the c-cold. I c-couldn't move. Then I l-lost you."

Daac nodded. "It's a freeze organism. Designed to kill anything living in the pipes. The suit is enough to protect you if you know what to expect. I thought if you were between us it would be all right."

Ibis stood beside us, grinning. His plump face seemed none the worse for the last hour or so.

"You gave me a moment, pet. Back there. My fantasy of being alone with you wasn't in a water pipe!"

I couldn't help but warm to him. The man had saved my life. Impulsively I hugged him.

"I don't know why you did it, Ibis, but thanks. Thanks a lot."

He tutted. "Don't let Pat catch you doing that."

Daac shoved a tube of sweet liquid into my hand. "Here. We have to keep moving. This will help. Did you get them?"

"What?"

"Her files?"

"You knew?"

"Not exactly . . . call it a guess."

Questions clamored over each other in my mind. Too many people knew what I was doing before I even did it. "Is that how you found me? A guess?"

"I never really lost you."

"You mean you followed me the whole time?"

"Not exactly *followed*." He got cagey.

"How then?"

"Did you get them?" he repeated impatiently.

"Why should I tell you?"

"Call it a trade. How I found you, for proof you've got Razz's files."

Something told me I'd regret it, but I had to know how he was able to follow me.

"Yes, I got them." I fished inside the cheesecloth to my leather tank and pulled out the wiper Lang had given me—the Zip disk lay snugly in another place. No point in giving away all my secrets!

The wiper lay small, wet and black in my hand like an oyster shell.

He restrained himself from snatching it—just.

I closed my fingers over it deliberately. "And you . . . ?" I trailed off.

He paused before answering. "My comm spike has a locator."

"Your comm spike!" I felt inside the tank again, this time for the spike. I had it close to my heart. Too close.

My hand trembled with cold and anger. Mainly anger.

I threw it into his outstretched hand in disgust. "How did you get onto M'Grey?"

"I have a permit." Daac shrugged. "If you'd told me where you were going . . ."

He had a permit! My head reeled with possibilities. "You mean I could have *walked* . . . What about the boat?" I demanded.

Ibis chipped in. "We . . . er . . . camped on it last night."

I shook my head in amazement. They'd been in it while I'd spent a miserable night between two concrete pylons a few meters away.

Life sucked!

"Let's go." Daac plucked a kit bag from the corner and threw it over his shoulder.

I thought mournfully of my own bag scattered on the bottom of the moat somewhere. Now I had nothing left but my pins and the garrotting wire in my G-string. It would take me a year to save enough for another sniper rifle, let alone the worm. And I'd used all my charms—the explosive ones, that is.

I glanced around at the basement. "Where are we?"

"Later," said Daac. "We move."

Ibis placed an arm around my shoulders, steering me to a narrow set of stairs. "How did you know which vertical to take?" he whispered.

I stared at him for a moment. "What do you mean? There was only one."

He shook his head slowly. "No. We must have passed at least a dozen after we lost Loyl."

Something tightened my chest. I remembered the Angel's voice in my head when I was in the 'copter. Then the image of it warming my frozen body. And the sense of urgency forcing me upward.

What was happening to me?

I smiled brightly at Ibis. "Just damn lucky, I guess!"

Chapter Fifteen

Ibis let us into a tiny, sparsely furnished condo unit in the medium gyro of the city shortly after nightfall. There'd been no Intimate in the lobby. Just some vandal-proof tissue recognition samplers and lots of deadlocked doors. The sorta place you never see your neighbors.

With a few muttered excuses that Pat would be worried to death, and a stern warning for us not to harm each other, he left us to it.

I wasn't exactly happy about being alone with Daac but fatigue dampened my finer instincts. And I didn't have any better ideas.

He went to the fridge and ripped open two beers. "San's in there." He pointed toward the bathroom door.

"You first," I insisted, not sure that I trusted him. Or myself.

He shrugged and took his drink into the shower.

The beer tasted wonderful. I gulped down most of the can and when I was sure the water was safely running, I slid the wiper out of my top and began to examine it. After a quick check to make sure the unit's PC had nothing much on it, I gingerly sleeved the disk. It was a clever piece of deception, for all intents formatted like normal storage—with fake download icons—while it actually erased.

"Couldn't wait, eh?" Daac spoke quietly into my ear.

I stopped the disk running and swiveled abruptly.

He pulled a side table across to sit on. Moisture from the shower glistened on his skin. It made me aware of how filthy my hair must be and that what was left of the caftan hung in clumps.

"I should shower now," I said nervously.

He shook his head. "I don't think this can wait any longer."

"OK," I agreed cautiously. "So start talking."

"I told you about Anna's research?"

"What's she got to do with it?" I frowned.

He gave the fleetest of smiles. "Didn't you wonder who might be funding it? How someone with my background had access to a fully fitted lab and an ultralight? How I could come and go so easily in Viva?"

I shrugged. "I guess I figured Anna had money herself. Hell, she owns *acreage*."

"She also has some advanced genetic research teknology available. Even Anna's inherited wealth has limits."

I thought of the body scanner. "So what's your point?"

He paused again, his flesh hand twitching. The man was wrestling with some serious discord.

"Knowing this will put you in more danger."

More danger! "Well, not knowing is definitely gonna get me killed," I said dryly.

"Razz Retribution is . . . was funding our research."

My mouth opened and closed stupidly for a moment. *Why would a media princess fund research to help the wasted?*

He knew what I was thinking. "She had . . . her reasons. But someone knew about the results. They figured if they snuffed out our financial backing then we would have to stop."

"Who?" The blood in my veins turned to ice.

"I'm not sure. At least I'm not sure why. But it didn't stop there. They've stolen Anna's research as well. The only other records of everything we've done *are on that disk*." His voice trembled as he nodded toward the PC.

My heart lurched. What should I tell him? That I'd wiped it? Or that I'd wiped *some* of it and saved the rest? How much did I trust him?

Easy answer.

Not!

I played for time. "Why did Lang hook me into this robbery?"

"My guess is he wants to hang something on Jamon. Everyone knows you're er . . . Jamon's . . . property. Any act you commit would be linked to him. And . . . Parrish . . . you're the perfect decoy. Enough smarts to look like a burglar. Expendable. What bait did he use to get you to do it? I bet it wasn't just cred."

His last statement galled. Made me want to scream. But hell, it was true.

I hunched on the chair, shivering, thinking about how Lang had scammed me. He'd promised me the files would see Jamon in jail. He'd neglected to say that I'd be there too.

If Daac hadn't pulled me out of the moat, I'd be quod fodder right now.

We sat for a moment in silence.

I felt his impatience—waiting for me to hand the disk over.

In the end I rose stiffly, not able to look in his face. "The disk is all yours." I pulled it out of the sleeve and handed it to him. "But it's a wiper. It was camouflaged. I erased her hard drive before I realized. I'm sorry. Looks like he played us all."

Daac's face shattered into disbelief and shock.

"I'm going to take a shower," I said.

In the bedroom I removed my pins and the Zip disk, and hid the Zip in my boots. Then I washed my leather tank, which had begun to resemble something dead and dried. Finally, I climbed into the san. Hot water was the best thing that had happened to me in a long while. As it drummed my tired, battered muscles and raw knee, I mulled over Daac's revelations about Razz.

I'd been cage dancing, it seemed, for people I didn't even know.

Much as I hated to admit it, Daac's little rescue mission had kept me from jail.

But what about him?

Instinct had made me keep quiet about the Zip disk. I had no idea how much of it was corrupted, and how much information survived—if any—but I wasn't sharing that news until I worked out Daac's angle.

He'd rescued me, sure. But he'd also tailed me, and then let me walk into an ambush with the idea of busting me out only so he could get hold of Razz's files.

I didn't know whether to be mad or obliged. So I stepped from the shower, still dripping, into a robe and searched for something to patch my knee. I found skin plaster in the bathroom cabinet. I flexed it a few times and stalked back into the small living area.

He sat, slumped and defeated, on one of the narrow couches, nursing another can.

"There's one thing you forgot to explain. Why are you so busy running around saving my carcass? Was it just to get the disk? Or do I serve some other purpose in your game plan?" I demanded.

He stared at his drink in a strange, disconnected fashion. It reminded me of the look I'd seen on Lang's face at Jamon's dinner.

"My gens have always lived in The Tert. It's our land. Long before Mondo and Lang's. Even though we don't exist as a tribe anymore—our task does."

"Your task?" His flat tone gave me the creeps.

"Our land is poisoned and sick. Our Task is to reclaim it, bring it to health, bring its people to health. I'm not the first to want it. But I'm the one that will succeed."

He said the last with all the conviction of the Godhead.

"What gens?" I retorted. "The Tert is a rubbish dump of people and waste."

A sneer ghosted his face. "You're from Viva, aren't you? Originally, I mean. You wouldn't understand about family and place. When people return to one place over generations, it becomes part of their soul's code. No matter how mean or putrid it is."

My eyes widened. "You're a native of the continent?"

Daac laughed harshly. "Maybe once. Genetically I'm as much a mishmash as you. But gens is a complicated thing. Hard to define. Those of us that carry the thread of *l'origine* know and understand. We've kept records."

"*L'origine.* Who else shares this crazy notion?"

He focused on the blank wall opposite. "There are many. Some you even know."

"Yeah," I said skeptically, "try me."

His gaze burned like a blowtorch. "This information is not given lightly, Parrish. Treat it with respect."

My shivers came back. "OK," I said. "Cross my heart and all the rest . . ."

He didn't look satisfied. But it was the best I could do. Today—this week—had been too weird. I waited, mopping the drips from my hair on the robe, while he decided what he would tell me.

"Raul Minoj," he said, finally.

"Minoj!" I yipped.

The last half an hour had ripped my understanding of my world in half. Now Daac was handing out free facelifts to the people I knew.

"But I asked Minoj if he knew—'"

"He is my gens, Parrish, not my friend. There is a difference. He may not speak well of me. Or speak of me at all. But he would always help me. And he would *never* betray me."

"Oh." I sank down into the opposite couch. "So Anna's research will heal your gens?" I said, speaking slowly.

"Yes."

"But where do I fit in?" My voice trembled in a manner that I positively did not like.

He levered himself up and joined me on my seat, wedging his torso and thigh against mine. Then he reached his real hand out and cupped my face.

"What *exactly* did Lang hire you to do?"

I thought for a moment. There seemed no harm in telling him now. "He said if I secured files from the PC at this address I would get a reward. Seemed easy enough. I had no idea it was Razz Retribution's house."

"Lione. Her real name was Lione Marchand," he said.

Emotion caused his hand to tighten on my jaw and something told me not to pull away. I stilled, fighting the trapped feeling.

"What was your reward, Parrish?"

"He said he'd get Jamon off my back."

"And now?"

"I guess he set me up. Told me to download the files and gave me a wiper instead. He didn't figure

on the cavalry coming to bail me out." I tried a grin
but he had my cheeks in a death grip. "Thanks, by
the way."

"Those files were my only chance to save what
we've learned. Without them Anna must begin
again. Only . . ."

"Yes?" I encouraged.

"Only now most of the money has also gone."

I could see grief and frustration in his eyes.

"Why didn't you go and get them yourself?" I
asked. "You said you could get onto M'Grey."

"For the same reason I had to help you get out. I
couldn't risk being turned into the scapegoat. I didn't
murder Lione. But they want blood. Nobody kills
media and stays free."

Then who did? The question hung unanswered between us.

"I should hate you for using me," I sighed. "But
I'm too tired and hungry."

"I didn't exactly use you, Parrish. When I returned
to The Tert, Sto needed protection and I needed time to
sort things out. You kept him safe while I got in
touch with my people. There was a purpose to that.
When you're meant to do great things there are always people who help you."

I stared openmouthed at his rationalization and
wondered how he could sound so plausible one moment, and so insane the next.

His hand dropped from my face and he traced the
line of the robe where it crossed over my breasts. I
could have slapped him away but the scent of his
body overpowered me. The deeper I inhaled, the further I sank.

I remembered his tongue in my mouth.

His next words came slowly, like a man unwind-
ing his self-control in tiny movements. "I need you
now."

I laughed shakily. "Sure of yourself, aren't you?"

He nodded. "On this, yes."

I couldn't think of a comeback. I mean, what do you say to that?

I knew I should run. Or shout, "No way, not in twenty lifetimes."

Call it weakness.

Call it vanity.

Call it downright confusion.

Call it the cobra paralyzed by the sway of the charmer. But I did nothing.

He leaned forward and ran his tongue over my lips. "Kiss me," he whispered huskily, *"please."*

His appeal was irresistible. Like his scent, and his smile, and his strange, brown eyes.

Tentatively I did what he asked. Feeling the warmth as his mouth closed around mine.

He kissed gently, drinking me in.

The sensation was heady, tantalizing. Driving away my hesitation.

He made noise in the back of his throat. His flesh hand slipped to my breast. It was warm and too damn good to push away.

Without warning he tumbled us both to the floor and pulled my robe apart, levering himself off me to gaze at my body.

His voice trembled. "Parrish, you are beautiful."

I am not beautiful.

Strong. Adept. Athletic. But not beautiful. Somewhere in my hormone-saturated brain a warning bell rang. But it got buried under an earthquake of need.

Instead of trying to enter me, he bent his head to the top of my thighs and tongued wet strokes across them. Then he parted my legs and settled himself between them, his face pressed up tight and hungry.

My body ached and my knee stung, but I lay there, totally seduced, and to my chagrin, orgasmed in seconds.

He drew back and smiled. Triumph? Amusement? Take your pick.

Then he slowly got to his feet.

"You can have the bed," he said.

I felt the loss of his body heat like a blow. I wanted to reach out for him, tell him to stay. Bring his strange intensity back to me. But I couldn't. Didn't know how.

So what's new?

Hours later I woke with the condo's mean bedroom windows casting a pale, narrow light into the room. When I enquired, the time display told me it was five thirty in the morning.

I climbed stiffly off the bed, tired and tender. My stomach complained noisily. I couldn't remember when I'd eaten last but it seemed a long time ago. The last few years I'd gotten used to living on small amounts of food, but it never stopped me wanting more.

I limped out of the bedroom to find the living area empty.

My insides churned when I took in the empty beer cans and the floor between the narrow couches.

"Having a vision?"

Daac had let himself in the front door quietly and stood behind me.

I pulled my robe tighter, turning to face him squarely. He wore a fresh set of jeans and T-shirt.

"You sneak around good for your size." I scowled.

He ignored my sarcasm, and my awkwardness, and threw a small case at me. "Clothes and *whatever* I owe you."

Owe?

I had to let go of the robe to catch it.

He set his other package down and began to unpack food. Involuntarily my mouth began to water.

"Hungry?" he asked.

"Maybe. Where'd you get your clothes?"

"It's not the first time I've been here. There are places you can buy things without questions, even in Viva. Eggs?"

"What?" I said, startled. "In the shell?"

He nodded and began pressing pads on the cooka.

After a second of indecision I picked up the bag and headed to the bedroom. "Five. Sunny side up," I called and disappeared.

The *whatever* made my eyes water and my pulse quicken. A bona fide Glock pistol—not like the repro Minoj had sold me; a concealable rifle, grenades and a collection of knives to excite any Mueno.

The clothes were nearly as good. I pulled out a set of fatigues, a black velour two-piece and mesh body armor. The body armor was light and flexible but tougher than anything I'd ever worn. I pulled on my clean leather tank top, replastered my knee and slipped into the mesh. Then I hesitated. Much as I wanted to wear the fatigues they weren't Viva. If I had to go out on the streets again I didn't want any extra attention. So I opted for the two-piece and stashed the fatigues back in the case.

Then I peered into the mirror and spoke sternly to myself.

He's gorgeous . . . but he's crazy. Remember that!

The smell of food eventually lured me back out into the living area.

Daac gave me a quick, appraising glance and then concentrated on dishing up eggs, cooked bread and a hot liquid that looked like muddy water and tasted fantastic.

I sat at the breakfast bar and took a sip. "Tea?" I murmured appreciatively.

He nodded.

"I heard you could get it again, in Viva. They've found a new way to grow it."

Daac slid a plate in front of me.

It looked great, right down to the little bread triangles and bits of green stuff for decoration. I prayed my stomach would handle it.

As I was about to take the first bite, I remembered the cuttlefish Jamon had tried to serve me. I paused midscoop. "Battery hens?"

He sat down opposite me and took a mouthful of his own. "Of course. I'm not trying to poison you with free-range stuff, Parrish," he said dryly. "Not after crawling through water pipes for the express purpose of keeping you alive."

He had a point there. I picked up my fork and began shoveling.

Daac ate more slowly, an amused gleam in his eye.

"What's so funny?" I asked suspiciously.

"When was the last time you ate?"

"Breakfast at the Emporium," I said, stuffing hot bread into my mouth.

"And before that?"

"A while." His attention was making me uncomfortable. In fact the whole thing did. Sitting, eating breakfast together, making conversation—it wasn't normal!

I tried changing the topic. "What exactly did Razz—Lione—have on her files?"

He sighed. "Anna's identified the genes that produce the genetic resistance to heavy metals. We were about to begin mass splicing of individual DNA. In fact we've already trialed some. In a generation or two the changes will be reproducing themselves more quickly than if we waited for the process to occur naturally. Our birthrate in The Tert is surprisingly high—but this way our children might actually stay alive a bit longer. We kept a backup of everything on Razz's PC. It was part of the agreement. Her security is so tight, it seemed a good idea."

Tight? Yeah, well I could vouch for that! "You seem to know a lot about this science gig."

He shrugged. "ALC."

Accelerated Learning Chip. Somehow I didn't buy that. There was something about his whole manner—at times it was almost . . . moneyed . . . educated beyond the normal Viva netschooler. Certainly not Tert scum.

"So how will you finance it now?"

"Maybe, in time, we can convince someone else to back the project. At the moment it's too risky—not knowing who we're up against."

"Where's this come from?" I tugged at my clothes and gestured to the case. "And this apartment? Who pays for that?"

Daac looked away from me, embarrassed. "People owe me . . . at least they owed Razz. I pulled in some favors. She had a lot of influence," he said finally.

His meaning struck me like a whiplash. "You were balling her, weren't you? *She owned you!*"

He didn't answer.

Unreasonable anger flared in me. Like a girl who'd just found out the guy she was smitten with was a porn star.

"Who else? I s'pose you're doing Schaum as well."

He leaned over the breakfast bar, no longer embarrassed. More like a thunderhead about to drop its load.

"And who the hell do you think you are? A vestal virgin?"

I stiffened, fists clenched. "I play it straight. That's who I am. Just trying to find a piece of air that no one else can fuck up."

"Can anyone join in, or is this a private show?"

Ibis's mild voice stopped us dead in our tracks. The plump man strolled into the room taking in the dirty plates. He threw me an outrageously flirtatious grin. "What are you complaining about? He cooked you breakfast."

I stalked off into the bedroom without a word to either of them.

Later, when Ibis finally tempted me out, Daac had gone.

I checked the condo city map and began plotting a route home. My new kit was packed up by my feet. I considered leaving it behind and then thought better. Daac owed me that much at least.

Realizing my intention to cut out, Ibis clucked around me. "You have to stay. There are too many people looking for us—for you. We'll get you out, but you have to be patient. Loyl's calling in some favors."

Patient? He had the wrong bod.

"What favors?" I raised a cynical eyebrow. "Grrl?"

"Tolly's not a girl," he objected. "She's a system and strategist tek. Anyway, there's a citywide search on. He's trading with her—a copy of the police search pattern model for—"

"Don't tell me!" I put my hand up.

Ibis gave a quick, semiapologetic smile.

I flicked out of the map and marched into the bedroom, glancing through all the net broadcasts. Ibis was right. Teknicolor Parrish. If I poked my nose out of the door, I'd be quod bait.

The knowledge depressed me. So did the fact that I was reliant on *Mr.* Tall, Dark and Certifiable.

Ibis pottered around the flat, tidying while I sat sullenly on the couch watching him. Eventually curiosity got to me. "How do you know him?"

Ibis poured two teas and brought me one. He sat opposite. "We're related, actually."

My eyes widened. "You?" He had to be joking. Ibis was medium height, soft-bellied, fair-skinned and playful while Daac was a strange, intense, dusky, humorless giant.

"Distant," Ibis acknowledged. "Loyl is obsessed with family. If you're blood then you're a brother. He *is* rather divine, don't you think?" He sighed heavily. "But straight."

"How did he meet Razz Retribution? Don't tell me she was related too?"

Ibis raised an eyebrow. "He told you about her?"

I nodded, lying. "Sure."

Ibis's eyes misted over and I couldn't tell if he was for real. "Loyl was devastated when she was murdered."

"You'd never know it," I bitched.

"She was a darling. But she was still media. She thought the world of Loyl. He persuaded her to keep investing in Anna's research. Even after the death threats."

"Death threats?"

Ibis stopped guiltily. "I'm talking too much."

Yes, you are, I thought, and it had opened a tiny window into Daac's mind.

Call me a cynic, but I've yet to meet anybody who wasn't motivated first at a personal level—even those with the grandest ideals. Everything else comes second to personal cost. Daac might believe in family and his "task," but I reckoned that right now he was working off gut reaction—guilt and anger.

His lover dead, his life's work smashed. Those, at least, were things I could understand.

This "higher purpose" gig, on the other hand, gave me nausea.

Or maybe it was those annoying creatures that had taken root in my stomach, flipping and fluttering every time Daac looked at me.

Eventually Ibis left to meet Pat. Or so he said. His worried look told me he'd gone searching for Loyl.

To keep my mind focused, I unsealed the neck of my body armor and fumbled for the Zip disk. Then

I shoved the couch against the door and sat down at the PC.

It came up with a scribble of symbols. Information was there, but I'd need help to retrieve it.

Teece!

I shut down the PC, tucked both the disks away, put the couch back and rummaged in the kitchen for some bread. Then I went and lay on the bed. One-World flickered on the wall screen but I didn't much feel like seeing myself in cross section. Instead I curled up in a ball with the Glock under my pillow, three knives strapped on, and the case with the grenades in easy reach. I drowsed, not really sleeping deeply, in case I dreamt something stupid—and blew myself up.

"Parrish." A deep, insistent growl in my ear.

"Mmm?" I muttered languorously to the familiar voice. Maybe I had been dreaming of Daac, a little.

It warned, "We've got company."

I sat bolt upright snapping the Glock into a draw. All I saw was my own mussed-up reflection in the mirror.

Daac was at my side, crouched, peering through a crack in the door.

Ibis's voice drifted through from the living area, flirtatious and calm.

"Oh my," the plump man cooed. "My lucky day. A big hard man."

"Military 43971A, Spirelle. This building is being searched. We suspect you may be harboring a dangerous criminal. Step aside."

Daac and I exchanged eloquent glances. The corny, tin voice was a "roustie." Mechanoid military. They were called rousties because they got to clean up the mess, the daggs, the deaders, like the roustabouts in shearing teams back when raw materials were still harvested from live animals.

That was a good and bad sign. Rousties were thorough and uncompromising—no humor at all. Ibis was wasting his time flirting. On the other hand they could be damn stupid if you knew how to mess with their logic.

Daac eased the door shut and crawled over to me.

"Pack up your gear," he whispered.

I was already doing it.

My mind raced through possibilities. The window wasn't one. Fifty-five storys down and anyway it didn't open. The laundry chute? At a pinch I might fit down it, but Daac had no chance. That left the contents of my case as my only hope. I could blow the whole unit off the side of the condo.

To my surprise, Daac was busy stripping off.

I smacked him silently on the bare shoulder. "What the—"

"They must have followed me back here. Tie me up," he whispered fiercely.

I stared at him. By this time he was down to his underwear.

Sweat collected on my brow. A weird mixture of fear and excitement coddled in my stomach. I wondered if he'd been with another woman. Tolly, was it?

"Quit sweating," he hissed, "they can detect it. After you've tied me, get into the chute. Slide to the first junction. No farther, or you'll end up going all the way. The fall will kill you, or the steam cleaners will blister your skin off. I'll drop this down when it's safe to come back." He held up a length of black nylon cord. "Now tie me up, but loosely near my hands."

My eyes stayed riveted to his body, as he peeled the last of his clothes off.

He tore the bedclothes down and lay spread-eagled on the bed, naked. Sculpted muscle and the finest matt of dark hair. His nipples were black.

Desire flooded me and my feet were rooted to the spot.

"Parrish," he whispered again, the barest hint of humor. "Later."

His soft sarcasm ripped me from the jaws of my libido. I had him trussed like a rolled roast in about thirty seconds.

"Promise me something," he whispered as I picked up my case and scrambled into the chute.

I glanced back at him, questioning.

"Promise me we can do this again."

I pulled a face.

Ibis raised his voice. "But I'm entertaining. You can't go in there. Don't you understand?"

The roustie would be online to the human-manned command module. Boy, were they in for a treat! I looped the case over my wrist and shimmied into the chute.

I reckon I did it with about a minute to spare. As I slid round the bend, Ibis squealed in mock outrage, then I couldn't hear any more.

The first branch was about five meters down and though I wedged myself to slow the slide, the Y-bend nearly cut me in two. I rubbed my offended parts and balanced there clumsily.

A load of clothes dumped down the left branch caught me by surprise and I nearly slipped. I wound up wearing underwear on my head and having to stuff towels and suits down either side of my legs.

A girl could get a disease in a place like this!

With the case protecting my head, I scrunched over to one side of the chute and siphoned things past. It worked, mostly, except for one very big drop that shortened my neck.

While I waited, I thought about Daac, tied up and naked on the bed. And me, stuck in a laundry chute, raining dirty washing.

The universe was a complete bastard!

An hour or more ticked by. Either there was a problem, or they'd forgotten me. How long can it take for a roustie to search an apartment?

I wiggled around in the chute and started experimenting. The sides were smooth and slippery and, unless I grew suckers, impossible to climb very far. I could probably puncture holes in the sides and use them as finger holds. But would the damage set off an alarm?

I filed that idea as a last resort.

At this stage going down was a lot more attractive than going up. But I needed something to slow me. Especially if a load dropped through at the same time.

The actual laundry was probably in the basement, which made the length of the tubes something that didn't bear thinking about. Fifty-plus tiers down.

Whew! Maybe I'd sit and wait a bit longer.

Then a humming noise started up below me. It grew louder by the minute. Service drone? Had to be! The chute had probably reported a blockage.

Me.

I'd never seen a chute drone before but my imagination did a great job. No doubt it had pincers to loose tangled garments. I pictured myself being skewered by claws and dragged down into the steam vats.

What seemed like the tame alternative to facing the roustie suddenly sent ripples of fear through me.

Hurry up, Loyl!

The chute vibrated as the drone got closer. I racked my brains for ideas.

Maybe I could confuse it, mislead it up the other chute. With any luck it'd have to go right to the top before it could come down again.

Carefully I opened my suitcase and checked over the contents. Rifle, knives, grenades.

Tempting!

I pulled open the velcro pouch. My new set of fatigues.

With a pang of regret, I pulled the pants free and unclipped the SOG. A more basic model than the one I'd had—but fine in a pinch.

Then I searched for a seam in the left branch of the chute. The nearest one—apart from the one I was sitting on . . . was just out of reach. Naturally!

With a steadying breath I dropped my knees carefully onto the narrow ledge I was perched on and stretched. The case was the problem. If I held it on my left arm it affected my balance. If I hooked it on my right, it was too heavy to use the tool. In the end I settled for clutching it between my thighs.

After a few minutes of scraping with the SOG, a sliver of aluminium ruptured and I snagged the pants firmly onto it.

Sweat poured off me.

The drone had shifted from a hum to a dull roar. Close. But judgment was everything. If I tried to wedge up the right chute too early I'd get tired and slip. Last minute only.

I breathed deeply and focused.

I can do this. I do not want to spend my life in a Viva jail. Survive! I told myself. SURVIVE.

I felt the vibration in my teeth. It must be only a few meters away.

I forced myself up into the right tube, higher than the first seam, and braced. But my wet palms slipped and I immediately slid back down half the distance.

As I scrabbled back up, I wondered abstractly how much it would cost for Doll to edit out my sweat response? Add it to the list. If I was going to keep this kind of stuff up I needed to take a serious look at my profile. A natural, pretty much unmodified girl could only do so much!

The drone roared to the junction and stopped, its bearded sensors flickering like long tongues up either chute. I held my breath while it sniffed the fatigues. It shot out an articulated hand to free the obstruction. The snag turned it into a tug of war, which threw the machine into confusion. I hoped it was programmed not to tear things.

Then I wondered if that would include me.

Eventually the drone won but it ripped the clothing in the attempt. It stopped still in its tracks and set off an alarm like a cold-blooded yowl. So much for my plan! My legs began to shake with the strain and I knew in a few seconds I'd slide right down onto those creepy sensors and drop my butt into the clutches of that articulated hand.

I'd already begun to slide, when a black cord slapped me across the cheek. I snaked it around my wrist and began a frantic, scrambling climb.

Muscles screamed.

Daac pulled me out of the chute at the other end. "What kept you?" I snarled.

He didn't reply.

Then I noticed his eyes. Shot to hell. His back and chest, still naked, were a raw mass of bleeding flesh. He trembled like a tortured animal.

Ibis was flaked on the bed, out cold.

"Jee-sus! What?"

"Boys in the command module thought they'd have some fun. Seems they were homophobic," he whispered.

I reached out a tentative hand to his chest. They weren't ordinary whip marks. They were burns.

"Bastards!" I cried.

He flinched. His eyes glazed over in pain.

How had he ever pulled me up that chute?

"There's a stinger in your case. Wake Ibis."

I nodded and snapped the case open. "What about you. Any opiates?"

He shook his head. "Can't. They gave me a derm of Crear. Can't combine it with opiates. Anna will have something to help." He stumbled over to near the bed and slumped down.

I whacked Ibis with the wake-up derm and he surfaced in a couple of minutes. Apart from having eyes as bloodshot as Daac's, he seemed OK.

Daac on the other hand was starting to shock.

Ibis helped me lay him on the bed. "It's too dangerous to bring Anna here. We'll have to get him to her."

"How long will that take?" I asked, worry gnawing in my gut.

"With a 'pede, only thirty minutes. If nothing stops us."

"Get one," I said.

But he was already gone.

Ibis wasn't long yet it seemed like a year. Daac tossed restlessly on the bed, complaining of thirst and moaning quietly as his wounds bled onto the sheets.

I tore the top sheet up and tried to wrap it around some of the worst burns, but he wouldn't keep still. Blood and a watery, yellow fluid stained everything.

Eventually he fell into unconsciousness. My worry blossomed into prickles of pure panic. Did people die from this?

I noticed his fingers had a bluish, bruised look. I crawled next to him and cradled his head in my arms, whispering to him, "Come on Loyl, we're taking you to Anna. You're the one who said she could fix anyone. Just hang on."

I don't remember how Ibis, Pat and I managed to get him to the basement 'pede bays. I do remember that strength wasn't an issue. If it was going to save his carcass, I reckon I could have carried him across a continent—ten continents—over hot lava. Aside from the mixed up feelings I had about him, he was too damn beautiful to waste.

We laid him in the back and Ibis and I stuffed ourselves in around him. Pat leapt into the driver's seat and set out for Anna's with all the finesse of an overdosed speed freak.

With the windows opaqued I couldn't see much outside. We sat tense, breathing each other's oxygen, waiting for the whine of an intercept 'pede or the slub of a police 'copter.

Either way I was in the mood for a fight.

I broke the silence. "Why haven't they stopped us yet?"

"I'm using the search pattern coordinates Loyl got from Tolly—and I'm skirting them. Seems most available mobile units are on the search for you, but they can't cover everything," said Pat. "Besides, once they start something full-scale like this, they get a lot of distraction. People who think they've seen you. And then there's all the ones they bust accidentally. Slows the whole thing down."

He pointed to the screen on the dashboard. I strained forward from where I sat, squeezed behind Loyl. The dashboard's virt map looked like a bunch of pissed-off ants deserting the nest. "But what about the rousties?"

"Could have been bad luck they followed him. Anyway, nothing linked him to you in the end. They were just having fun," Ibis finished grimly.

I sank back, sick with confusion and fear. How did I get into this?

Forever later, the 'burbs bled into the green-gray of the farmlets of the Outer Gyro.

Daac's moans tapered off, and as soon as he quieted I wished he hadn't. Anything to let me know he was still alive. I fixed my eyes on the quick heaves of his naked, bloodied chest and breathed every breath in time.

As Pat hurled the 'pede the last distance I could hear him on the comm. "Anna, track us in and drop the security domain at twenty meters. I'm not braking for pleasantries."

"How bad is he?" Static broke up the distress in her voice.

"Bad," confirmed Pat. "See you in the shed."

The shed?

I thought of her warehouse and its medical facilities. I hoped she had the right gear to treat him. Scientists weren't usually paramedics. But then Daac had brought me to her when he thought I was seriously injured.

Ibis must have read my thoughts. He squeezed my hand. "Anna knows what she's doing. She spent ten years in a combat clinic in the Territory."

I stared at him in surprise. His eyes were ruined, inflamed and heavy-lidded, but his smile was comforting and sincere.

"You're kidding me?" Maybe Dr. Schaum had some redeeming points. If she could save Daac, I might even cut her some slack.

Ibis turned his head toward me and dropped a kiss lightly on my cheek. I didn't smile back as I returned to my vigil of counting Daac's breaths—but ever so gently, I laid my head on his shoulder.

It took hours for Daac to stabilize.

The first couple of hours Pat, Ibis and I hovered, while Anna worked on rehydrating his body. Silent tears streamed down her face. My own emotions—raked raw already—were thrown by her distress.

"He'll be all right, now, won't he?" I begged for her reassurance as we all shared a late-night meal.

She shot me a look of pure hatred. "This is your fault. And you didn't even get what we wanted."

"Anna!" Ibis intervened. "You're upset. Please . . ."

She swallowed hard, like she was trying to catch hold of something, then got up and returned to her patient.

I should have left the compound then, but something stopped me. I had to know Daac would make it before I did.

Early the next morning I went for a run around the compound, to think. Ibis watched me from a peculiar structure he called a "gazebo."

I pulled up near him, sweating and buzzed, mind clear.

"My God, Parrish," he gasped in awe. "Why aren't you doing this for a living?"

I thought of Kat and shrugged. "It's just another type of prison, Ibis."

"But you could have been free of all this." He waved his hands in the air.

"Free? That's one thing I wouldn't have been. Athletes are paid meat with an expiry date," I said bitterly. "I should know. My sister is one. Five years tops, I give her, before I get the call to say she's dead. Performance enhancers get them all in the end. It has to be that way."

"And to think, one time they were illegal," Ibis said.

We shared a comfortable sort of silence for a while, staring out in the direction of Anna's "shed." From the outside it looked so ordinary. The sort of place you might store your garden fertilizer.

"I'm leaving soon," I told him.

"I guessed," he sighed.

"Will you help me?"

His nod was brief.

* * *

Still, I hung around until the evening, hoping for news, watching the others roam restlessly. I was alone when Anna Schaum stepped outside for a break.

She spoke first. "He's conscious."

I started eagerly toward the door, then I caught her miserable expression in the moonlight. It stopped me dead.

"Do you know what he wanted?" she said.

"Wanted?" I was surprised at such an irrelevancy. He was conscious. He was alive. Who cared what he wanted?

"You," she choked out accusingly.

I stifled a nervous laugh. Her misery was so apparent, her hatred of me undeniable.

Usually people disliked me for a *good* reason. Jealousy over a man was hard to swallow and something I wasn't used to. But I'd be damned if *I* was going to apologize for it.

On the other hand, Schaum had saved his life. I could forgive her a lot for that.

It spurred me to do the closest thing I could to actually being sensitive—I walked away without seeing him.

Sometime after midnight I slipped out of the main house and crossed the darkness to Anna's shed. Daac had been moved across to the house and the facility was deserted. It wasn't locked; there was no need now.

Kneeling before Anna's favored PC, I initiated a search through her work files. Somehow I couldn't bring myself to sit in her chair.

After my practice run at Razz's PC, Anna's keyhole was cinch. Even her password was stupidly obvious: *Loylmedaac.*

For a scientist, she was a real girl!

Once I was in, it took a while to find what I was looking for and when I did most of it was sci-speak and cryptic notes. I flicked through them looking for anything that made sense. When I found it, it didn't help a bit.

Observations of genetically modified trial group. Participants chosen by L-m-D:

> *Changes noted to the behavior of the chromaffin granules and adrenergic receptors.*
> *Neurotransmitter activity increased.*
> *Increased glycogenolysis noted.*

Patient Symptoms:

> *Enhanced muscle action, nausea, sweating, hallucinatory events: hearing voices and visions, facial—*

The screen dropped out before I finished reading; an inbuilt safeguard against unwelcome snoops. It was probably rigged to an alarm.

My cue to leave!

Within a few minutes Anna and Pat were outside the shed, turning on the lights. I hid near the door as they ran in and began checking the equipment for problems. While they argued over possible causes I treated the floor to my best belly crawl and slipped out and away.

I left the compound as dawn came, waking Ibis to disengage the buffer. Pat was still asleep and for all I knew Anna was warming Daac's bed. The thought didn't make me happy.

Ibis pulled me loosely into his soft embrace.

I stood in it awkwardly.

"Take care, sweetie," he said.

"Yourself," I replied, surprised by a tinge of regret.

I couldn't remember the last time I was sad to say good-bye to someone. Maybe Kat, all those years ago. "Ibis, I've got no right to ask this, but there's a kid somewhere in Viva. King Ban's family has adopted her."

Ibis's eyes widened. "The one that was all over the news. You know that kid?"

"Yeah. I need to find out the real story. See if she's OK."

I didn't have to spell it out, Ibis understood me right away. "I'll ask around. You come see me when you've sorted out your business. I'll have word."

We hugged briefly. This time it was mutual.

"Soon," I said.

"Soon," echoed Ibis. But I saw the doubt in his eyes.

PART THREE

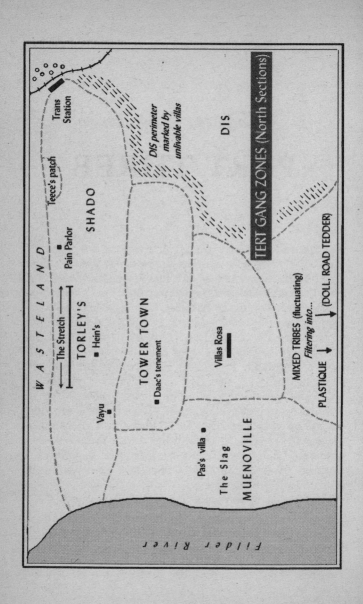

TERT GANG ZONES (North Sections)

WASTELAND

Trans Station

Teece's patch

SHADO

DIS

DIS perimeter marked by unlivable villas

Pain Parlor

TORLEY'S

← The Stretch →

Hein's

TOWER TOWN

Villas Rosa

Vayu

Daac's tenement

MIXED TRIBES (fluctuating).
Filtering into...

→ (DOLL, ROAD TEDDER)

PLASTIQUE →

Pas's villa

The Slag

MUENOVILLE

Fiilder River

Chapter Sixteen

In the end I walked most of the way to the outskirts of Viva, resting in a storm-water drain the first day. The Militia wouldn't expect me to hoof it, but I still had to dodge several 'pede patrols.

Ibis had lent me a battered old fake fur coat, stifling hot in the mild weather, but it helped me blend in with the rest of the homeless that roamed on the fringe. I hung my case over my shoulder on the inside of the coat. It rubbed reassuringly against my body armor.

I found another storm-water drain, about five in the morning, just a klick from Viva's outer limits and the main access to The Tert. 'Pedes full of rousties clustered around the checkpoint and a Prier hovered overhead like a vulture's mother. For a second I thought enviously of Daac's ultralight, until the black fear of flying flooded back.

I'd have to sprout wings before I flew again!

I sat in the mouth of the pipe, peering outward. "Where's your manners? You should knock 'fore you come in."

I jumped at the gravelly voice.

Down the other end of the drain, a pile of rubbish

grew arms and a head. In the mounting light I caught the gleam of a throwing knife.

"Just passing through. Figured this was vacant," I said carefully.

The half a body elongated slightly. "You was wrong. Not from round here, eh? There's a waitin' list. You gotta earn your drain." The knife moved subtly from one hand to the other. "On t'other hand, mebbe you're one of Trunk's mob."

"Who's Trunk?"

I slipped my hand inside the coat and fumbled the lock of my case. Normally I wore knives or pins. But at the moment advertising a walking arsenal was not a great idea.

"Put your hands out in front of you. Where I can see 'em." The voice sounded dry as Tert dust. "You prove me you not one of Trunk's. Mebbe I not kill you."

I ran through a list of possibilities. If he only had a knife I could probably overpower him. He might be an amputee. Teece warned me to watch for them round the border.

Yet something told me to tread gently. Enemies were easy to make—friends harder. I settled on the truth as my angle.

"Militia and media want me for something I didn't do. I gotta get back to The Tert. Save my arse."

The pile of papers and rags considered what I'd said. "Come close. Slow. Real slow."

"What's your name?"

"Me ask questions. You answer."

His clipped talk reminded me of Bras. "Sure," I said.

"Stop. Close enough. What under ya coat? Show. Careful."

I reached slowly inside and snapped the case off its strap. "You want to trade?" I asked.

He laughed. A wild, high-pitched sound. "What about, me take, you go. That's my trade."

"Look, I need cover till dark, then I'm gone. Maybe I can trade you time in your place for something I've got." I was close enough now to see the outline of his face and shoulders. His knife was aimed at my eye.

"Open case, put down," he ordered.

I did as he said, sliding it forward. Greedily he leaned for it.

As he moved, I rolled, snatching the largest knife cleanly from its slot, bringing it hard against his throat, knocking his own blade away. At that same moment I felt the muzzle of a semiauto slide against my belly.

"Fun, fun," he whispered with rotted-meat breath. "What do we now?"

I thought fleetingly I might faint from the stench.

"My finger quicker on trigger than your stab. I win." He cackled again.

I hesitated a second then forced a grin. "You win."

At my surrender his hand slackened, just a fraction—maybe fatigue, maybe poor judgement. I kneed the muzzle sideways with all the force I could muster. It clattered away.

Quickly I increased the pressure of my knife hand. "No ammo, was there?"

I could distinguish his features now. Long nose and sagging, lined cheeks. Eyes like a dirty pavement.

He shrugged. "You win. How much Trunk pay you to take my home?" One hand stroked the culvert wall tenderly.

Slowly, with great care, I took the knife away. Then I crawled backward keeping it raised. "Nothin'. Like I said I need some cover till dark. That's all."

His stared at me, uncomprehending. "You not kill me?"

This time I grinned for real. Keeping the knife in clear sight, I said, "I'm Parrish."

He responded with a gush of stinking breath. "Gwynn."

I dragged the case back closer to my body and rummaged through the compartments with one hand. I sent a quick thanks to Daac when I found what I wanted. I tugged an ammo clip free and waved it under his nose. "This fit your rifle?"

Gwynn studied it. He nodded hungrily.

"When I go, you can have this. As payment. Help you keep your . . . place safe. OK?"

I edged back to the other end of the pipe. "I'll keep out of your way until I go."

With that Gwynn seemed to fold back into himself, like someone had stepped on him. From where I crouched it looked like he was shaking. How the hell does he get food to eat? I wondered.

Half an hour answered my curiosity. A skinny figure crept into the opening of the culvert and up to Gwynn. The old man seemed pleased with their whispered conversation. After a quick exchange the figure crept away.

He spoke then, catching me by surprise. "You want food, Par-rish?" He held out a handful of scraps.

I was starving and inside my coat was a package of decent food from Anna's well-stocked kitchen. I felt suddenly ashamed that I hadn't offered some to Gwynn. Instead he was trying to share something that a rat would have passed up.

But then, he had tried to rob me!

"No thanks, Gwynn."

He seemed relieved and gobbled down the handful in a matter of seconds. The food sparked a mood of conversation in him. "What they want you for, Par-rish?"

I hesitated. How much did I tell this old creature?

Again, I settled on the shortened truth. "They think I killed a media hound."

Gwynn gave a tuneless whistle. "Bad."

"Yeah. And wrong," I added irritably.

"How you gonna stay out of jail?"

I smiled grimly. "I don't know."

"You know who did it?" he asked.

"Maybe."

We sat in silence for a while. Gwynn appeared to have gone to sleep.

My thoughts drifted to Anna Schaum's compound. Had Ibis gone back to the Emporium? How quickly was Daac recovering?

"You not know Trunk?"

Gwynn's voice interrupted my thoughts. I stared at him. "No. Like I said before. Who is he?"

"Trunk wants what's mine. But there's only one way he get it."

The old man was telling me he'd die for this filthy culvert.

What was it Daac had said?

Something about a place being part of your soul's code, no matter how mean or putrid it was.

Maybe that was just a fancy way of saying you had no other damn place to go.

"Mebbe I show you a way out then." Gwynn caught my attention again.

"Another way?" I held my breath.

He cackled, tapped his forehead. "Gwynn the Grate Keeper. Anywhere you need. I can show you how."

"What do you mean, 'anywhere'?"

"Those Militia out there . . . phh," he made a sound of disgust. "Gwynn show you underneath ways."

"Underneath?"

He held out his hand. "You give me ammo. I show you way to Tert."

I studied him in the shadowy light. "Should I trust you, Gwynn?"

"No," he said simply.

"Yes" would have been a lie. I fingered the clip for a moment then I threw it to him.

In seconds he had it loaded in the chamber of his semi. With a deep sigh of pleasure he settled back against the wall. "Now we wait. Be ready."

The waiting took hours. Time enough for me to doubt Gwynn's sanity—and my own, for giving him live cartridges. Gut instinct could be cool sometimes. Sometimes it could be witless.

I brooded over the times I'd been wrong and wondered if this would be one of them.

Then on some unbidden cue Gwynn stirred from his pile of rubbish and dragged his body along past me toward one end of the culvert. He was old and dirty but his shoulders looked like a weightlifter's. I guess chair aids weren't much use for drain dwellers. Nor synth legs.

I crawled behind closely, without touching him. He stopped meters shy of the other end and scraped away rubbish from the floor. With a grunt he began to strain. A slab of concrete ground freed and he easily shifted it to one side.

"Gwynn is strong," I said, impressed into comment.

His old face brightened. "Gwynn Pan-Sat medal. One time."

He dug around in his tattered shirt. From inside it he produced a vaguely silver coin on a grubby ribbon, the Pan-Sat symbols still clearly visible.

My mouth dropped.

Somehow I caught myself before the obvious question fell out of it. If Gwynn had been an ex–Pan-Sat athlete, then I guessed he wouldn't want to be discussing his current living arrangements.

He tapped his head sadly. "They look inside here. See what makes Gwynn strong without pharma. Gwynn not same after. Ever."

"You mean you won a medal *without* enhancers?"

"Gwynn born that way. Then they take me. Then they take my legs."

"What? They cut your head open and your legs off to see what made you so strong?"

"No. Cut head open to see. Then legs don't work properly anymore. Gwynn get sick. Medic have to take legs," he said.

"Who did that to you, Gwynn?"

"Don't matter, Par-rish. Past is done. Gwynn got food. Got job. Gwynn the Grate Keeper."

He sucked in a lung full of air and expanded his chest proudly. Then he poked a finger at me. "Now you go down. Go south. Pipe goes three ways. You follow east, left. To Tert. Canrats hide there too. Be careful."

I reached inside the coat and pulled out the food Ibis had given me. I gave it to him. "Here, old man. Thanks. Maybe I'll come see you again one day."

He smiled. At least I think that's what it was.

I glanced back at him as I slipped down into the gloom. But he was already sliding the grate back across. Another minute and I was in pitch-black.

Small spaces are damn awkward when you're my size. Fortunately the first few klicks of Gwynn's pipe were big enough for me to walk along in a semi-crouched manner. But even that, after a while, sent drilling pains up my legs and back. I settled into an alternating pattern of exhausting duck waddling and hunched walking. I drew the line at crawling.

I had my coat wrapped tight, and hood up, to avoid skin contact with the soil.

The hairs on the back of my neck prickled as I stretched my senses to detect canrats. I cursed the fact I'd given Gwynn all my food.

The pipes, I decided, trying to distract myself, were a maze of obsolete sewerage pipes. In sections tree roots broke through like claws. In other parts the pipes were smooth apart from a coating of dirt and mottled fungus. Some of the fungus may have been edible but I wasn't willing to risk it. Not yet anyway.

I wondered how many people knew about and used these pipes. The possibilities for undetected movement in and out of The Tert astounded me.

Periodically, smaller pipes ran off at angles. So many that I lost count. But it wasn't till my legs and stomach had clenched into a permanent cramp that I found the major junction.

Muscles screaming for relief, I sank down to rest. A brief hunt through the coat's pockets turned up a choc bar Ibis had left in there. Brilliant!

I formed a mental picture of my pleasure and sent it out to him, tagging a hug on the end.

Then I felt stupid.

Ibis was the closest thing I'd made to a friend since . . . well, ever, really.

If you didn't count Kat.

Kat was making top cred from pro ball somewhere in Eurasia. Living and playing hard. I didn't blame her for picking that option, really. A short life, but good. The last time I cried—I think—was when she left. Her choice.

At least she had one!

Gwynn's story, on the other hand, made me spit. If I ever managed to sort out my own problems and stay out of jail, I'd come back and see Gwynn. See what I could do for him. Maybe get this Trunk guy off his back for good.

There I go again!

If I didn't watch out I'd begin to sound like Daac—deciding who needed help and when.

I rubbed my lower back for a last, long moment, urging blood into it. Then I shuffled forward down the left fork of the pipe.

The first canrat appeared soon after. You don't exactly see them in the dark, more like feel them. And with my particular augs, smell them. The first whiff of damp dograt fur sent me fumbling for the Glock that I'd left loose in my coat pocket.

It was handy to be able to smell in the dark, if only I could see as well.

See what? Great golloping ropes of saliva hanging from mutated fangs—maybe not.

I aimed the Glock low.

"Let me past. No harm to you," I called out.

Canrats couldn't talk much, but most of them could understand a little. Man's best friend and nature's best scavenger combined.

It growled. Low and menacing.

How many others lurked behind it? I sensed their heavy presence close in, like a fog rolling down the pipe toward me.

I racked my brain for an alternative, one that didn't include wasting my entire ammo supply shooting the first couple of canrats I'd come across. Who knew what would happen later?

I tried a long shot. A deluded sort of idea.

Canrats had an organized community. A pecking order and a communication network. Maybe they'd heard something about my bout with "the Big One."

"I killed the Big One!" I shouted into the darkness.

The growling intensified into a cacophony of terrifying noises. Snarling. Barking. Preparatory to disembowelling and chewing.

One canrat—according to my olfaugs—had grown quickly to a dozen. I could smell their hunger.

They could smell their food. Me.

I shouted above the noise, determined to be heard, "The Big One. *I killed the Big One.*"

The snarling grew like an earthquake.

Then it came to me in a flash.

"Oya. I am Oya!"

Silence. In one eerie accord.

To my astonishment I sensed their presence withdraw. Within five minutes my olfaugs told me they'd gone completely.

I wound myself in knots over their reaction. It gave me something to think about as my back stiffened and my thirst and hunger pangs reached a critical level.

I took frequent rests. The pipe seemed grainy—or was I near to fainting?

I wanted to go back to Gwynn, but I figured I'd been crawling for six or eight hours. Way too long to return. Outside it would be night again.

Endless smaller pipes speared off the main. I began to fear wandering lost until I died.

Then, like before, in the water pipes under M'Grey Island, something attracted my attention above me. I noticed the tiniest difference. Not an opening as such, merely less fungus and filth. I concentrated on it.

I rubbed my hand over the area, protecting my eyes from falling debris with the other hand. My fingers traced three sides of a roughly chiseled square. Like someone had started fashioning a way in and stopped.

Or was it a way out?

I pushed that thought from my mind and with a surge of energy, scrabbled and scraped and pushed.

It remained stuck fast.

I thought about going further on. If others used these passages there had to be an easier way out. But Gwynn hadn't mentioned where and I, stupidly, hadn't asked.

Sometimes when you're tired, you just get damn pigheaded. I wanted to get out *now*.

I am not *going to die down here!* I told myself.

Slipping a knife from my case, I gouged and chipped along the unformed side of the square. Then I pushed and shoved until my arms turned leaden and refused to raise above my head.

Had it loosened? A fraction, maybe? A slight shift?

Spurred on, I slid down onto my back and pushed my legs upward, planting my feet inside the outline of the square.

I kicked, using my stronger leg muscles, and rocked repeatedly upward. My neck felt like snapping and my back stung with the imprint of sharp rocks, but I refused to give in.

Without a warning, the square gave way. My feet disappeared and then rebounded, throwing me on to my side.

My neck hadn't broken—I could still feel my toes. Things were improving!

Shakily I got to my feet and thrust my head up through the hole into a low, lengthy, foul-smelling space with a set of rough steps at one end. A bug-filled, grime-splattered fluoro gave out wan light. I levered through, hands and knees scraping on a carpet of filth, and crawled past rows of boxes to the steps. Gagging, I tried not to think about what was in them that could smell so bad. It clung to me like hideous cologne.

At the stop of the steps was a hatchway. Hope flared again. *Maybe an empty villa?*

The hatch moved on the third shove. A halo of bright lights and animal noises sent shooting pains through my head.

Maybe not an empty villa.

Inhaling the fresher air and blinking crazily, I waved my hand like a white flag. Right now I had no more fight. Wherever I was, I knew I'd have to talk my way out of it.

"Want no trouble," I croaked into the light.

No reply.

I squeezed through the hatchway until my head hit something. It forced me to contort sideways and slide the rest of my body horizontal, keeping my head low. I lay there panting, trying to make sense of the surrounding shape. My eyes took moments to adjust. My brain took longer.

I was in a cage.

In a smallish room.

The noises came from a group of punters caught up in some hardcore torture in the next room. I could see them through the open door.

I'd crashed a pain party.

Crap!

I'm no killjoy on this type of thing—each to his own. But I had my own brand of torment going. I didn't need barbed wire, meat hooks and electric prodders.

I tried to find a gate to the cage but there wasn't one—only a long chain and a heavy winch mechanism to lift it up. The lever was on the other side of the room.

"Let me out," I rasped, rattling the cage.

No one heard.

I rested for a few seconds, summoning my remaining energy. *"Fire,"* I roared.

Half a dozen bodies—those who weren't strapped or tied—spilled through the open door toward me. Some glazed-eyed, some drooling, some crying.

One I knew.

Stellar, the bodyshop bitch. Alive still. Barely.

That made two of us.

I recognized her fingernails and her pasty complexion. The rest of her was bondage-clad bones.

Unfortunately, her dead eyes ignited with cunning at the sight of me. She took in the open hatch and my filthy state.

"Bitch," she mouthed in welcome.

I scanned the crowd wildly for Jamon, but couldn't see him. Major mercy!

"Who is she?" The whisper spread amongst the audience.

Stellar saw an opportunity and grabbed it. She wobbled forward on absurd, crippling heels. "She is . . . Jamon's gift. He hid her in the crypt." Her arm swept toward me with a grand, trembling gesture. "A sacrifice to seal our pact."

Crypt! Eeuch! My empty stomach twisted.

"This should have been discussed," frowned a freakishly tall man with bowed shoulders, large hands and a harsh face. "He knows my rules, Stellar."

"He wanted to surprise you, Master Jayse." She knelt down in front of him, head bowed in a submissive gesture.

"But she's dirty," complained a blond woman, looking me over. Barbed-wire restraints tracked lines of blood across her body.

I tried to hold on to my calm, but it deserted at the word "sacrifice."

"Stellar!" My voice edged to the hysterical. "Over here!"

She stared at me. Curiosity entered her dull eyes. "May I be excused for a few minutes, Master Jayse? Please?"

Big Hands cupped his huge ornamental codpiece like it was a trophy. "I suppose so. Sort out how you're going to present her, Stellar. Personally, I prefer her dirty."

He turned back to his business. In seconds the next room was sick with moans.

Stellar crawled over to me. It looked prettily submissive, but she obviously had trouble standing.
When she got within reach I grabbed her arm, pulling her close to the cage.

"Get me out of here," I whispered fiercely.

"Why should I?" I saw the familiar pout, but it
lacked life. The same way her breath came in
chopped-off gasps. " Jamon will be here soon. He's
been looking for you."

"You're ill, Stellar." I tried for sympathy and fell
short.

She trembled. Sweat appeared on her upper lip.
She licked it nervously. *"La morte vite.* Who told
you?"

I shook my head. "Jamon fed us mercury-poisoned
fish that last night I saw you."

"But you . . ."

"I didn't eat mine. Lang warned me."

Her face crumpled. Something between anger, distress and disbelief.

"You'd already eaten it," I explained. "I'd have
stopped you if I could. Believe me."

I meant the last. Much as I despised Stellar, she
was a Jamon Mondo casualty.

"Why would he do that to me?"

I shrugged. "Because it pleases him. Suffering
pleases him."

She might have doubted any other answer—but
that she understood.

We sat, leaning against the wire of the cage, cheek
to cheek, while she digested what I had told her. Her
breath was sour.

"He's changed," she said. "He's making deals with
jerks like . . ." She gestured toward Master Jayse.
"And training night after night on fight sims."

Fight sims were basic battle strategy. "What are
the deals about?"

Her eyes were out of focus. I could see her struggling to think. "He says the Gentes want his turf. So he's going to get them first."

"Gentes?" I asked the question, but I feared I already knew the answer.

"Local families. Long-termers." She turned away and vomited bile.

It had me gagging again. I wanted to close the hatch behind me to stem the other smell, but at the moment it was my only way out.

"You're dying because of him, Stellar. I can see he pays for it."

A tremor ran through her.

Was it the mercury? Or emotion?

She crawled across to the lever. Tears spilled onto her hands as she worked the handle.

Emotion.

It shook me.

The cage raised on a well-oiled chain, high enough for me to roll underneath.

She lowered it down again and crawled back.

"You'd better hurry," she whispered. The tears left dirty stains on her cheeks but her eyes seemed clearer. Sadder. "Before Jamon comes. I'll tell them you beat me when I tried to wash you. Take the other door. It leads to the main corridor."

"Will they let me out?"

"Out is easy for you." She smiled weakly.

I wanted to say thanks, and that I was sorry. I could have helped her walk away from him instead of hating her. I could've . . .

But Stellar didn't want thanks. She struggled to her feet and tottered back to join the party.

Chapter Seventeen

Big Hands's pain parlor turned out to be midway between Teece's bike biz and Shadoville.

I backtracked to Teece's on the last dregs of my endurance, well disguised under layers of filth.

I found him staring miserably at the empty space in his bike shed.

"Sorry about the bike, Teece," I said, huskily.

"Parrish," he yelped, turning. "What in the Wombat are you doing here—smelling like that?"

"Need water." My tongue stuck to the roof of my mouth and my legs buckled.

He crossed the floor in three strides and scooped me over his shoulders.

"Into the tub," he ordered. "You stink worse than a canrat carcass."

He carried me to his bathroom, a small, plain two-by-four with one undeniable luxury—a bath—and stripped my clothes, piling the case on the top of the filthy coat and suit Ibis and Daac had given me.

Then he dumped me in the tub, not even waiting for it to fill or test for scalding.

He disappeared and returned a couple of minutes later with a jug of water. He set it down on the floor within my reach.

"Drink slowly. Don't drown," he muttered darkly and left me to it.

Revived a little, I soaped. As quickly as the bath filled, I emptied it and started again, not relaxing till the water lost most of its grimy tinge. Finally I sank down into its salubrious warmth.

I stayed in it for hours—hoping it would soak away my thoughts of Stellar, the pain parlor, Gwynn and Loyl-me-Daac.

It didn't. So I climbed out, took the disks from my tank and dropped them in my boot. Then I rinsed the bath clean and staggered into the bedroom.

Teece was waiting for me, bare-chested on his bed, feet up, in a faded aqua silk robe the same color as his eyes. He held a semiauto loosely in his lap.

"For me?"

"You're hot property at the moment. I got eyes out along the border. Everyone wants a piece of you."

I sighed. I had nothing on but a towel and I was too tired to care. I just curled up on the end of his bed like an oversized and bedraggled alley cat.

"C'n I borrow a piece o' this?" I slurred.

He nodded.

"Teece?" I yawned.

"What?" He leaned forward keenly.

"When I wake up, could I have something to eat?"

"Now hang on a little minute, Parrish. You're not going to sleep until we talk . . ."

I didn't hear any more.

I woke sometime later, stiffer than a corpse. The room was dark but not the pitch of night, more the grainy gray of early morning. Teece snored gently at the other end of the bed, the semi still tucked under his arm.

I lay wondering whether to slip away before he could grill me. Hungry as I was, it seemed like a better option than having to explain myself and atone for the loss of his bike and helmet.

Quietly, and as fluidly as I could manage under the circumstances, I slid off the bed.

Got as far as the door.

"Going somewhere?"

I stretched, turned and grinned at him in the half-light. "Didn't want to wake you, Teece. But I could eat an army and their boots."

He pointed to the side table and a tray laden with cold food. Cheese, pro-subs and bread.

Guilt tweaked my conscience. Teece treated me well. And what had he ever got in return? Trashed bikes!

I sat back down on the side of the bed and hoed into the food. "Thanks," between mouthfuls, "I really mean it, Teece. Thanks a lot."

He lay, propped against his pillows watching me eat, curiosity on his face. As the pile on the tray dwindled, he asked softly, "So what's going on, lovely?"

I steadily chewed every last crumb, playing for time. How much could I trust him? I wondered. He'd talked about love once. Did "love" last more than a few weeks or months for anyone? I didn't think so. Not in this town.

But I guess I owed him something. "Someone's trying to put me away. For life."

He laughed. "Tell me something I don't know. Your face is all over the nets." His brow creased. "But what happened? When you left here you told me you had a chance to make things better."

I shook my head. "Things changed." My voice trembled, just a little bit.

To make matters worse Teece touched me, lightly on the arm, a comforting pat. The simple gesture was too much. I suddenly found myself spilling the whole story.

"Lang hired me for a job, said if I got him some files from a certain place in Viva it would put Mondo in jail for life. How could I refuse a gig like that, Teece?"

He nodded, understanding. Jamon was part of the reason Teece didn't come to Torley's anymore.

"Turns out Lang set me up to take the rap for Razz Retribution's murder."

"Why would he want to hang it on you?"

"Messy story, and I'm not sure I know the answer. Yet. See, Razz Retribution had been financing some research. Genetic immunities to heavy-metal poisons. Apparently the research came up with stuff that could help a lot of Tert people. But someone took her out, which stopped the money supply, so the research stopped."

Teece opened his mouth, as if he might say something, but my words kept galloping out. I told him everything.

When I finished he didn't seem all that astonished, more troubled.

"But you said they got wiped?" he asked.

I grinned. "Not exactly."

I got up, went to the san and pulled the disk from my boot. Then I returned, tossing it onto the bed in front of him.

"When I realized what was happening, I bailed. What I saved is on here. I need to find out what it is. Will you help?" I tried awful hard not to plead.

He didn't rush me with an answer. "Why does Lang want you pinned for the murder?"

I shrugged. "Dunno exactly. Seems I was convenient."

"What would Lang gain from stopping this research?"

I shrugged again and pointed to the disk. It lay between us on the bed like a grenade. "That's what I want you to tell me. And there's something else

you should know. It might help you figure things
out. Lang can alter his physical appearance—shape-
change. Not with med-tek or cosmetics or anything
like that." I snapped my fingers. "He just does it."

This time his eyes narrowed in disbelief. Or maybe
at the state of my sanity.

"I've seen it, Teece. I think it's something to do
with the side effects of this research. They've done
trials using Tert people."

Teece gave a low whistle. "Heavy shite, Parrish."

We stared at the disk for a while, contemplating it.

"So how'd you manage to get so dirty?" he
asked eventually.

I told him about Gwynn, and Stellar and the
pain parlor.

He laughed.

"What's so funny?" I hiccuped.

"You. How do you find such dirty sandpits to
play in?"

He leaned forward and spread his fingers across
my shoulders where the muscles were taut and sore.
The warmth soothed them and involuntarily I
groaned.

"It takes talent," I murmured. "Mmm, that's
good."

He tugged at my towel, loosening it and slid his
hands around my stomach.

"Parrish?"

It was a question that didn't need words as an
answer. It might even clear my head of Loyl-me-
Daac.

But a frantic hammering at the door took the decision out of my hands.

"What?" he called gruffly.

"Sorry, Teece." The voice was seriously apologetic.
"It's important."

"Coming."

I grabbed his hand. "Will you do this for me, Teece?"

I was asking a lot. Too much! But then, just coming here was that.

He picked up the disk and put it in his pocket. His faded blue eyes filled with longing. "This time you'll *really* owe me," he said softly. "And I'm collecting."

"Sure." I smiled brightly. Bravado.

When he left I scrounged through his closet for something to wear and found an oversized T-shirt printed with a faded 3-D holo of the Beach Boys.

I took my tank top from the side of the bath and slipped it on. Then I donned the T. It covered my backside—just. But there was no point in trying to wear any of his pants. We weren't even close to being the same shape. I retrieved the wiper disk and forced my swollen feet into my boots.

Uggh! Not a good look. Or a good feel.

Pushing vanity aside, I smoothed my hair, picked up my case and went to find Teece.

He was sitting in his comm cache looking tetchy.

The face on the screen wore an expression easily as pissed off, and twice as scary.

Shit and double shit.

Loyl-me-Daac.

I stepped back out of comm viewer range. Too late!

For a split second Daac's eyes swept across me. I read things in them—surprise, annoyance, and something else . . .

From a corner vantage point I peeked at him again. He looked weak, but resolute as always.

His focus had shifted back to Teece. "Tomas."

Tomas? Was I missing something here? Since when had Teece ever been called Tomas? And since when were these two on comm terms?

"What is it, Loyl?" Teece rasped.

Loyl? I held my breath. What could Loyl possibly want with Teece?

Daac gazed at him: an intense, zealot's stare.

I shivered. The look I'd come to loathe.

"I wanted to warn you, Tomas," he said distinctly. "The Gentes are at war."

The air seemed to rush out of the room with his words. Teece sagged forward like he'd been punched in the gut, and the present rushed away from me with a whistling roar . . .

Angel, rejoicing, dancing. Wings fluctuating color, shining golden to warm bloodred. Chanting with a fiendish ecstasy. WAR! WAR! WAR! . . .

I came out of it seconds later—horizontal—with Teece eyeballing me at short breath's distance and Loyl shouting tinnily through the speakers.

"What's your problem?" I blurted, panic climbing my throat.

Teece hauled me up like a sack of dried beans. "What's yours?" he demanded.

I'd just had a full-scale hallucination. Half the world was chasing me. Now the man I most lusted after and trusted least was buddy with the man I didn't desire and trusted most.

I couldn't stand much more.

I ripped Teece's fingers from the shirt and without another word I bolted.

Wandering half naked through The Tert is not sensible. Judging by the attention I attracted, I had to do something about it or Jamon would know I was back long before I hit Torley's.

If Stellar hadn't already told him. Somewhere I'd stopped thinking of her as the bodyshop bitch—right about when she cried all over the winch mechanism.

I bartered Teece's Beach Boys shirt for some baggy

duds and a muscle top with a stoned-out Slummer and hoped it didn't get him killed on the beach in Fishertown.

Feeling a bit less conspicuous I skirted Shadoville, avoiding the district around the pain parlor, and mulled over what to do. Though Teece had fed me, my stomach ached for food already, and I was flat strapped for credit. There was no way I could get near my room stash unseen. Having run out on Jamon I doubted he'd be very forgiving. He might have wanted to poison me along with Stellar, but that was his pleasure. He wouldn't let anyone else take it.

As for Lang, well, stick his name at the top of my list of people to piss off! Whatever his game, I wouldn't play sucker for him again.

All this confusion left me nowhere to go. I'd lived pretty low before, but never totally without means or a place to sleep. It didn't feel good.

I slipped around the back of a tequila cum coffee-house and hunkered down between the rubbish chute and an enormous steel vat of cooking oil.

Note to self: Don't eat in here. Who knows who had their paws in the oil after hours?

Methodically, I went over what I knew. Lang had double-crossed me. He'd set me up to be police bait when I broke in to Razz Retribution's home. The more I thought about it the more I was convinced Lang's shape-changing ability had something to do with Anna Schaum's research.

Lang wanted me convicted for the murder. And the media had locked on to the idea. Coincidence? Or was there a link between the two?

The whole deal made that old expression, between a rock and a hard place, seem like silk sheets and gel pillows.

And what of Mr. "dispensable" Stolowski? He'd somehow got hooked up in this courtesy of Loyl Daac.

Part of me still wanted to protect Sto. He was on the sharp end, no matter what way you looked at it. His only sin was being in the right place at the wrong time—that, and believing in a zealot. Guilt by association with Loyl-me-Daac—self proclaimed messiah and pheromone-saturated hunk.

I crouched in the alley amid the squalor, and dithered.

Daac talked of war. What in the Wombat did he mean by that? Whose war? Why war?

According to Stellar, Jamon had been preparing for it.

Questions piled on top of me faster and thicker than answers. And now, to complete my perfect picture of chaos, I was having visions. My symptoms were uncannily like the ones documented in Anna Schaum's files, but I couldn't see how. I wasn't one of her lab rats.

Still, the similarities scared me. It sent a quiver through my insides, like a deep, vibrating note. My temples throbbed and my mouth began to water.

Another vision crept unasked into my head.

. . . *bleeding, battered bodies. Bodies strewn across pavements, hanging from windows of buildings. Salty, metallic warmth in my mouth. Sliding down my throat . . .*

Shaking my head I forced the images away. With horror I realized I was biting my own arm, sucking at the wound for blood.

I gagged and vomited.

Then I calmly stood.

I knew one person who could help me.

Mei.

But Mei meant Stolowski. Sto meant Daac. Daac meant my insides flip-flopping and some explaining I'd rather not do.

Since when did I get to be such a coward?

I sighed and scraped vomit off the tip of my boot.

There was no point in agonizing over Daac and his family obsession, or which media 'Terro was going to shoot me in the back. If I didn't stop these visions I'd save everyone the trouble and shoot myself.

One thing I can't stand is stone-cold crazy people.

Mei, I figured, would be hanging out in one of two places. Either my old room or Daac's medi-facility. Since my room was definitely off-limits unless I wanted to wind up back in Jamon's grasp, I decided to try the other.

I reviewed my compass memory from the day I'd left Daac standing on the roof pointing to Fishertown, and set my direction. With all going well I'd be there the next day.

The Tert reeked of its usual unappealing odors and strange noises as I followed my bearing east. Normally I would take the route along the northern perimeter of Torley's. Instead I cut south of east, passing behind the places I knew well.

The Tert had no strict divisions, apart from tolls, on the everyday walkways. The change of territory was just something you learned—like left from right. There were some obvious signs.

Muenos tended to decorate things with gaudy colors. Torley's, Shadoville and the northern strip were easy to identify by the ratio of bars to everything else. In Plastique you found the results of some of the more extreme surgical makeovers. Where Teece lived on the eastern edge was populated with part-time Fishertown squatters who brought to it their own peculiar stench.

The way I was headed—southeast of Torley's—increased the risk of encountering some first-grade crazies. They gravitated there inward, acting like a buffer zone to Dis and the black heart of The Tert.

Walking along a cramped, disintegrating side path

of one villa set, I felt the prickle of attention. Someone watching closely. Slowly and deliberately I peeled a broken plank from a makeshift barricade, making sure the nails were still attached. The watcher stayed with me for some time but made no move.

Shame. I was nearly back in the mood for bother.

I consciously drifted to more crowded thoroughfares and, as the day wore on, lost all sense of being followed.

By late afternoon the rear of Torley's district gave way to rows of units with their plethora of lumpy cocoons and spiderlike antennae on each roof.

I holed up on a rooftop in an empty cocoon, sleeping fitfully through the night. By midmorning the following day I began to recognize the architecture near Daac's patch.

Now I had to sniff out his enclave. My stomach nagged at me to feed it, but I'd gotten good at ignoring it. Palatable water was the main problem. Most people drank from communal rainwater tanks. Some had their own small ones. Clean running water was a thing of history in Tert Town.

I fought tiredness and despondency.

How could I get water, food and information with no cred?

I rifled through my case and closed it again, unable to part with anything in it—even for water. In desperation I searched the pockets of the Slummer's pants.

Nothing. I ran my finger along the tattered seams. Tucked in the hem, I found something. I ripped it free and examined it.

A fish hook?

What else would you expect from a damn Slummer?

I hastened to the nearest hockster, a family-run stall with a rash of feral kids hanging around it. Without preamble I asked for a price.

The trader laughed derisively.

"I need money," I insisted.

He stared hard at me. I saw a glimmer of recognition.

"You're the one who tried to save that feral kid. I saw you on *LTA*. You got a damn 'Terro after you. And Militia."

LTA! Live to Air. I held my breath wondering what he'd do with the knowledge.

"My woman says youse a saint. Here. Staysharp hooks are pretty rare." With a big wink, he gave me a handful of cred for the tiny hook. Not a fortune, but enough for a meal and some.

"Thanks," I said. "I'll remember. What's your name?"

"Fleshette. But don' you go mentioning it to anyone. You're dangerous tackle. Keep your head down."

I thanked him again and headed straight for a food stall.

"Tabbed water and three quesadillas. You know where can I find a shaman named Mei Sheong?" I asked the woman.

Her brow creased in concentration as she slopped the quesadillas together. "Don't know that one."

I thought for a moment. "What about a dealer named Styro? Plastique type." Surely Daac's buddy would be well known.

She slapped the debugged water and the food onto the tiny counter. "I know that one. Cred first."

I sized her for a minute and passed it over. She tucked it safely into her greasy apron and continued raking lumpy mincemeat with a long-handled fork.

"Hey!" I objected. "What about Styro? Where can I find him?"

She spared me the most fleeting glance. "Turn round."

I did. Quesadilla halfway to my mouth.

Styro leaned against a makeshift smoking booth about ten feet away. Gone was the piebald skin, replaced with something smooth and olive. But the boots were still thigh-high and pink, and the hair molded into a Gothic castle complete with ramparts. He smirked at me as if he'd been enjoying the show.

Note to self: Teach Styro some manners.

I strolled over, munching my way through the food.

"You want something?" he asked slyly.

I hesitated, suddenly paralyzed by the thought that Daac might be nearby. Then I remembered his warning to Teece. *The Gentes are at war.* Surely Tall, Dark and Hormone was busy preparing for his own bit of excitement.

I didn't want to think about what his bald statement meant—even the memory of it sent blackness swarming across my vision. No way did I want to do the horizontal hallucination thing in front of Styro.

"Chichi boots," I murmured.

He stared suspiciously at me.

"Truly," I said.

"You weren't looking for me to admire my boots."

"No. Where's Mei Sheong?"

Styro affected disinterest, picking at his stiletto-sharp nails. "Why should I tell you?"

I swallowed the last of my quesadillas and grabbed his frilled shirt. The frills tightened like a noose. This close, I could see he wasn't stoned. The best dealers never were.

"What do you want from her?" he gasped.

I caught something in his look, the mere flicker of softness in a bitter, narrow face. Styro had feelings for Mei. I released the pressure on his neck a fraction. "I'm not going to hurt her, Styro. I need some advice."

His eyebrows arched at the word "advice." "What happens if she doesn't want to give it to you?"

I considered his question. "She owes me nothing. If she has no advice, then our business will be over." I smiled silkily and smoothed his frills.

He nodded in doubtful agreement.

Implied violence was an art, really. You didn't have to be big, although it helped. You just had to mean what you said. I remember an islander I'd met in my first months in The Tert. A small, heavyset guy with a baby face and tight curls. People either respected him or they avoided him. "It might sound stupid, Parrish," he told me one time, "but nothing scares me. Nothing. Punters can tell. When I go up against someone they *know* it's not bluff."

Right now I cared for nothing except getting a handle on these hallucinations. I certainly didn't care about a weed like Styro who'd maxed me out on sedatives. Perhaps he could read that in my eyes.

I followed him amongst the rows of identical units that one time must have been hard to tell apart. They still were, only now patchwork alterations and tacky decorating touches gave them their uniformity. Barely sloped, gutterless roofs designed for torrential midsummer rains made them ideal flooring for the thousands of sleeper cocoons. Every now and then whole sections of roof collapsed under the weight.

Some Mueno influence had crept across from The Slag. Dirty, multicolored mats hung across open windows and doorways. In places, tangles of ugly gray-leafed lead-resistant vines curled along broken stair rails. Canrats and smaller Tert hybrids sometimes came down to hide among them.

Styro led me into one building, and then through to another along an unsteady connecting passage. We climbed a set of internal stairs until we came to a

long corridor that looked vaguely familiar. Glimpsing into rooms as we walked, I recognized the medi-
facility where Sto had been.

How long ago that seemed.

Several doors down, Styro stopped abruptly. Two
scrawny figures lounged outside playing a card game
called Brand. The winner notched a series of burns
on his arms and legs. Like initiation scars.

Styro whispered them aside and knocked on a
door. They went back to their card game as if they
had no interest. It didn't fool me.

I hung back in the dark of the corridor, curious to
see how Styro handled things.

Stolowski answered the door, bleary-eyed, hair
bleached and mussed like a bird's nest. His face had
altered too, the freckles gone. Daac must have arranged a makeover to help keep him safe.

The air between the two men crackled. They
wasted no time on pleasantries.

"What?" grumbled Sto.

"Mei there?"

"Yeah. What if she is?"

Styro's face purpled.

Any other time I would have found the whole
thing amusing. Right now I was in a hurry.

I stepped out of the shadows, keeping the bodyguards in clear sight. "I need to see Mei, Sto."

"Parrish," he gasped. "I thought . . ."

"You thought what, Sto? That I was dead? In
jail? You should know better than to listen to
rumors."

He swallowed rapidly, like he might choke. Then
he held the door aside for me to enter.

I stepped past Styro and shut the door in his face.
Then I snipped the locks and looked around.

It wasn't much of a home. A bed, built out of the
closet, a badly peeling mirror—glass, not even a

synth—and a sink that doubled as a san unit. But surprisingly clean. Jasmine incense wafted through.

Mei crouched on the window ledge, fussing over a burner and aluminium cooking cup and staring out on the street. Only someone as small as her could fit up there. I wouldn't have had a hope.

"Mei," said Sto nervously. "Visitor."

" 'Lo, Parrish." She didn't even turn in my direction. She was probably still pissed off at me from the last time.

"Sto? Get some exercise," I said quietly.

He glanced between us both, waiting for Mei to tell him what to do.

I sighed. Some women don't know how lucky they are.

Mei glided off the ledge like a small exotic cat and prowled over to rub herself against Sto's shirt. "Go for a walk, honey."

Sto gave her a quick hug and left obediently.

As the door clicked behind him she rounded on me, hands on hips, feet spread. For a little creature she had mettle.

"So you want to know what's causing your visions, eh?"

She had me there. Openmouthed.

"How did . . .?"

She went on, "It's a sort of possession. I could sense its presence there before but I wasn't sure. This time I could feel it even before you came in the room."

"A sort of what?" I didn't like what I was hearing. *Possession was for the stone-cold crazies.*

"I'm not certain. Sit down on the floor," she instructed. "Drink this. It's the only way to know."

I hesitated then sat. I didn't trust her, but what choice did I have?

Cross-legged we faced each other and she gave

me the cup she'd been warming, waiting impatiently while I rolled the bitter fluid around my tongue. Psylocybe or datura, I thought at a guess. Hallucinogens for the hallucinator.

I swallowed and she reached her hands out for mine. Hers felt small and warm, mine felt large and roughened against her soft skin.

"I can't promise anything, but I'll try. But you should know, Parrish, it'll feel bad," she warned.

I stared into her cool almond eyes, forgetting the ridiculous pink curls and haughty act. "Why are you helping me, Mei? Do you want money?"

"Who said it would help?" She shrugged. "Anyway, this is my work, Parrish. I'd do the same for most anyone."

Her honesty was vaguely comforting.

"Now concentrate," she ordered. "I'm going to piggyback there with you. Think about what you've been experiencing. Let the visions fill your mind. Don't be afraid, I'll be on your shoulders. And whatever you do, Parrish, don't throw me off. Got that? I'll take care of the rest."

I nodded, terrified at the thought of summoning images of the Angel.

Did I ever mention I hated voodoo shit?

Mei began a toneless hum, swaying. She performed an elaborate set of hand movements and the scent of jasmine intensified—the last "real" world thing I remembered . . .

Images slammed against my face. So fast I lost my breath. Half creatures, half places blowing past me into a vortex. Vertigo—so steep and intense that I whimpered, curling into a tiny ball. Even with my eyed pressed tightly shut I could still see things. Memories. Shouts in anger. Color, leaking into the sides of my vision no matter how hard I pressed my eyes shut. Magenta bleeding to brown. Brilliant fluorescents bound by chains of silver and gold.

*Chains that descended, wrapping themselves around my
arms and legs. Tightening, pulling away in opposite directions. Dragging my arms and legs in different directions.
Tearing my body apart until my screams became the colors
in front of my eyes.*

SILENCE.

The screaming had stopped.

*My body squeezed out into a place, fresh born and new.
The Angel lapped lazily up and down, swimming in a
flowing river of my blood; luxuriating . . .*

I heard a gasp in my ear, a sharp intake of breath.
Shock. Someone else was here with me.

Speak to it, the someone else said.

I tried to see who it was but it hissed in my ear,
*I am too small to see. Turn back or it will become
suspicious.*

I felt foolish, but the voice in my ear compelled me.
"Hey!" I called.

The Angel soared upward, droplets spraying in all
directions, like a magnificent bird shedding water
from its wings. It swooped toward me, landing
lightly.

I tried to look into its face but my eyes hurt, so I
settled for staring at the tips of its wings where my
blood dripped in long, coagulating strings. The
sound of a hundred synchronous drums assaulted
my mind. I resisted the temptation to clap my hands
over my ears and stifle the sound.

Though I couldn't see its face, I knew how terrible
it must be.

Terrible and beautiful.

Its body, uncovered before me, was sculpted muscular perfection. It took my breath away.

Distract it! hissed the someone in my ear.

"Who are you? Satan or Mamba?" I gibbered.

It laughed—a hideous sound—arching its wings
in disdain.

Where feathers should have been was a swarming,
crawling mass of data. Scrolling past at a frantic rate.

Words filled my mind, gradually ordering themselves into meaning like a voice, but not.

*"Mamba. Satan. The names mean nothing. They
are vehicles for us. We have been waiting a long time
for release."*

Confusion slowed my thinking. "Waiting for
what?"

I stared at the Angel's wings, fancying that I
glimpsed snatches of stories—from the Bible and
folklore. Names as well: Jesus, Thor, Zeus.

What strange creature inhabited me? Or—had it
always been there?

Keep it up, whispered the someone else. *I need
more time.*

Time?

The Angel filled my mind again with its words.

*"Our need is purely to feed and grow. Your race
is rich in nutrients. Here we can at last fully evolve."*

"E-evolve?"

*"We are so deeply rooted in your physiology that
you believe the violent compulsions you feel are your
own. And yet we have never managed to fully birth.
Our scouts miscalculated the ferocity of your immune system. We've been trapped, waiting for our
time. Now all we need is much blood to be spilled
and we will grow."*

A strange sensation built in the back of my neck.
My skin prickled and rippled and stretched.

*"We are a race whose building blocks is the epi-
nephrine manufactured in your bodies. Fear and
anger are our food. There is no right and wrong to
us. It merely is."*

"You mean you're a p-parasite?"

*"Would you call yourselves parasites? Consider
those things essential to your survival. You consume*

water, food. What if they were needs destructive to another race? What if just utilizing them would bring about the end of that race? Would you stop drinking or eating?"

I tried to consider the question much more calmly than I felt.

"Perhaps not. But then what do you mean by 'consume'? Practically speaking, if you consumed all those things, it would in the end deplete you of your resource for living. Then what would you feed on?"

The Angel clanged in mimicry of laughter.

"We won't destroy you. We will train your bodies to feel constant fear and anger. Some—the stronger ones—will be selected to prey on others. Those hosts will have special qualities."

Special qualities? What the frig did that mean?

"Why do you look like an Angel?"

"That is your doing, not mine. We are anything you imagine. But you have not really seen us yet."

"Then what do you call yourselves?"

"Our ancient name is unrecognizable to you. Some have known us before as Eskaalim. Rejoice, host. We will evolve you into something much more than you are; something that is us."

"But what changed?" I shouted. "What freed you?"

I'm ready now. The someone else again, in my ear.

For what?

"Go now!" the Angel commanded.

The substance beneath my feet began to shudder. I struggled to stay upright, falling one way, then the other.

Don't throw me off. Not yet. Not yet! Someone else.

"I'm trying . . . not to," I whispered desperately. "But I need to know . . . *what changed?"* . . .

The skin across my shoulders ripped open in a

spray of fluid. It drove me to my knees in agony, but I still strained to see what was happening.

I glimpsed a bird flying free. Whorls of energy shaped like a curlew with thin legs and a long curved beak. With an outraged cry, the energy-bird scaled the giant outline of the Angel like a thrown spear, up over the wide shoulders, along the curve of the neck. It fashioned its body into an arrow, with its beak as deadly and sharp as a sword point.

Eyes.

It was going to pierce the Angel's eyes. I followed its flight for as long as I could. Until it reached the curve of the Angel's jaw. Until the pain across my back forced me from consciousness; the cry of the curlew swirling in the distance . . .

When I came to, a fire burned across my shoulders. I lay on my stomach, panting.

A hand shook my upper arm urgently.

"Don't touch me," I growled.

"Parrish?" It was Sto. He sounded panicky. "What happened, Parrish? Something's wrong with Mei."

I swiveled my head to the other side, ignoring the stabbing pain along my neck. Sweat ran down my back. Making a monumental effort not to whimper, I hauled my carcass upright.

Mei lay across the floor from me, her neck skewed at a funny angle. "Don't touch her, Sto. Get your medic! *Hurry!*"

He left in a stumbling run.

I crawled over to Mei and gently felt her wrist pulse. Faint, but hard to tell over the thundering in my own veins. Whatever the crazy hell thing went on just then, I knew Mei had been trying to stop it.

Seconds later the med-tek was at her other side. Sto and Styro hovered anxiously over our shoulders.

The tek threw me a quick, puzzled look. "What happened?"

I would have shrugged if I could have moved my shoulders. I settled for a slight shake of my head. "She's a shaman. She—we . . . were in some kind of trance. When I came to . . ."

He slipped a flat pillow under her neck. It molded and inflated to support her.

"Looks like you tried to break her neck."

Not me. "She's alive, right?" I asserted.

"For the moment," he murmured. Then to Sto, "Bring it over."

Carefully, he smoothed creases from the stretcher. His preciseness irritated me. Med-teks always seem to have all the time in the world. Eventually he signaled Sto to help him lift.

They eased her out through the door, Sto whiter than it was humanly possible to be and still have blood. Styro, hanging on his right flank, wasn't much better.

The med-tek glanced back at me for a second. "You better come along as well. Before you bleed to death," he added as an afterthought.

I realized then that the trickling feeling down my back wasn't sweat, but blood. It had begun to pool like oil on the floor. I clamped my hand onto my neck, searching to stem the flow with pressure. A wave of dizziness and nausea swept me and the temptation to lie down was impossible to fight. I rolled backward onto the floor . . .

"Parrish!" A beast roar roused me. I tried to rub my eyes clear and only succeeded in clogging them with sticky, drying blood. I could smell it.

Yeuk.

Hands fell upon me, feeling the length of my body. I knew I should be pissed off that someone was running their hands over me, but actually it felt quite nice. Warm.

As if reassured by what they found, the hands

suddenly grabbed my shirtfront and hauled me up-right.

I squinted through sticky eyelashes into Loyl Daac's furious face.

"What's going on?" he demanded.

I tried to free myself, noting in the back of my mind that my shoulders hurt a lot less than they had. "Why are you shouting at me?" I asked, dazed.

He shook me as if he might get the answer he wanted that way. "I thought you were dead."

I smiled, I hoped, sort-of-nastily. "Nope. Just resting."

He bared his teeth as if he might bite, then he let go abruptly.

I sagged back onto the floor. He knelt in silence beside me while I wiped my eyes clear and gathered my thoughts. Actually, I felt surprisingly OK and had a suspicion that it was only due to whatever the thing was inside my body.

I couldn't bear to think about what had happened, like trying to forget a bad trip.

"How's Mei?" I croaked.

Daac turned away, the curve of his lips and nose perfect in profile, despite his harried expression. "I don't know if there's anything we can do. The medic has pumped her full of everything he can think of but her neck is fractured and she seems to be in some sort of coma. Her neuro readings are showing the weirdest activity. Nothing like we've ever seen before. What in the hell happened between you two?"

My skin went cold and clammy at the thought that I was alone and Mei couldn't help me. And yet I knew one thing with absolute certainty . . .

"You've got to stop whatever you're planning," I insisted, clutching at his sleeve. "There must be no war. *Blood must not be shed.*"

He turned back to me—almost defiant—his hands

spread wide. "It's too late, Parrish. It's already begun."

"No!"

"What happened to you? For Chrissakes tell me!"

I hedged. "It sounds too crazy. Besides, you've only been partly honest with me."

He raised his eyebrows, and I hit fair and square between them with my next question.

"Who in the hell have you been experimenting on?"

He jerked away, but I wasn't letting him off lightly.

"I know there are side effects. I've seen her records."

"That was you! Anna said it must have been, but Ibis said no."

Ibis covering for me? "You expect me to just accept you using me to get your precious backup files. I want to know what's going on. It's my arse the whole world is chasing."

He paced some, then answered slowly as if he were choosing his words. "There have been some other effects. Yes. The tests showed an amazing resistance to pollutants. But some of the test group began showing some unusual symptoms."

"Test group?"

"We chose a random sample. They were paid well."

"What were the symptoms?"

"Headaches, hallucinations. Some claim to be possessed by a creature. We're not sure why. Without Lione's—Razz's—backing we can't continue the research."

Possessed by a creature? Sweet! "And now someone has stolen your data."

He frowned. "Lang sent you to destroy Razz's files. But I can't see the connection. Why would he want that?"

I thought about Lang's meeting with Jamon, Road and Topaz. What deals had been struck that night? Who'd discounted their souls?

I took a deep breath and expelled it heavily. Every time I added two and two, I came up with forty-five. It was really starting to piss me off.

Chapter Eighteen

A Tert war is bizarre and wholly terrifying. People starve rather than go out of their front doors. Those that do travel in gangs, armed with a deadly mixture of primitive and tek weapons. Bats, spears and biopouches filled with contaminants.

I stood staring from the window in Loyl Daac's room as light began to fade on the deserted alleyway below. At both ends huddles of restless guards minded their territory.

"Jamon started this?" I asked Loyl without taking my eyes from the scene below.

He sat murmuring quietly into his comm hood. The flicker as he changed visuals strobed in the corner of my eyesight.

"Just a minute," he muttered.

When he'd finished, he ripped off the hood and came to stand behind me. Preoccupied as I was, I could feel a prickling awareness of him. I wondered whether he thought I'd been with Teece. Or if he cared.

"You look cleaner," he breathed into my ear.

I laughed shortly. Without humor. My second wash in a man's san in three days. It was getting to be a habit. "Don't you like women covered in blood?"

He grunted in annoyance and shifted away.

I glanced at him briefly. It was more than enough. His eyes shone with that feverish, evangelical fervor I hated.

"Jamon started the fighting." His look hardened. "While I was in Viva he began his raids, murdering my people, one by one. Ritual slayings." His hands opened and closed with anger. "Parrish, he slit their throats."

"Their throats?" I echoed dumbly.

"What could we do? We have to protect ourselves against him and his like."

"His like? You mean the Muenos, and . . ." My stomach tightened. "What about Doll Feast?"

"Only if she supports him."

"This is a stupid fight, Loyl." I tried not to shout but my voice edged. "How would Jamon know who is your gens and who is not? You said yourself that you were a mishmash of racial types. A bunch of hybrids."

"I lied," he said flatly. "I know exactly who my ancestors are. My family has been collating a bloodlines register for years. Now Jamon has a copy of it."

"But what you're doing . . . war or genocide. There's no damn difference between the two."

Stubbornness settled on his face. "We know who we are. And this is our place. What would you do? Let your own people be murdered?"

He had me there. But then I wasn't trying to own a people. "But what will you gain from this war? You don't win. Haven't you spent years supporting research to save your people? Now you're going to get them killed."

"It was always going to come to this. It just happened earlier than I thought. Some loss is fated."

"Fated!" I spluttered. "It's not only Jamon. Can't you see that? He'll bring in the others. If Lang is involved then the politics of things here are blasted to hell. The Muenos will kill for the sake of it. Doll will use the opportunity to whittle down Road Tedder's numbers. Chaos. How can chaos profit your gens?"

"Chaos. Yes, I know," he said.

His eyes lost some of their fervor. But his mindset was crystal as Viva water. He wanted this war. Nothing I said would change that.

He moved closer. "Decisions had to be made, Parrish. Less than perfect ones. That's my *task*. My gens need me to be a leader. Chaos is not good for us—no—but it never lasts. Humans crave order in the end. And someone to follow."

I'd heard that argument before—from Teece. I wasn't buying it as an excuse from him either. "That's what all the power-crazed say."

Daac locked me in his arms.

I wanted to move away . . . and didn't. "What do you want from me?"

He held his flesh hand a fraction above my skin, yet it was as though we were touching. "We have something."

I felt the strange pull between us, had felt it from that first instant in Hein's bar. It would be so easy to soften and yield to him. Instead I forced myself to think.

"How do you know Teece?"

"Teece is gens. I need him. He knows people in Fishertown. With their help I can close Jamon in on all sides."

"So he's useful?"

"Yes."

My heart contracted. Teece had Razz's disk. Had he told Loyl about it? Should I have trusted him?

"And I'm useful as well?"

His hands tightened on me. "Useful is not a word I would apply to you, Parrish. Unpredictable, stubborn. But when I saw you with Tomas—"

Suddenly his lips descended on mine.

I stood passive to his kiss, not trusting myself to breathe.

His comm chimed crazily in the background.

"Wait for me here. Until this is over," he whispered. "We'll talk more."

I watched him settle behind the hood, his attention drawn irrevocably back to the fighting.

He'd asked me for time. Another thing I couldn't give. I had my own problems, secrets to unlock, scores to settle. My . . . fascination . . . for Loyl-me-Daac didn't change those things.

Soon, a stream of stealthy figures began tapping at the door. One of those knocks was Stolowski packing a Remington like it might bite him. Loyl dragged him inside.

"Sto, stay with Parrish. This building is safe. Unless the Militia get it into their head to nuke us," he joked.

Neither Sto nor I laughed. "Why would they want to do that?" Sto asked.

"Ask Parrish," he muttered. "The whole place is swarming with Priers. I gotta go out for a while. Stay here with her, you'll be safe."

He opened the door, turning his strange eyes on me. "Wait. Please?"

Before I could think of my reply he joined the procession of shadows in the corridor outside.

Sto stared after him then shut the door.

"How is she?" I asked.

"Coma still. The medic hasn't got time to spend with her now. Injuries are starting to come in," he said.

I shivered. "Has she said anything? Anything at all?"

He shook his head. Tears brimmed and fell. "What did you do to her, Parrish? What happened?"

I shrugged at him helplessly. "I don't know how to explain it, Sto. I've been having these . . . visions. They got worse, so I came to see her. She said she already knew. Said she could sense them. There was this thing . . . an Angel . . . only it wasn't really. A creature made up of information. A construct of some sort. It wants this war real bad, Sto. It's going to use us to grow and evolve. Mei . . . well, she turned into some sort of bird and flew straight at the Angel. Tried to peck its eyes out. That's the last thing I remember."

I stopped, tired with explaining something that made little sense, and waited for his blank look. If anyone had told me that story I would have shot them full of lead and dropped them in the Filder River without remorse.

Stone-cold crazy.

But Sto nodded slowly like he was churning it all through his mind.

"Mei's been saying to me that something's changed. Something big was gonna happen. Said she sensed changes in the flows. So did the others."

"So you don't think I'm insane?"

Sto gave me a watery grin. "Yeah, sure I do. But not about this. Parrish, I'm scared."

I stepped toward him. "So am I. Where can I find the other shamans, Sto?"

He rubbed his hand across his hair. Sweaty pale fingers through a mat of yellow white. "I shouldn't be telling you this, but I guess I still owe you in a way. Find Vayu, around Torley's."

I squeezed his arm, smiling as warmly as I could manage. "Keep safe."

He held the door open and the Remington out.

I took it from him and walked on through.

Nobody looked twice at me in Daac's safe house. I hurried along the corridor and down to the nearest way out. The first one I came to was crowded with eager war-johnnies and heavily guarded. Gens, no doubt.

I wondered if Minoj had holed up with his arsenal of weapons. Who was he supplying? Probably everyone. Making a killing in cred.

Minoj made me think of Teece.

Daac had gotten Teece involved in this. *How involved? Enough to betray me?*

No.

I slipped back upstairs and scouted the other entrances. They were all the same.

I sighed. That left the attics.

I headed up the next flights of stairs, picked a top-floor room at random. I turned the handle and let myself in. It took no hard guesses to work out that the inhabitants were probably downstairs playing soldier.

By design all the upstairs rooms in The Tert villas had attic hatches. This one was no exception, though it hadn't been used in a while. Knowing Daac, he'd probably booby-trapped the entire roof area.

I would have.

I dragged a crate over, stood on it and tweaked the lid the tiniest fraction. A device winked back at me. An image of Gwynn flashed into my mind. If I got my arms blown off I might be good company for him. I lowered the lid again, losing my nerve.

What the hell was I doing? Going out to find a shaman who lived in the same district as the man I most despised, most wanted to kill and most wanted to avoid—in the middle of a gang war!

Wouldn't it be easier to ride the whole thing out here and see what happened? Get some psy-spook to help my visions when the war was over. At least here I was out of the Militia's and the media's grasp.

Or was I? What was Daac's crack about them nuking us?

On impulse I got down from the crate and fiddled with the room's comm. It only took a minute to tune in on a news bulletin.

A Prier giving a panorama of The Tert was the main image of the news footage. Any which way. The accompanying audio reports beat up the rumors of gang war. Pinch-faced sociologists discussing the possible implications for the citizens of Viva. Blah. Blah.

The very last segment, though, had me tripping over my own jaw:

". . . rival gangs in the Tertiary sector are said to be responsible for the current unrest. A racially motivated group thought to be led by Parrish Plessis is making a bid for control and racial supremacy. Plessis is wanted in connection with the murder of news anchorwoman Razz Retribution. Plessis, having made a Mission-Impossible type of escape from a robbery on M'Grey Island, is back in the Tertiary sector directing her gang effort. Any information . . ."

My brain screamed a protest at the distorted truths. Was this what Daac had meant by the Militia nuking us?

I stared at the screen, not hearing any more. Not wanting to.

How did this happen? How did this get so bad?

The more I tried to take control of my life, the more out of control it got. I didn't know whether to cry, or laugh or crawl away and hide.

All of the above.

Yet all of the above wouldn't solve a frigging thing!

With a mental cuff I slung Sto's Remington over my shoulder. Then I walked over to the window and began removing the mesh.

It wasn't hard to get onto the roof from these unit blocks. They only had short overhangs and no gutters to accommodate for the torrential summer rains. My main worry was being shot in the back while I hung there.

As I scrabbled up I expected any second to feel a searing pain between my shoulder blades.

It didn't come. Maybe the dimming light covered me, or maybe there was too much to watch out for on the ground.

I crawled up the slight incline of the roof, weaving carefully between the mic dishes. A hand reached out and grabbed my ankle as I stepped between two sleeper cocoons, nearly upending me. I stomped down as hard as I could with my other heel and swung the nose of the Remington into the narrow opening. Comm drone drifted out.

"Let go," I growled over the noise, "or I'll blow you off the side of the roof."

Whoever it was took me at my word.

I scrambled as quickly as I could to the peak and looked around.

The Tert's sea of roofs hadn't altered from the time Daac and I had stood there together. There were no signs to show the turmoil below, save for black and brown smudges here and there that I took for packs of canrats keeping well out of the trouble, and the wasp buzz of Priers.

The strip of sea to the east and the dull, oily glint of the Filder River to the west were where they should be.

Only I was lost.

I checked my compass and took a bearing north-east that would take me back to Torley's. All I had to do was stay alive long enough to get there.

I shuffled to the other edge and light-footed over a makeshift rope bridge to the next roof. From there I used the roof-dwellers' rope-down to get me to the ground. For all the effort I was probably only thirty meters better off. But at least no one had tried to stop me.

The alley was uncannily quiet. Occasional bursts of handguns and the whine of machinery punctuated the silence.

The evening felt heavy with the usual stormy cloud—what I could see of it—and the air fitted around me like a dank, tight jumper. Cooking smells were strangely absent. As if people were afraid to eat in case someone else took advantage of their dis-traction from the war to turn them into a casualty.

I slipped from corner to corner, remembering how easily Bras had navigated her way around in the dark. I wished she were with me now. For my sake. For her sake she was a whole lot better off with King Ban and his family.

Under the cover of darkness everyone was danger-ous; and vulnerable.

Several times during my long night I came face-to-face with armed groups of strangers carrying glowers or light wands or fire torches. They wore no colors, no identifying marks.

Neither did I.

It saved me on more than one occasion. In a battle where the opponent's lines aren't clearly marked, hesitation could be a friend. More than once they whispered warily amongst themselves. Who is she with? Is she one of us? Sometimes I talked my way around things by guessing their alliances. Other times I used their indecision to vanish into the dark.

A few times I turned into blind alleys, where patchy constructions coupled buildings together, blocking the thoroughfare. In one alley I stumbled upon four young gangers torturing their captive. One of them hummed. Another raped while he held a knife. They performed their act in the pinprick of a hovering Prier's spotlight.

Without stopping to think, I kicked the rapist so hard in the back of his head that he was unconscious before he hit the pavement. The singer I shot in the thigh. The remaining pair ran, dragging their injured friends.

As I helped the woman to her feet the Prier lifted and swung away. I fired after it but it was a useless gesture.

The woman was old. Like my grandmother would be if I'd had one.

"What's your name, girl?" She clung to me with desperate gratitude.

"I'm Parrish. Did you know who they were?"

Tears ran down her face. She nodded through them as if she could barely say the words. "Boys from my block. I know their families. They wanted my food."

She moaned aloud—a wail that chilled my blood. "This fighting is turning them into animals. But what's it about? I don't know what's happening."

I carried her across the alley to a squat that was boarded up. I knew the occupants must have seen what had happened, but were afraid.

"Let me in," I shouted. "The woman needs help and shelter."

Eventually a light flashed across us from a window and the door opened a crack. "Please take her." I handed her gently into the arms of a woman about my age with shaved hair and tattoos on her face.

"You did a brave thing," she said. "I would have helped. But I have children . . ."

I nodded, understanding what she meant.

"Them Priers are everywhere with their cameras. It's creepy."

"Stay inside," was all I could think to say, and left.

This fighting is turning them into animals.

The old woman's words burned into my mind as I continued on my way. Maybe because deep down I felt a sensation that I didn't like and refused to own. A churning excitement at the blood and the danger and the ugliness.

Like two people living inside one skin. *Not enough room.* I shivered.

One of us was definitely going to have to go.

Sometime well past midnight, I noticed the outline of the buildings had changed, telling me I'd reached Torley's and the Shadoville strip.

I moved along as silently as I could, but soon I was surrounded by a band of hostile shapes waving light wands. I slid the Remington around till it hung loosely in front of me.

One magazine would take some of them. Then again, from the gleam of steel and the flicker of LED displays, they packed some decent hardware of their own.

One of them stepped closer. A stocky, mongrel female with a semi. She waved her wand in my face and squinted. "Who have we got here?"

I decided to try talk first and took my hand off the trigger. "No one. Minding their own business."

She stared hard. "Seen you before, haven't I?" Falling back she whispered to the figure on her right.

"You're Mondo's woman." Then she stepped toward me again and smiled. It wasn't a smiling kind of night.

"Figure you might be worth something," she said.

"You figure wrong."

"Heard he had a price out for you."

"You heard wrong too."

Three of them came at me from the front. They were easy. I arced the Remington and it answered sweetly in a rattle of fire that took their legs out from under them. But it's hard to see everywhere when your enemy is in a barely lit circle. As I turned to watch my back, another wave came from the front and the sides. I was down on my knees sucking pavement way too quickly.

Ten or more. The Wombat knows how many in the shadows.

The mongrel with the semi rammed her piece into the side of my neck and spat into my face.

It dribbled down the collar of my shirt. I would have wiped it away, but someone was tying my hands behind my back. I scraped my face along the ground to stop the spit getting in my eyes.

They hauled me up and stretched me over an old water hydrant. Greedy hands tore at my top; catcalls ricocheted around me.

"Strip her," ordered the mongrel.

It was happening to *me* now. The same as I'd seen earlier in the night. Rape, maybe murder. Or worse than that—delivered to Jamon for bounty.

No.

As they tried to tie my feet to my hands I kicked and jerked, rolling free of the hydrant.

Rough hands grabbed me again, pulling me onto my back, but they couldn't contain my legs. I caught one of them under the jaw hard enough, I hoped, to shatter bone. I roared and kicked and kicked.

The mongrel leapt astride my chest, ordered others onto my legs.

Trapped.

I lay still, smelling her anticipation. She put her face down close to mine. "Do that again and I'll blow your brains out," she muttered hoarsely.

My eyes seemed to be playing tricks in the darkness. One side of her face, distorted and crawling with dark whorls.

"Be my guest," I offered. "Better than your filth on me."

But I lied. I didn't want my life spread on a Tert Town pavement. I didn't want to die.

I wanted to kill her.

I want to kill her!

That thought crystallized pure and clear.

My ears filled with a throbbing sound. Pressure gathered in my head, so fierce I thought I was dying anyway. A roar erupted. A sound I could never make. A battle cry, bloodcurdling and vicious.

Yet it came from me. The pressure built steadily until my skin stretched to bursting. Crimson ran before my eyes.

With a crack I exploded.

At least I thought so.

Time passed.

I groped around dazed, my hands free from the ropes. Bodies lay strewn around me. Other shapes backing away. Scared. I touched the nearest corpse. Hot flesh. Burnt. Sounds overtook the echoing war cry in my head. Sounds of fighting. Young voices. Young bodies with homemade weapons—finishing the job I had started.

More bodies. Around me like torn scraps.

"Oya?"

I stared into a child's face. Filthy, feral and alight with hope.

"Oya. We fight for you."

I licked my lips. With immense effort I framed a word. "Me?"

More of them came. Clustering around. "Oya, we were watching."

I shook my head in confusion.

Daylight was coming.

They helped me up, two tall, skinny boys under each arm. One blind, the other smiling broadly.

I only looked back once as I limped away.

A drink and some crumbling pieces of pro-sub and I felt less surreal. The ferals had taken me into a building; an attic protected with movement sensors like the ones in the attic above my room.

They swung on rafters and perched on beams around me like little primates. Watching and listening. I wondered if Jamon knew about them.

"Why did you help me?"

"The Muenos feed us because of you, Oya. The Muenos talk about you. Light candles for you."

Pas! He had kept his word.

"What happened back there? When you found me?" I asked one of the tall boys. "What did you see?"

He looked puzzled. "We saw you, Oya. You burnt them because they were going to hurt you. You are fierce." Around me they began to clap and cheer.

The boy confirmed my fear. It had come from me. I'd killed twenty or more people with some type of electric charge from my body. Burnt them alive.

Shivers racked me. "A-are y-you sure?"

He nodded, his long hair falling across his eyes. "One moment they are on top of you. The next . . . Psss!" He made a noise like food sizzling in a fire.

Nearby, an explosion sent dust spiraling around us. The crossbeams groaned.

The ferals silenced in one accord. The tall boy fixed me with serious, worried eyes.

"Oya. Can you save us?"

Chapter Nineteen

Too many people, too much.

But how could I stop now?

For someone trying to climb out from under the pile, I seemed to have gotten responsible for everyone else in it.

I forced myself to think. "Do you know a shaman named Vayu?"

The tall boy pondered. "Where from?"

"Here. Torley's."

"We can find out. The Pets will know."

He clicked his fingers, a succession of staccato noises, and a small, pale girl with pure white hair crept alongside him.

"Tina will go."

Tina smiled nervously as if the act itself might get her killed.

I tried to smile back, but my mouth seemed to be suffering rigor mortis. "Thank you. What would you like in payment?"

The tall boy shook his head and pointed high to a rough shelf attached to the roof. Two young girls armed with small, sharp spears guarded either end of it. The shelf bulged with stale bread and dried meats. "You've paid. Many times over."

"Is this what the Muenos gave you?"

"Yes. But with the fighting there will soon be none for them to give. They help us, but not if their own bellies go hungry."

"Then tell Pas you have spoken with me. Tell him no matter what he must give you some food."

"But he will not believe me."

"Then I will find him."

"Thank you, Oya. Thank you," he said beaming.

I slept for the rest of the day and through the night, dimly aware of bodies pressed closely around me. I woke in the slim light of dawn and discovered a tiny girl no more than three or four, still asleep, clutching my shirt and sucking her finger. As I eased away from her I nearly rolled on another, an emaciated boy who tossed and turned restlessly, unable to find comfort for his bones on the hard surface.

Children lay littered around, moaning as they dreamed; whimpering and calling out in fear. The sound shook me.

Treading the beams carefully in between young bodies, I moved toward the manhole.

Tina sat nearby, gnawing on hard bread and sipping water from a container, waiting for me. Exhaustion and apprehension showed in her white face.

I kneeled next to her. "Tina?"

She broke off some bread. "I will take you to Vayu now?"

I hesitated, weighing my promise to the ferals against my desire to find someone who could help me with my visions. Yet from the moment I'd woken to find their bodies pressed trustingly alongside me, I had my answer. "I need to speak with Pas first."

She nodded.

We ate together silently. Then left.

* * *

Timid though she appeared, Tina led me through
The Tert with surety. Her innate sense of direction
reminded me of Bras.

Outside seemed quieter with daylight dawning,
but the remnants of the night's excesses were evi-
dent. Drying bloodstains, ransacked hovels, dismem-
bered Pets.

Tina searched their remains for faces she knew,
stopping to sprinkle water on them from a little jar
she gripped tightly in her hand.

"Holy water?" I asked, curious.

"No. Acid. So nobody eats their eyes."

I flinched at her matter-of-fact tone.

"How did you come to be alone, Tina?"

She stared back at me, cruel shadows under her
eyes. "How did you?"

We walked south, almost the way I'd come, toward
Mueno territory even though I itched to be going east
into the heart of Shadoville. We kept on the major
walkways. It was dangerous in the open but more
dangerous using the cover of back alleys.

"Have you got a weapon?" I whispered, fearing
for her as the weight of watchful eyes traveled with
us. The Remington, rescued by the ferals and back
in my hands, didn't fill me with great confidence.

She nodded, pointing to a tiny pouch around her
waist.

"Rasta virus," she whispered back. "Killing radius
of a hundred meters. The . . . potency weakens after
that." She seemed disappointed at the thought.

No wonder she moves with confidence, I mused.
She was a walking biobomb.

We barely spoke again until midday, when the
building facades displayed gaudy threadbare ban-
ners, bundles of feathers and roughly made dream
catchers. Silent, knifed-up Muenos began to mark our

progress—whether as protection for them, or for us, I could only guess.

Without hesitation she took me to a door smeared with dried blood.

"Pas thinks chicken blood wards off evil spirits," said Tina.

"What do you think?"

"I think it's a waste of food."

Her pragmatism almost made me smile. Almost.

We spent a day and a night with Pas. He was less obese than he had been and more confident. An energy of purpose seemed to rage through him as he flicked his long hair about.

"Topaz strays from our ways," he spat. "He is like *this* with Mondo from the Stretch." He made a rude gesture with his fingers.

"How does he stray, Pas?" I asked, curious.

He lowered his voice. "I have heard, at night, he takes a woman's form."

Shape-changing? I didn't know whether to laugh or be troubled by Pas's words.

"No matter. Oya is our true leader now." He stopped short of prostrating himself before me, but I could sense his impulse to do it.

I thrust the image away before it got me shaking. "This fighting must stop, Pas. You must tell the Muenos to resist it. Secure your territory. Mondo wants this fighting to spread something evil. Much blood will mean much evil. More than Oya can stop."

"There is nothing Oya cannot stop."

This whole conversation was ridiculous. I'd come here to convince Pas to keep feeding the ferals and wound up acting as the Muenos' favorite godhead again.

Next thing there'd be an anointing ritual.

*   *   *

An hour later I was perched awkwardly on something that felt and looked like bones, with a swathe of chicken feathers on my head.

I should have split when Pas started filing his men past me for benediction, but I couldn't bring myself to crush Tina's wide-eyed belief.

Pas recited the Mueno faiths, including the legend of Oya. I learned that Oya was a powerful female voodoo deity. A witch who invoked great changes. By the look of all the hundreds of Oya dolls cluttering Pas's living room she also had some bad-hair issues.

Where was the likeness?

Truthfully, the Oya association scared the jeesus out of me. Not only was I hallucinating Angels, but now half of The Tert reckoned I was a femme voodoo warrior. I'd thought to use it, but it was getting way out of control.

After the litany, the room filled with shaven-haired Mueno women bearing dirty trays of food. Tina ferreted whatever she could carry into her robes.

Confined to my bone throne, the heat of the bodies and the overwhelming smell of blood made me dizzy. The graininess of a vision threatened.

I fought it with every ounce of self-control, and lost . . .

Angel. Slitting throats, dancing in blood. Scalps piled on my body. Suffocating me . . .

I came back, draped indecorously across the bone throne with fifty Muenos prone before me. The sight nearly blacked me out again, yet my behavior seemed to be what they expected.

Tina told me, as we made our way back west at daybreak escorted by a small Mueno guard, that I had *glowed*. She related it matter-of-factly, as if it was something Oya would naturally do.

I tried to hide my shaking hands from her and didn't ask any more questions. *At least Pas will keep feeding the ferals,* I thought.

I insisted the Muenos leave us on the edge of their territory, feeling relieved when it was just Tina and I again.

The weight of being a savior made me totally nauseous.

We reached the fringe of Shadoville by late afternoon, dodging skirmishes as we went. Tina led me to an inconspicuous building sandwiched between a semicircle of villa units. It was only two stories high and about one room wide. I couldn't remember ever seeing it before.

She pointed to the building: her pale eyes filled her face.

"Don't kill any children," she said simply, and turned and left me standing.

Don't kill any children!

What had my life become?

Chapter Twenty

I stepped toward the narrow building in a hurry to get under cover and off the street.

The front door wasn't barricaded and I moved cautiously amongst the lower rooms observing the sparse furniture and bare kitchen. A noise above drew me to the stairs. The Remington lay loose in my grip, comforting.

I flicked away a crawling sense of foreboding as if it were an insect and squeezed my finger against the trigger.

Upstairs was more typical of a spirit house: symbols painted along the staircase, the scent of incense drifting down. It reminded me of Mei, and I wondered if she was still alive. I hoped for Sto's sake that she was.

The last door at the top of the stairs was shut. I hesitated, balked by a sense of foreboding.

I had to go on, but what if the shaman, Vayu, couldn't give me answers?

I was running out of options and into lunacy.

I flashed on the face of the mongrel woman, and the disfiguring, black whorl. What the hell had caused that?

I reached out for the door handle a second before it opened. A slight woman with a weary expression stood there. Her beaded red hair fell almost to the floor.

"Come in, Parrish. We've been waiting for you."

I should have been surprised. But to tell the truth, I was beginning to think there were no more surprises left for me.

"Vayu?"

She nodded briefly in acknowledgment.

I stepped inside.

Candles littered the perimeter of the room, and holo statues for warding off bad spirits. Cross-legged on the floor sat a group of people—a mixture of races and ages, but similar in other ways. A wave of energy coursed around them as if I'd somehow stumbled into the swirl of an electrical storm. My body hair stood on end.

Vayu glided around behind me and took her place in the circle. She beckoned me over to sit by her side.

"Put your gun away," she instructed in a quiet voice. "We won't harm you."

I believed her—most shamans are pacifists—but shook my head anyway. "Sorry."

She sighed heavily and nodded.

I sat next to her, leaving the Remington loose in my lap. It seemed a crude gesture on my part. But heck!

They sat in an intense, heavy silence, waiting for me to speak, but the words stuck in my throat.

In the end Vayu took pity on me. "Mei is still alive."

I nearly asked *How do you know?* but that would have been stupid and pointless. So I settled for, "Good news. I'm glad."

She smiled then, a beautiful, shining thing that made me feel stained.

"I don't know that we can help you, Parrish Plessis. The creature growing inside you is already strong."

"Can you explain it to me?

"Perhaps. But first you must tell us what you know. We can sense the earth's energy flows are changing, transforming in ways we have never seen before." She shivered.

I began telling my strange story. "I went to Mei Sheong for help. I'd been having visions—of an Angel. We both took a drink. Mushroom, I think. Then I had the vision. I spoke to it. It's—it's a parasite feeding from my body. It's somehow been trapped by my immune system but now it is free."

"How so?"

"I'm not sure. I know a man who has modified genes in locals . . ."

"I've heard talk of him. But Parrish, what do you think this parasite seeks?"

"It told me we would evolve into something else."

Vayu paled. The others shifted and whispered among themselves in grave, low voices.

"We feared something, but not this. What can we do? It's outside our understanding, our capabilities," she said.

It wasn't what I wanted to hear. "You mean it's not a hallucination? This creature is real?"

"Yes. True shamans have always been able to contact the spirit plane with the assistance of hallucinogens. What you have encountered on your pathway to meet with the spirits is different. An interloper— a parasite you call it. But others have come to us with similar stories. To those unaffected by the visions it may seem like madness. But we shamans see further than the material world. We see energy."

Vayu's revelation floored, terrified and relieved me

all at once. I *wasn't* crazy but I *was* possessed. I don't know that it made me feel any better. "But how did this happen? Where is this creature from?" I gasped.

"We don't know," Vayu said.

"Why is it in me and not you?"

She shook her head helplessly. "You must find the answer to that."

"What can you do?"

She hung her head in ready defeat. "We can only wait and watch."

My bewilderment quickened to anger. "You mean you've given up already!"

A ripple passed through the group—embarrassment, perhaps? Enough, hopefully, for me to prick their guilt, not combust their fear.

I homed in on the opportunity. "I can tell you this much. It's some type of information creature, feeding off the epinephrine—the adrenaline—in our bodies. You deal in energy, don't you? Isn't information energy?"

"Energy trapped within flesh? But how can this work?" Vayu's eyes widened.

I shrugged.

"For a human body to confine such energy, the creature must be providing some mechanism to protect the flesh. If we knew what that was, perhaps . . ."

She looked intently around the circle at each shaman. One by one they nodded briefly in unspoken agreement.

She took a breath. "Parrish Plessis, the others have agreed to try another journeyback if you are willing? Perhaps with more of us we will be stronger and can learn more. But it will still be dangerous."

I grimaced. "What's a little danger between total strangers?"

No one seemed to share my humor.

They joined hands and began a low chant accompanied by precise but fluid movements, similar to the ones Mei had made.

I knew what to expect this time and prepared for the rush as I swallowed from the receptacle Vayu passed me.

This time, though, the rush was gentle: a slide into a white haze . . .

I floated above the stream of unformed images, buoyed in the air on the wings of a large, brown eagle. I nestled in amongst the feathers, conscious of nothing but rhythmic movement and the exhilaration of freedom.

We covered an endless, featureless distance before the eagle dived slowly toward the ground. The river course it had been following changed slowly from a thin black line to a dull brown and—as we swooped closer and closer— a viscous red. Blood. My blood.

Without warning the sky darkened from the cast of a huge shadow. Something attacked the eagle from behind, viciously ripping its tail feathers apart. The eagle wheeled, raising its talons in defense, but it foundered like a vessel without its rudder.

The attack came again, an intangible enemy, tearing flesh and bone.

Underneath me the eagle's solid back shredded, scattering into single, tiny flames, souls who together had formed something solid but independently were snuffed out, sucked away into darkness. One flame flickered brighter, lasted longer. Vayu. I felt her reach for me with a brief, impassioned thought.

"Stop the change. Stop the man who seeks the change."

Then the shadow grew as if gorging on her light until I could see nothing, feel nothing . . .

Consciousness found me on the floor in Vayu's room, on my knees, hands outstretched. Around me the shamans lay—lifeless. I crawled frantically from one to the other listening for heartbeats. The only one I heard was my own; wild, frightened and confused.

When the door was flung wide open and bodies crammed through, I was thumping Vayu's chest and screaming at her to breathe.

Dreadlocks and incisors dripping saliva answered me instead. A slight figure followed them in, wearing its snake smile. Eager for me.

Jamon.

"Well done." He stroked the lead 'goboy on the head. "You were right." Then he addressed me, a sweeping gesture taking in the bodies of the shamans. "Parrish, what have you been up to?"

I stared at him, incapable of speech.

"My 'goboys have been tracking you for a while," he said conversationally, holding up the remnants of the Beach Boys T. "I hope your friend doesn't want this back?"

Teece's shirt. What happened to the Slummer who wore it?

"Take her home!" he instructed with a twitch of his tattooed cheek.

I staggered to my feet, swinging the Remington up, firing. The first shot took the closest 'goboy, but it ended there. The magazine was empty.

I swung the barrel as a bat.

But Jamon knew not to risk his men in hand-to-hand combat against me. They shot me with a paralysis derm from a few meters.

I ducked sideways to avoid it. Two more were already on their way. One struck me in the hip. In a matter of seconds I collapsed, unable to move my legs.

"Excellent," he said. "The effects remain localized to your legs, Parrish. It will fade. In a few days."

A few days! He might as well have shot me in the head.

They came then and bound my hands, touching me all over with the eagerness of grave robbers. They bore me back to Jamon's rooms like a trophy, through the confusion and craziness crippling Torley's.

Everyone I saw was armed. Many were bleeding or staggering hungry. I glimpsed familiar faces, and they me. No one spoke or offered help. I didn't blame them. They were too busy surviving.

Jamon's villa was unchanged—the polished table and scores of heavily scented candles; hand-cut crystal glasses on the sideboard—except for a large rectangle of clear plastic that stood against one wall. It was shrouded in a velveteen cover with only the edges jutting out. I wondered at its size, as Jamon's hounds dumped me on his sofa.

He followed my gaze with a strange, almost dreamy, expression. "You ran away, Parrish. You shouldn't have done that," he said.

Then he swung and punched me.

A direct uncontested hit that rattled my teeth and sent a hot skewer of pain across one cheekbone.

Hate consumed me. I twisted away, spitting blood from my mouth. But my legs flopped uselessly, like dead meat, and I slid sideways on the sofa.

Through the doorway the babble of his comm network mocked my uselessness. In the middle of a war, tied up and semiparalyzed.

Like Loyl, Jamon directed his fight from a screen. And yet he had left his comm to come and get me? And they say there's nothing like a woman scorned!

Blood trickled from my mouth, staining the silk covers.

"I'm not yours to have to run away from, Jamon," I whispered hoarsely.

"Brave words," he said, "but that's all they are. You see, now Stellar is gone you'll be living here with me."

He was right. They were brave words. In truth he

terrified me. But live with him? Not in this hell or any other!

He smiled again. "Now make yourself comfortable, Parrish. I have business to attend. If you attempt to escape, they will stake you for my pleasure."

Stake me. I knew what he meant. The image of it mushroomed in my brain. I stared across at the door. The same four 'goboys that had paraded me through Torley's were posted outside it.

Jamon disappeared into his comm room, leaving two more guards watching his back. Even paralyzed, with half my face shattered, he was taking no chances.

I was flattered. Enough to tear him limb from limb. If only I could feel my legs and feet. And if only my face didn't hurt like someone had scraped half of it off.

Time spiraled.

I lay helplessly on the couch, in a strange world of numbness, pain and despair.

Eventually I dozed, woken again by Jamon's restless prowling and a change of guards. They squeezed tubes of water into my mouth, and held me laughingly over a bucket to pee. Once they bothered to turn me so that my view rotated between the plaster wall and the candle-strewn mahogany table.

When I was awake and lucid, I listened to the incoming accounts of the fighting. It helped distract me from the throbbing in my cheek and the depressing reality of my predicament.

Even though the reports were conveyed in a kind of panting 'goboy shorthand, I gleaned enough to know that although Jamon had enlisted Topaz's support against Daac, the Muenos weren't cooperating.

A furious Topaz wept repeatedly over the comm to Jamon. "My hands are tied, Señor Jamon. The

Muenos won't fight for me. One of my men, Pas, is leading a revolt. My informants say they are waiting for word from someone they are calling Oya."

Reports also filtered in, that small groups of Jamon's 'goboys had been set upon by feral children armed with bioweapons. One attack in particular had claimed more than fifty. The feral, a girl about ten years old, had released a quick-acting virus in the barracks while one whole shift of 'goboys slept. The girl was found dead near the entrance.

Tina!

I wept then—unashamedly. Like never before in my life. Until my soul was dry and hard.

Then came the strangest of all the accounts.

Jamon's right-hand 'goboy had vanished at the same location as Teece's business, west of Torley's. He'd been on a night scout, disappearing near an uncovered manhole. Search attempts underground had only revealed scores of hostile canrats.

Underground? The canrats? Or could it possibly be Gwynn?

An ember of hope ignited in my chest; and resolve. The Muenos, the ferals and now Gwynn. I couldn't let them down.

Occasionally I heard Daac's name mentioned. Jamon wanted him bad.

I thought a lot about Teece. As long as he's alive, I thought, I can cope with the rest.

If he wasn't I'd never forgive Loyl. Or Jamon.

Or myself.

Sometime after the report on his man's disappearance, Jamon emerged, grimly, from his comm room.

He sent the two internal guards away, leaving only the four outside. Then he came and sat next to me, holding a set of wired-up restraints. Lifting the waist of my shirt he rubbed them across my bare skin. The charge prickled mildly.

He lowered his mouth and ran his lips along the same line then he mounted me, awkwardly, tearing the rest of my shirt away. His face contorted with frustration and anger.

With the tips of the restraints he administered a series of electric shots across my breasts. I spasmed in pain but clamped my teeth tightly together, willing myself not to give him the pleasure of my screams.

Every now and then he stopped to survey the marks on my skin and smile in satisfaction at the tears streaking down my face.

"Why have you started this, Jamon? Why are you killing all these people?"

He frowned, his eyes dark with madness. "Loyl Daac wants my territory, Parrish."

"Who told you that?"

"Lang."

Lang! I squeezed my eyes shut, feeling the grainy-gray beginnings of a vision. The parasite was swarming my consciousness. I let it come. With it came an excruciating burning, heralding the sudden return of sensation to my legs.

I strove to control my reaction to it, and as Jamon shifted position, moving his weight off me to tear away my pants, I kneejacked him in the throat.

He gurgled and flopped forward onto me.

We wrestled for a few seconds before crashing off the sofa, into the large plastic block. The shroud fell from the block and caught up between us. He tried to strangle me with it but I punched him in the face with both fists.

The sound alerted his guards. They crowded in to surround us.

"Call them off," I screamed, gripping his throat.

Something was wrong. My knee blow should have knocked him unconscious.

The 'goboys circled us, frantic, unsure what to do. I tightened my hold, pounding Jamon's head against the floor.

"Call them off!"

"Back," he ordered them, but his eyes, coldly furious, were on me.

I pinned his arms with my knees and fished out the small Beretta strapped under his arm. I shoved the barrel between his eyes. "Untie my hands. Carefully."

While he fumbled to comply, something caught my attention. A shape. A human foot.

I glanced quickly across.

Inside the acrylic block, clear as Jamon's best high-ball glasses, naked and absolutely dead, was Stellar. Preserved in the act of kneeling.

"Charming. Isn't it?" Jamon gasped as the last knot unwound. "A taxidermy teknique. Shame her body wasn't better to look at. You, on the other hand, will make a marvelous sculpture."

Sculpture! My stomach heaved at the atrocity and my hand tightened on the trigger. It would be so easy to kill him now—here, like this. Then the 'goboys would shoot me and it would be mercifully all over. No more struggle, no more visions.

But if I died the war would continue, maybe escalate.

I couldn't let that happen. Too many people were dying for me.

With the Beretta aimed at his head, and taking care to shield myself from his bodyguards, I hauled him to his feet and inched backward into the comm room.

They followed at a distance, not daring to attack without their master's word.

When I reached the doorway, I pulled Jamon through, slammed the door shut with my foot and locked it. Like all paranoiacs he had the room well reinforced.

"Sit!" I moved the Beretta to the spot right behind his ear.

That's when I noticed it. A black whorl, curling behind his ear like a slug. The sight of it sent my stomach crawling up the back of my throat.

"What do you want, Parrish?"

I had to admire how readily he regained his composure.

"Call your troops off."

For a second the composure slipped. "Are you crazy?"

Now it was my turn for silky smiles. "Likely," I agreed. "Get on the comm and call them off."

He stared at me, trying to guess my motive.

I thumbed the trigger on the Beretta just to let him know I was serious. "Don't waste time, Jamon. Call them off. Then broadband a statement to say you are withdrawing. You can't win this."

He whitened, then tapped a shorthand code to his troops.

I prodded him harder. "So that I can understand it."

He repeated his orders in plain speech. His voice was cold and tight.

"Now broadband. To Viva as well. I want the media picking this up. Identify yourself as the instigator of this gang war," I said, steadfastly ignoring the howling as the 'goboys in the next room hurled their bodies at the door.

He shot me a look of pure venom then turned back to the comm. The blackness behind his ear began to ooze along his neck like molasses.

He was changing—but into what?

"Hurry," I screamed at him. "Tell Loyl Daac you'll meet to discuss territorial issues."

He unclenched his fists and opened the audio links

to all nets. "This is Jamon Mondo. I have ordered my people to withdraw. Loyl Daac. Let's . . ."

I stabbed the muzzle into the skin on his scalp.

". . . meet to talk about territorial issues."

I let out a breath of air. For a few minutes we watched and listened as the Common Net blitzed out. Eventually a message came through on Jamon's P line.

"Answer it with visuals," I instructed.

Loyl's face filled the screen. "Mondo?"

A ripple of antagonism played along Jamon's slight body. "You heard it," he snarled at Loyl.

"Why?"

"Let's just say . . . it comes down to current choices."

I couldn't resist leaning over his shoulder to study Daac's face—make sure he was in one piece.

Stupid mistake!

The same one Gwynn had made with me in his drain. The distraction caused me to drop the muzzle of the Beretta a fraction.

With the swiftness of a death-adder strike, Jamon snatched it away and shot me at point-blank range. I managed to deflect his aim by my own reaction. The shot burned along my left side, missing anything vital.

I struggled to stay upright but Jamon was out of the chair raising the pistol again. I kicked his legs as hard from underneath as I could, but my wound hampered my movement.

"Parrish!" I could hear Daac shouting from the comm.

Jamon righted himself and leveled the Beretta for another shot. His face had nearly totally transformed now, his flesh crawling with darkened whorls like leprosy rapidly spreading.

I froze, appalled at the sight of him. "What are you?" I whispered.

My horror must have penetrated his mind. Pistol poised, he moved away to glimpse his reflection on the screen.

I could hear Daac again. "Parrish! What's happening? *Get out of there!*"

His cries mobilized me. I scrambled for the door, frantically working the locks. They sprang open and I catapulted into the embrace of half a dozen 'goboys.

"Out," I shrieked, pointing back at Jamon.

They howled in confusion and fear. I shoved against them but they held me fast in a wall of sweaty fear.

Jamon stepped toward us touching his own face, his voice awed. "Lang said I would change."

The 'goboys ran from him then: instinctively frightened.

I felt the same. But I couldn't move.

"Lang?" I croaked. "What else did he tell you? That he would make you invincible? Did you really swallow that crap?"

Why wouldn't he? I nearly had.

He stopped as though my words confused him. "I'll be able to shape-change. I'll live longer. Can't you see the advantages?"

"No!"

He wiped blood from his lip and held it toward me. "You could be transformed as well."

"What are you doing?"

"My blood will change you too."

"Your blood . . ." I gasped with sudden comprehension. *The feathers. Dripping with blood. Blood in my mouth.* Had I somehow been infected that evening in the Muenos' villa? *No!*

"It's a parasite, Jamon. Using you for food. It'll leave you nothing. No 'self.' "

"Self?"

"Surely even you want to retain that!"

"Come, Parrish, aren't you tempted?"

"You're offering me that, and yet you tried to poison me," I accused.

"What do you mean?"

"The swordfish you served Stellar and me was contaminated with mercury."

He shook his hideous head. "Impossible. Lang provided the ingredients for the meal. He insisted. That's why he ate it without concern."

Then Lang tried to poison me. But he stopped me from eating it!

Threads of reason tied and untied in my head.

No! He wanted me to think Jamon had, so I would do his errand. Which meant . . . Stellar had died in order to make a convincing story for me.

It seemed unbelievable and yet . . .

"Parrish, help me stop your Cabal kin."

"Cabal kin?"

"Didn't you know? Loyl Daac is Cabal Coomera."

My mouth dropped. Daac. *Cabal Coomera!* "Liar!"

Adrenaline roared through me, sending the world into fast rewind. I spun back to that moment when I met Daac at Hein's bar, when the strange heat passed through me. I'd put it down to attraction. Chemistry.

But it was Kadaitcha work.

And from then on—his constant lies. My mind ran over them.

"Then why are you in his bloodlines register?" snarled Jamon.

I felt dizzy at the layers of deception. Vomit rose in my mouth. I was down on one knee when Jamon came for me. His inhuman snarl reeled me back to the present.

I threw up fists to ward him off, but he never reached me.

An explosion deafened and he convulsed then

slumped over like he had fallen asleep. I crawled back from him, shaking.

Between his shoulder blades a jeweled spear protruded. Streamlined, sophisticated and deadly. Explosive tip. Minoj special.

Chapter Twenty-one

They helped me to my feet. Four dark-skinned men with tribal scars and markings, dressed in worn leather coats. As much as I dared to look into their faces, they bore a resemblance to Loyl-me-Daac. Although older and leaner and with an aura of dignity.

The tallest held out a cloth for me, then averted his glance while I wiped myself clean of Jamon's blood.

When I'd finished, he spoke in a quiet, accented voice. "Parrish Plessis, you now owe us *goma*—blood debt. To repay it you are required to perform a task. This done, you will be offered sanctuary with the Coomera."

Sanctuary. I tried to control the chattering of my teeth. The thing I had dreamt about for so long was before me—and yet my very reason for wanting it was dead on the floor at my feet, his heart pierced by a tribal spear.

I drew myself straighter, trying to muster some dignity of my own. "Th-thank you for your s-service." Another shudder rolled through me. "He—he was infected with a parasite."

"We know of the Eskaalim. It concerns us. Many things concern us."

"W-what do you want from me?" It was getting to be a tired question.

There was a heavy silence as if the four were communing silently. I'd felt something similar before, with Vayu and her shamans. Understanding without words.

"There is a traitor amongst the Cabal who has taken something of much value for his own devices. With it he seeks the shadow path—to change what should be untouchable within us. Parrish Plessis, you will stop Loyl-me-Daac."

"Loyl," I gasped. "But he's one of you. Can't you—"

Another of the four stepped forward. Older, I thought, and painfully gaunt. His words came hesitantly as if speech was something he rarely practiced.

"Tradition . . . makes such a task . . . difficult. It is better done by . . . other hands."

"He won't do it, though. He won't stop."

"Then . . . you must . . . send him to . . . the other side."

The other side. The very thought set me shaking violently again. "A-and if I don't?"

The four faded back, as if they might suddenly vanish before my eyes.

"You would forfeit *sanctuary*?" They exchanged looks—confident smiles, I would have said, if their lips had moved.

"First I want to know if you murdered Razz Retribution." I blurted the question without thought for the consequences. It was at the root of so many things.

A solemn shake of heads and a *"Look further"* was all I got. They prised the spear free from Jamon's lifeless body and were gone.

I sank to the floor.
The Cabal wants me to stop Loyl!

I almost laughed aloud at the irony.

Even they had their dirty politics and they wanted me to wash it.

It occurred to me then that Loyl had been well named. But his loyalty didn't belong to the Cabal, or Razz Retribution, or me. It belonged to his obsession with recreating his gens—his craving for immortality.

Jamon had risked everything for the same thing.

Desire, whatever form it took, was the real energy of the human world. The Eskaalim would use it and twist it and bloat on it.

Right now my desire was to have a wash. Followed by painkillers and food. Then I wanted to crawl into bed for a week with someone who didn't have plans for me other than to rub my back.

But life was ever the bitch and never the good fairy. So instead I re-covered Stellar's body with the shroud.

I felt I should pray for her, or cry.

But neither came to me.

Instead I dragged myself back into Jamon's comm cache. One-World was alive with news that the war was over. I switched the babble down and focused the remaining fragile shreds of my concentration on hacking into Jamon's personal files.

My side throbbed every time I moved, but stubborn determination kept me at it.

That and an overriding desire to know if Jamon had spoken the truth.

Was I really linked to Daac's gens?

The idea seemed ludicrous, and yet I'd been drawn to live in The Tert. Maybe there was something to Daac's romancing about "place."

An hour later and I'd found part of what I was looking for. Daac's bloodlines register, a genealogical spreadsheet casting back a hundred years and further. I skimmed page after page searching for my name.

The entry came up with my old address in Viva, a brief history of Rene and my natural father's breakup. It also had a genealogical tree constructed of Rene's ancestors.

The revelation left me dazed.

Rene always acted like she'd been born in a reproducer. I didn't even know who her mother was. I didn't think she did either. But she must have. I felt a wave of anger and frustration toward her. The secrets she'd kept.

I zipped the entire register, dumped it onto a disk and continued searching for anything else of use until my eyes felt swollen and strained. In the end I powered down the PC, disconnected it from its peripherals and stuffed the drive and the disk down my pants. Then I closed the door on Jamon and his polished mahogany table for the last time.

In a matter of hours the place would be looted. I hoped someone would burn him.

Outside, above Torley's, Priers still swarmed, camming everything. Their drone filled the background like net babble. I wondered at the level of interest, and which one carried the 'Terro with my name on it.

Why hadn't it come for me yet?

Meanwhile punters surfaced from their hideyholes, cramming the bars to find out what was happening. Snatches of conversation floated to me.

"Oya ended the war."

"Mondo is dead."

"Cabal work."

"Renegade Cabal . . ."

"—saw a feral girl take out a heap of them. She was glowing, like them holy icons."

Wearily, I climbed the stairs to my room. There

were no dingoboys guarding it now. Someone had even repaired the door. With relief, I pressed the lock shut and fell onto the bed.

I gave myself long enough for a large hiccup of self-pity, then I stashed the disk and drive in my best hidey-hole and forced myself into the san unit before my wound opened its own bacteria factory.

By the time I'd washed, found my oldest set of fatigues, done a patch job on my side and scrabbled around for my last pro-sub, my mind started to tick. With a clarity born of relief at my unexpected survival, I suddenly knew what I had to do.

I just didn't know whether it would work.

As insurance I slipped a couple of Tempo tabs in my pocket. The though of feeding the parasite what it liked best—adrenaline—worried me, but my body had its limits and right now my flesh was redlining with exhaustion.

I checked the credit on my comm with Merry 3# and found enough left for a few calls.

Minoj's face came up, greasy and old on the screen. No synthesized image this time.

"Little thing," he rasped tiredly, "you *are* a survivor."

"Better than that, Minoj. I'm a player." I said it with total conviction and a hard face.

His look got suddenly cagey. Age melted from his face and a spark lit in the depths of his jaded eyes. Minoj loved Tert politics.

"Jamon Mondo is dead. I claim salvage rights," I said.

"Who supports this?"

Bluff was not my game. I usually told it the way I saw it—but sometimes you have to cheat. "You."

He blinked. Only once—enough for me to see the surprise.

"Think, Minoj. Jamon is dead. I take this stretch,

hard and fast with your support. I give you exclusive selling rights. Only your weapons. You can open up shop here."

"The 'goboys will never work for you."

"I don't need them. I have my own muscle." That was a lie, but I kept my expression tight hoping he'd heard enough rumors about Oya to buy it.

He turned the idea over in his mind—the list of Jamon's possible successors. In the end he came to the conclusion I guessed he would. *Back Parrish and then manipulate her.*

"What do you want me to do?" he asked.

"Spread the word, loud and quick. Jamon Mondo is dead. Parrish Plessis claims salvage. Minoj Armaments second her."

"You'll be challenged. You'll need protection."

I smiled. "No. They will."

His indecent smile mirrored mine.

"One last thing, Minoj. I want you to give Lang a message." I felt sure Minoj had some way to contact him. What arms dealer couldn't source a big client in an emergency?

"No, Parrish. Claiming salvage is one thing. Taking on Lang is something else. I won't back you on that." He lowered his voice. "He is not what you think . . ."

"Tell him I figured out about the wiper and I have a copy of the research. I want to negotiate at Torley's. *Directly.*"

Minoj sighed.

I placed three more calls. One to Pas.

"Oya. You have ended the war. The people are rejoicing."

I cut quickly across his religious fervor. "I need you *now*, Pas. Bring some men to Torley's."

He beamed. "Of course. We leave immediately."

"One thing, Pas. Tell me. The Feather Crown . . . was it chicken blood?"

There was silence, as if the question surprised him. "No, Oya. It is part of our custom that the Crown is dipped in human blood."

Human blood. My heart sank. It had been a futile hope, and now even it was gone.

My next call was to Teece.

"Parrish!" He looked relieved. "Why the hell did you run out on me like that?"

"Had to take care of some things. Have you got anything for me?" I hung on his answer, trying not to hold my breath. Was Teece with me or not?

"Yes. I saved what looks like some gene sequences. I'm not sure exactly. And some of her diary."

"What did the diary say?"

"Looks like she didn't trust Loyl's scientist. She had her watched. Seems Dr. Schaum must have some sort of conscience because she had a regular visitor to her place. A preacher."

A preacher!

My adrenaline spiked as a bunch of suspicions met and melded. I could barely keep the tremor from my voice.

"Teece, I owe you something for this. Bring the disk to Torley's pronto. I'm claiming salvage on Jamon's stretch."

"You're *what?*"

I cut him off before he could rant. A shiver ran deep through me. Thrill. The parasite liked what I was doing. But it didn't know the half of it.

I placed my last call.

"Parrish?" Loyl's face lightened. "Where the hell are you? I'll send someone—"

"I don't need your protection, Loyl. I'm claiming salvage on Torley's, the Shadoville stretch and everything Jamon owned. If you want to do business with me, you'll find me where we first met."

His expression was nearly worth the heartache he'd caused me.

Nearly.

I cut the comm line and armored up.

There was hardly anything left in my weapon stash. A couple of throwing knives, a garrotting wire and a real old-fashioned Luger with two packets of ammo. I holstered it to my thigh. Now was not a time for subtleties.

Hein's bar looked pretty untouched by the war.

Larry Hein spotted me the instant I entered. He gave a nervous, beckoning wave and I strolled over.

"Larry."

"Parrish."

His acknowledgment was short and loaded with angst. I wondered what had twisted his panties. His deep-set eyes were hard to see on the best of days. Now only the clumps of mascara along his lashes were visible.

"Just passing through?"

"No, Larry, I'm claiming salvage."

He swallowed hard. "The 'goboys are prowling. Riko says the place is his now. He's trouble. Using my place as his *office* and Mondo's not even cold."

I didn't know Riko particularly, but I could read Larry's displeasure like a beacon. "Get me a tequila! And send Riko my way."

I took a seat, back to the south wall. The usual.

Sipping on the tequila, I swallowed a tab and tried not to jitter. I'd cast my net wide and I prayed to the great freaking Wombat that I could haul it in when the time came.

In less than an hour the smell of 'goboy interrupted my nervous reverie. A waft of Larry's chiffon-clad arm sent his servitors scurrying to secure the tables. Battening down.

Still edgy, punters saw the drill and clasped their drinks. Things quietened.

A howling followed hard on the 'goboy scent as a handful of them sauntered through the doors. The patrons at the bar shifted. Magically a clear path opened between the 'goboys and me.

That was the best thing about The Tert. People understood the rules.

Riko was easy to pick, dressed in red synthetics and smelling like carrion. The others wore synths in blues and grays and stooped just a fraction lower so that he appeared to be the biggest, even if he wasn't. *Dog rules.*

Saliva glistened on their chests like beads.

Larry leaned across the bar to talk to Riko. In a matter of seconds their untidy heads swiveled in unison in my direction.

Group snap, guys.

I swallowed a private laugh and pushed back from the table.

Not hip to the art of polite conversation, they converged on me in a mass of stinking fur and wet, gaping mouths. Five of them, with Riko reclining at the bar to watch the fun.

I had a knife in each hand as the first one leapt across the table. I could have used the Luger but I wanted to make them bleed—for show—and, if I was honest, because they could repair themselves more easily from knife wounds than a hole in the head.

Yeah, OK, I didn't really want to harm the dog part of them. It was the human bit I was after.

I sliced the first one in a thin line across his stomach, dodging his poisoned finger- and toenails.

Number two was nearly on my back when I

launched upward and sideways. He collided with
number three coming in. I creased their necks with
blade and scrambled away. The remaining two came
at me from different sides, but I dodged between
them as if they were standing still and headed for
Riko. I'd been born with quick reflexes and the parasite seemed to be sharpening them. The tab helped
too.

A vision swarmed.

I realized suddenly that my real problem was the
smell of their blood. I held my breath as I lunged
across the room. An arm's length away from Riko I
took a quick gulp of air, just to clear my sight.

But Riko rolled a second before I contacted the
space he was occupying. Quicker than I expected, his
fist caught me on the corner of my jaw.

I stumbled and spun awkwardly. He was baring
his teeth, pleased with himself. Sprouking. Flanked
by the pair I'd dodged.

"This place is mine now, girlie."

Girlie! The term raged like a scrub fire through
my brain.

He stretched his hands out, beckoning. "You work
for me. I pay you. I look after you. Not like Master."

A garrotting wire was in my fingers before I knew
I'd even reached for it. I bridged the gap to Riko in
one blurred stride, looping the wire around his hand,
twisting, severing the skin like it was jelly.

Blood spurted and Riko howled. The wound
gaped, baring the wrist bone. I could have sliced that
as well but I didn't want him to lose the hand
permanently.

"Bitch," he screamed.

Then he began to cry.

The 'goboys clambered around him, pressuring the
wound, licking his face in comfort and, I suspected,
for the taste of his blood. They carried him out. If

they didn't hurry up and find him a medic, he'd bleed to death.

From the corner of my eye I could see Larry sending his Pet cleaners to deal with the mess. Larry didn't like blood. In ten minutes Hein's would be like nothing ever happened—the beauty of running a bar you could hose out.

I glanced around at Hein's silent patrons, some pinch-faced and scared, others grimly entertained: all careful.

My voice rose harshly. The wire stretched taut from one hand to the other. "I claim Jamon Mondo's territory. Any disputes will be settled by me. Larry Hein will post new lore and act as my broker. Spread the word."

Some punters cheered. Others stayed silent.

I could feel Larry's concealed pleasure. He'd warned me about Riko, I'd remember that. Besides I needed some allies.

Parrish Plessis. Twenty-first Century Warlord.

Shite!

I waited in my room for Larry's call. Tremors racked my body—a combination of gut-deep fear, the bad end of the speed and the parasite's gluttony. Partially severing Riko's hand had made me nauseous, and the parasite ecstatic.

All up it didn't make for sangfroid.

Possible outcomes of the next few hours frayed my mind. Timing would influence everything in the end. And I had no damn control over the timing at all.

Lang would come, because he couldn't risk me having a copy of the research he had gone to such lengths to destroy. But how would I know him? His shape-shifting made him the most dangerous of all.

Daac would come. Out of aggravation with me and

concern at what I might do with his bloodlines register.

Pas and the Muenos would come because I was Oya.

Teece would come—because he loved me.

Poor Teece.

I dozed on the bed, shivering, and listened as The Tert came out of hiding. Gunshots sounded occasionally still, but it was mostly just shouts of drunken, celebratory relief.

Once or twice the Angel swarmed across my vision but I breathed it away in slow meditative breaths. The effort left me with a tearing headache.

To distract myself I dialed into Infonet and read what I could about the adrenal glands. Where they were. How they worked.

Larry's call came a little before midnight.

"Parrish, there's a guy called Daac here demanding to see you. He's got half an army with him. They're making the punters *real* edgy."

"On my way, Larry."

I stood and stared for one long moment at Merry 3#, wishing I could change places with her. Then I swallowed my last tab.

Hein's was stinking Fishertown sardine material. Torley's punters shoulder to shoulder with thirty or more of Daac's men.

I could pick them now. They had a lean and hungry look, like the war would never be over.

The hum of conversation persisted when I entered, but like before a gap opened for me to the bar. It seemed my days of going unnoticed had gone the same way as my finer feelings toward Loyl Daac.

And there he was. Drink in hand with a face like hell. Stolowski was next to him, pale-faced and jumpy. On his other side, to my annoyance, stood Anna Schaum.

I stopped a couple of paces away, feeling the weight of his men around me.

"Loyl. Sto." I nodded toward Anna. "What's she doing here?"

"She wanted to come."

"To check out the lab rats in their natural habitat?" I looked her over casually. Something about her seemed different. Not right. I heightened my olfaugs but alcohol and body odors and the smell of fear crowded in, confusing me.

Daac slipped a protective hand on her shoulder. "She's safer with me."

Somehow I didn't think so but I hesitated at spoiling his delusion—yet.

"Parrish, I'd like to talk. Privately," said Daac.

"Here's fine." I stood, legs apart slightly, one hand on the Luger.

Irritation flashed across his face. I was forcing his hand publicly—he hadn't expected that. He looked around uneasily, gauging the situation.

The Muenos hadn't arrived. Some of Hein's punters might back me in a fight—but not all. I hoped I wouldn't have to find out how many.

"Jamon Mondo is dead. I've claimed salvage on his territory."

"Mondo stole information of mine. I want it back."

I shook my head. "My insurance. I'll keep it safe. You stay out of my face."

"It belongs to *my family*."

"And the Cabal wants it back," I said calmly.

My words stopped him dead. "What do you know about the Cabal?"

"She's bluffing, Loyl." The girlish voice turned my attention to the slim woman next to him. She seemed unusually composed for a scientist in the same cage as the lab rats.

"Does she even have what she claims?" she said. "Get her to prove it."

Daac nodded slowly. "I could take this place now, Parrish," he said. "Give me a reason not to."

I took two steps closer. I could almost reach out and touch him. Wanted to, really. "An army of Muenos." *Pas, where are you?* "And if you touch me, I've arranged for the entire contents of your blood-lines register to be wiped."

"What do you want?" he whispered dangerously.

Outside Hein's, shouts erupted.

The word "Mueno" rippled through the bar like a menace. A dozen or more of them forced their way inside, hair braided for action, knives on parade. I looked for Pas, frantic that he didn't start anything— or worse, prostrate himself in front of me.

I underestimated his savvy, because they fanned out in front of the doors, blocking escape.

The tension in the room reached roulette. My vision swarmed and blood pounded in my head like metal rock. A mistaken gesture could send us all to hell.

Or were we already there?

"Stop your experiments, Loyl," I told him. "They're endangering everyone."

His eyes flicked from me to the Muenos, calculating risk. "What are you talking about?"

I lowered my voice. "The side effects you found are symptoms. You've released something inside those people. A parasite that alters human biochemistry."

"What would you know about biochemistry?" Anna Schaum scorned me.

"I don't have to *know* about it, I've seen the proof. You see, Loyl, I *did* save Razz's files. She knew who wanted them and why. That's why she's dead."

The enormity of my lie sent me spinning toward a hallucination.

Not now! Not . . .

I never got there.

Anna lunged at me with precise, unnatural speed.

Somewhere in my hindbrain, I was waiting for it. Had been from the minute I'd identified the smell on her as caustic.

I shot her point-blank in the torso. Right about where the adrenals nestled onto the kidneys.

She keeled over and spasmed at my feet.

I made myself watch, gripped by an unholy fear that I'd made a terrible, terrible mistake. *Please, please let it be . . .*

Around me guns and knives jacked out in all directions.

But as the convulsions subsided so her appearance altered.

Instead of Daac's precious scientist, Lang lay dead at my feet, as Jamon had only hours before.

The tension drained from the room, replaced by a grim reality. Shape-shifters. Non-humans. *The whispers, the stories . . . were true . . .*

This time I couldn't control my reaction. I'd killed someone. *Something.*

I turned away and threw up my insides until they threatened to desert my abdomen for good.

Some warlord!

"Parrish."

I stared up groggily, through blurred eyes, to Loyl. There was no compassion in him. Only stiff shock. And anger.

"How did you know?"

I straightened. "Razz's diary. She was having Anna watched at the compound. Seems she had a regular visitor you didn't know about—a preacher. I guessed it was Lang. He made the mistake of using the same form with me."

"You knew he could shape-change?" His wire hand convulsed like he might strangle me with it, but I plowed on.

"That's why you must end your work. It's loosed something vicious. The shamans can't fight it. Nor can the Cabal."

I searched for an appreciation of the danger in his face. But I got cold and calculating—obsession meeting opportunity, how he could use the knowledge.

My resolve to stop him hardened.

"Where is Anna?" A tinge of awkwardness crept into his voice.

I looked away. I didn't know the answer to that. And, frankly, I didn't care. How long Lang had been in Anna Schaum's form was Daac's problem.

"You took a big gamble, Parrish."

"I cast out the bait. I knew he'd come. I just didn't know what shape it would be in."

I didn't tell Loyl that I'd recognized Lang by his scent. *And* by instinct—the way one parasite can recognize another in its human host.

Nor did I bother to explain how the Eskaalim are similar to us. That they like to dominate, and fight, and they'll sacrifice each other to get what they need.

"I made a mistake about you. You're dangerous and you're ambitious," he said softly. "But you'll give me what I want—in the end."

"Then you've just made another mistake," I promised.

He turned his back on me without another word and took his men with him.

Hein's suddenly seemed enormously empty. I told Larry to feed the Muenos and put it on my tab. Then I thanked Pas—who bowed and mumbled worship-type utterances. I put up with them because he'd come when I needed him. I patted his shoulder awkwardly and told him that as long as he kept feeding the ferals I would, on my oath, make sure he supplanted Topaz Mueno.

He bowed again and went to find food.

Some of Hein's punters came up and shook my hand, Tert-style. Others just came up close and stared at me. So they'd remember who I was.

I bore it for as long as I could and then, just as I decided the floor looked as good as any place to pass out, my prayers were answered.

"Parrish? What the—"

"Teece!" I whispered.

He hurried to my side, tired and filthy but, I hoped, in better condition than me.

"Mondo?"

"Dead. And Lang." I nodded to the body that Larry's servitors were busy removing. "You missed the show."

He spat. "Good riddance! Wish I'd been here, but I had a little bit of trouble of my own. There's been Priers out everywhere shooting *LTA*," he admitted sheepishly. "You're all over the Common Net. Breathing down Jamon's neck. Forcing his surrender."

I noticed the blood on his arms. "You're cut?"

"Yeah. But the fighting has stopped. Everyone's talking about this Oya. They're saying Oya has saved The Tert—even though it was really you." He laughed. "I guess it's about time we had a savior."

I didn't have the energy to explain to him that Oya *was* me. Instead I let him help me to a tactile. Around us Hein's recovered its rhythm. People in The Tert liked to get on, but they wouldn't forget.

Someone put a drink in my hand.

"Where are you going now?" he asked, gently slipping an arm around me. "You look like shit."

I laughed weakly. "I'm going with you."

The surprise and pleasure on his face was worth more than a week's sleep. Maybe, with a bit of luck, he might even forget that I owed him a bike and a new helmet . . .

Then again, maybe not!

I wasn't in love with Teece, but he'd earned my respect. And trust. Sometimes that means a whole lot more.

When I'd recovered, I still had a lot of business to take care of; a media image to fix—like how to convince the world I hadn't killed Razz Retribution.

Then I had a kid with no arms I had to see and an army of Muenos and ferals to repay. I also had to make that promised visit to Gwynn and get Trunk off his back.

And there was no forgetting the Cabal! Would I do what they wanted me to if Loyl didn't stop his experiments?

I didn't know.

Daac had gotten under my skin. He'd also lied to me at every turn. The jury was still out on what that meant.

But first, I had to find the complete set of research data. I'd realized one thing today. Lang was a minor player, like Jamon, when I'd thought he was *the* player. My real enemy still lurked in sinister silhouette.

Besides. It was the only hope I had for undoing the genetic changes in me.

Perhaps, then, I had a chance.

Perhaps, then, we all had a chance.

Or maybe I was just delaying the inevitable. While the Eskaalim mixed cocktails with my basic chemistry, the war inside me would continue. I didn't know if I would win it, but I wouldn't back down. I wouldn't give in.

I wasn't on the run anymore.

I was on the hunt.

"Teece, I need some air."

He nodded, understanding, and headed toward the bar. "I'll come and find you."

I drained my drink and staggered outside.

Torley's hummed a soothing business-as-usual tune. It settled my overstrung nervous system better than a wack of benzos. I needed some time alone. I'd killed a man and staged a gang coup—it was more than enough for one day.

I made it down an alleyway half a block from Hein's and collapsed onto a set of rough steps. Leaning back, my eyes closed without my permission and my mind clouded with exhaustion.

Despite the cracked plascrete sticking into my back, I dozed a little—maybe a lot—until something jolted me awake.

"Parrish Plessis?"

I opened my eyes. Recognition hit like a slap.

Aah, finally!

I jerked the Luger clear of the holster and whipped out my remaining garrotting wire, but neither would do much damage to the 'Terro crouched a body's length away.

After a helluva long moment it periscoped its lens to within a hot breath of my face.

I glared straight back into the iris, and directly, I hoped, into the face of its Prier journo. I had no juice left and I wasn't gonna get far on an ugly look. A wild urge to shout *you'll never take me alive* flashed into my head. I stifled it and dredged up some dignity.

"What?" My belligerence easily matched my gaze.

From the side of the lens unfolded another, smaller arm. The bud-end mic snaked toward my head.

I stilled, and let it settle in my ear. Visions of my arrest being broadcast on the next *LTA* suddenly evaporated. If it wanted to kill or detain me, it'd be over by now.

Seems, instead, though, it had something to say.

I sighed. Didn't everyone?

The connection crackled before the journo's voice came through from the Prier.

"Ms. Plessis, I need work done. Privately."

Acknowledgments

First books are a huge, collaborative affair. How else could the writer ever get to the end of something written wholly on faith and borrowed time? So here are heartfelt thanks to my collaborators . . .

Linda Curtin for starting it all (yes, Linnie—I blame you!). Robyn and Kerry Smith for reading very early Parrish when she was still Loretta. The ROR-ettes: Maxine McArthur for putting up with the hysterics, Rowena Lindquist for Scallywags, Trent Jamieson for consoling e-mails, Tansy Rayner Roberts for being beautiful, and Margo Lanagan for fire-lighting skills and telling it how it is. Lyn Uhlmann, Adrianne Fitzpatrick and Lu Cairncross. Kath Holliday for the "Attitude," and the long drive down with the Bolly. The Vision Writers Group, Brisbane, for carrying the speculative fiction torch, especially Kate Eltham and Grace Dugan. Dr. Ros Petelin for teaching me about excellence (still learning, Ros!). Peter Bishop from Varuna Writers Centre, NSW, for pulling me out of the pile. Tara Wynne, my agent, for being such a delight to work with and for taking a risk. Ben Sharpe, my dazzling editor, for letting Parrish loose.

Rose, Nicci and Lorna, my *real-Life* heroines. All my family, de Courtenays and de Pierreses, especially cher frère, Paul, and my boys. And lastly, for Nick, unquestionably the light and love of my life.

Need your Parrish fix?

Turn the page to see
who's got her
in their sights now. . . .

CODE NOIR

*Coming from Roc
in July 2006*

Two thin streams of water drilled into me like a needle gun. I told myself it was as good as a massage and jumped around under it like a dancing grrl in a cage. One arm, then the other. One breast, then the other. One buttock, then the . . .

"What the hell—" I spun around as the water suddenly cut off.

The man standing in the doorway of the san with his hand on the valve had the pleasure of my best side. He didn't look impressed.

I stepped straight out and into his face, too annoyed to be embarrassed. "—are you doing?"

"We have immediate need of your service, Parrish Plessis," he said.

Those words had become too familiar. First the Prier pilot, now this. I couldn't remember hanging out the sign that said "gun for hire."

"Our Clever Men have been taken. You must find them."

He didn't even try to make it sound vaguely like a request. But then the Cabal Coomera were like that. All somberness and threat.

This one seemed to shimmer—a dark-skinned figure with tribal scars on his bare chest and face, and an assassin's bleak, hooded eyes. His open leather jacket and titanium-capped boots were the only tangible part of him.

The ancient ceiling fan extractor of Teece Davey's bedroom—my current home—struggled to disperse the steam that curled around him.

You didn't invite the Cabal into your home. Certainly not into your san.

Behind him a couple of paces stood an identikit. Except older, leaner.

"How did you get—?"

The pointless question died on my tongue. These guys were Kadais. They made it their business to sneak around and scare the whatsit out of everyone.

Already I had a creeping urge to prostrate before them and beg for mecry.

Jeez, Parrish, get a grip!

The younger one slid forward without stepping— or so it seemed.

Spooky.

Legends said they once wore feather feet, and sang tribal lawbreakers to their death. These days the tribes were pretty damn diluted, like all the other nations that lived in The Tert, but a flavor of tradition survived. And the Kadais were the ones who ran the hits.

He handed me a crumpled tee.

"Remember you owe us *goma*."

I struggled into the shirt, using the time to think.

Goma. Blood debt. They'd killed my ex-employer, Jamon Mondo—before he killed me. *Goma* was something you didn't reneg on with the Cabal. In repayment they wanted me to stop Loyl-me-Daac, a renegade from the Cabal, from experimenting with genetic manipulation.

I figured there was only one way to do that: execute the guy.

Simple. But there was a downside. Daac happened to be the only person in this world I had deep feelings for. Not to mention serious issues with. Either way I didn't think I wanted him dead.

"Your *goma* is . . . difficult for me," I said cautiously. Then I ventured, "He is your dirty washing, after all."

I saw a flicker of amusement cross the younger one's face.

The Cabal wanted rid of Daac. He'd strayed from their code of beliefs. For all their sinsiter ways, they weren't hell-bent on genetic supremacy. Trouble is they didn't want to soil their hands with it. Or couldn't, due to some old custom.

The older one frowned a gully. "The matter of the *karadji* is more pressing. You will attend to it before you repay *goma*."

Karadji. *The Clever Men. The ones with spirit power.*

"W-will I?" I stammered. There's something about the Cabal. An aura of dignity, and a cold, hard belief in what they did. It brokered no quarrel. Even from me: Parrish Plessis, pugilist and self-styled warlord.

"Four of them have been taken from us. Those remaining are in hiding. And it is not just our *karadji*. We believe others are in danger as well . . . shaman of all beliefs."

A couple of months ago I would have whimpered aloud at the thought of taking on such a task. Right now all I felt was the heavy resignation of someone who only ever gets deeper in it. "I'm—uh—pretty busy."

It was worth a try.

"When you find them, we shall return to you the research that holds the answers you seek, Parrish Plessis. This we pledge."

An answer to the Eskaalim! The creature that invaded and tortured my mind. The creature that changed me— that would eventually possess my body and soul.

My heart high-jumped at a chance to survive.

See, I was infected by an alien parasite that was working overtime on perverting my humanity. Sounded weird, but the reality was weirder. I didn't have long and I wasn't the only one.

I blamed Loyl Daac for it. My theory was that his genetic fooling had loosed this creature on the world after it had been dormant for eons. Maybe he could reverse what he'd done, except now he no longer had the splicing codes—they'd been stolen. The Cabal were telling me they knew how to get them back.

They watched me, adopting an implacable take-it-or-leave-it-and-suffer-the-consequences silence.

Find our karadji, *they said. Find them! Like that was easy? Welcome to The Tert, boys—haven for the rather-be-lost-than-found! Sanctuary of secrets and zipped lips.*

"You have Loyl Daac's stolen research?"

"We will."

I hid a sigh. It was as good an answer as I'd get. It meant I had to trust them. And for some reason I did. Call it misguided respect.

The older one did the spooky thing and slid alongside his partner, his expression bleak and cautionary. "There is one condition. If the *karadji* are not safe before the next King Tide, Parrish Plessis, the deal is off."

King Tide? I swallowed my qualms and nodded in agreement.

With the slightest swing of his shoulders he threw a dagger in a low arc. It stabbed the floor at my toe tips.

I didn't even have time to twitch.

Hotly, I bent down, jerked it free and waved it at them.

Too late! The doorway wore nothing but air.

I moaned aloud, letting the built-up fear and anger

stream out of me and then subside. With only a tiny tremor I handled the dagger. The hilt shone like steel-colored marble. *Polished iron ore.*

The Cabal spear that had killed Jamon Mondo had been jeweled. Opal inlaid and glittery.

I fingered the handle of this one. It felt cold and warm at the same time.

The sensation sent a shiver.

Worse than any premoniton.

Marianne de Pierres's short fiction has appeared in a variety of anthologies. A film and television graduate from Curtin University, she writes reviews for *The Courier-Mail*. Marianne is a cofounder of ROR—wRiters On the Rise, a critiquing workshop for Australian professional genre writers—and was integral in the development of the Clarion South writers workshop. She lives in Queensland, Australia, with her husband and three sons.